The Literature
Express

The Literature Express

Lasha Bugadze

Translated by
Maya Kiasashvili

DALKEY ARCHIVE PRESS
CHAMPAIGN / LONDON / DUBLIN

Originally published in Georgian as *Literaturis ek'spresi* by
Bakur Sulakauri Publishing, Tbilisi, Georgia, 2009

Library of Congress Cataloging-in-Publication Data

Bughadze, Lasha.
[Literaturis ek'spresi. English]
The literature express / Lasha Bughadze ; Translated by Maya Kiasashvili. -- First
Edition.
pages cm. -- (Georgian literature series)
"Originally published in Georgian as Literaturis ek'spresi by Bakur Sulakauri."
ISBN 978-1-56478-726-2 (alk. paper)
1. Short stories, Georgian. I. Kiasashvili, Maya, translator. II. Title.
PK9169.B84L5813 2014
899'.969--dc23
                        2013037373

Partially funded by a grant from the Illinois Arts Council, a state agency

Georgian Literature Series is published thanks to the support of
the Ministry of Culture and Monument Protection of Georgia.

www.dalkeyarchive.com

Cover: design and composition by Mikhail Iliatov

Printed on permanent/durable acid-free paper

Table of Contents

For Sophie

1. TBILISI

The Russians bombed us in August. Elene broke up with me in September. In October I went to Lisbon.

I knew I'd be taking the Literature Express as early as spring, but I could have never imagined the Russians would shell us in August. Neither had I taken Elene's threats seriously. I never thought she'd be so adamant. Everything seemed to be happening at the same time. First I was told I was to travel along with one hundred writers across Europe, then it looked as if the Russian bombs were about to kill me and finally it transpired I wasn't such a wingless angel as Elene had believed earlier. "I'm sorry for the time I wasted on you," was the last I heard from her. Then she switched off her phone. I sent her two miserable messages and gave up. I didn't beg or plead with her. The Russian bombs drained me of all energy. But prior to that someone called Koka phoned me, mentioned the Literature Express and summoned me to the Ministry of Culture.

It turned out the Literature Express was actually a train. One hundred writers from various countries were to board it and cross half of Europe over a month.

For some reason the invitation had arrived at the Ministry of Culture. Koka frankly admitted he had thought of me only when the poet Khavtasi (one of our senile ones) refused to go. There were two invitations. Koka told me initially they'd planned to send two poets (apparently, the Minister had said poets would add a certain charm to the entire trip), but then they decided to make room for me, a prose writer. In the end, it was me and a poet chosen for the trip.

It still baffles me how Koka and his superiors had come up with me and not someone else. Whose idea was it to send me to Lisbon? Others have dozens of books published while I've got one single collection of short stories . . . Who considered me a bona fide writer in such a kleptocratic organization as the Ministry? I suspect Koka (who I guess was something like the Deputy Minister)—an effeminate, mildly aggressive provincial with sideburns. Apparently, when I was awarded the prize (I've received a local literature prize for my short stories), he was there at the ceremony, bought my book the next day and enjoyed it tremendously. That's what he told me.

The very same day I wrote to Heinz, the organizer of the literature trip. In reply, I received a semi-formal letter with the enclosed trip itinerary. His missive started with *Dear Mr. or Mrs. Zaza.* He seemed unsure to whom he was writing—a male or a female. Completely confused by my first name. I wrote back saying I was a male and that Zaza is a solely male name in Georgia. Needless to say, I added some smileys (you know, these buttock-like faces).

The train journey sent me into a state of light shock. The idea of the Literature Express packed with poets and writers traveling across seven European countries confounded me even as I tried to envision the trek.

I remember sharing my fears with Elene who, in her typically motherly manner, chided me:

"Don't say a word! God knows when you might get another chance like this. You must be completely inane to miss it!"

I also remember Elene and I studying the route on the map. We'd taken my grandpa's old globe to bed with us, placing it between us as if it were a baby. We looked closely at the cities the Express was to go through.

The train was due to leave Lisbon and pass through Madrid, Paris, Brussels, Frankfurt, Malbork (which we failed to find on the globe), Kaliningrad, Moscow (to which I immediately bade farewell as no Georgian was allowed into Russia: we were refused visas), Warsaw, and finally, Berlin. In short, we were to cross half of Europe. "In future, we plan to organize a European-Asian trip," Heinz said later. "This time the money only covers half of Europe."

Incidentally, at the time the Russian plane dropped a bomb on Makhata Mount we were in bed too.

It was five in the morning. Elene and I were woken by a deafening noise of a blast. I thought the TV transmitting tower had been blown up. It was right there, above our house and I imagined the metal monster falling on our tiny house in an infernal blaze ...

Elene had opened the window and was looking out.

"No," she said. "It's still there."

"Where did it drop then?" I asked happily.

She stepped onto the balcony, shaded her eyes with her hand for some reason and looked up in fear.

"I'm not sure. I can't see," she replied.

We got dressed, threw our passports into her handbag and sat down to watch TV.

"If we're shelled again, we'll hide under the stairs," Elene decided. I put my head on her shoulder.

"It's crucial for the mobiles to work," I said.

I recall trying hard to stay calm: I yawned noisily and joked, telling her I'd never imagined we could dress so quickly. Basically, I was overexcited with dread.

"And all the while you were worried about getting tired on that train. Aren't you daft?" Elene told me.

True. I hadn't counted on being killed by the Russians in August ...

Later that morning we found out the bomb had fallen across the river, quite far from us, in the vicinity of the Tbilisi Sea.

That night I believed I had no one in the world as precious as Elene. That's how we'd fallen asleep in front of the working TV. She had her little handbag in her lap, I had my head on her shoulder.

We split up in a month.

As a rule I don't drink often, but if I do, it's something *alarming*. I don't get sour or vicious. I just laugh a lot and don't want the day to finish. In short, absurd as it sounds, I'd been talking in my sleep.

In the morning Elene was waiting for me in the kitchen. Sitting at the window, she eyed me with a mixture of disgust and irony.

"Who's Maka?" she asked.

I thought she'd read a message or something.

I'd got acquainted with Maka over Skype during the August war. She was scared stiff but hysterically coquettish at the same time. I'd never come across anything like this in my life. She used to write texts like: "When the Russians march into Tbilisi, I'm going to commit suicide . . . But don't tell me you don't care for blue-eyed girls. By the way, what color are your eyes?" She sounded somewhat simple and unrefined, but was a real looker.

In a nutshell, I had a kind of therapeutic and sad sex with poor Maka. True. She was on the verge of tears all the time, while I felt pangs of guilt for treating Elene in such a ghastly way.

All in all, Maka and I met three or four times. Hard as I tried, I couldn't make her come even once. Maybe that's the reason she felt like crying. I'm not sure.

"We need to get to know each other better, much better," she used to say over and over again.

How much better was I supposed to know her?

If I hadn't talked in my sleep, no one would have found what I'd done. As far as I know, it hadn't happened before. Apparently,

I was so drunk I readily answered all of Elene's questions—what's easier than getting me to talk? I'm not a medium. Unfortunately, I failed to realize where I was and who was conducting the fatal interrogation.

In the beginning I found it hard to believe no one had informed her. She might have seen an incriminating message in my phone. But then I stopped caring. Come what may, I thought. Down deep I knew perfectly well the crisis in our relationship wasn't caused by that night's prattle.

"I'm sick and tired of having to drag you," she said a year earlier, at the seaside. She must have considered splitting up at that moment. What she had initially found appealing in me (my oddities typical of a writer, my lifestyle, my lovable infantilism) by then had turned into a tedious, depressing reality. Some produce piles of books and still don't earn enough, while I had published a single book two years earlier with only four hundred copies sold. So how on earth would I make any money? "At least a thousand copies need to be sold in order to get a bestseller rating," my publisher had told me. My salary was just enough to buy me cigarettes (while I still smoked). I did receive a literature prize, but still live off my parents. I go to bed at four in the morning and wake up at midday, but only as a courtesy because I can easily sleep till later. Looking through Elene's eyes, I used to find it awkward, but now it's this novel I find embarrassing. I go to work twice a week, write a couple of ads, mess around a little and come back. And now, on top of everything, it's someone called Maka I'm after. In short, I seem to be a complex problem for Elene. Or rather, was. Not anymore.

"I always feel down with you," she admitted that morning, "because you've always got some problem or another which I'm obliged to solve for you. You're not an angel, strictly speaking, so it's not worth sacrificing my life."

The house we rented at the time (chosen by me but paid for by Elene) had withstood the August shelling together with us. But I vacated it two weeks after she left me.

"You can stay if you wish," the owner told me. "You might find someone to pay for it."

I didn't want to stay because everything there reminded me of Elene, so I moved in back with my parents, into my teenage cell.

I sent her only two messages. I didn't persist.

And in October I flew to Lisbon together with the poet Zviad Meipariani.

He had brought along a literary newspaper in which some poet-critic vehemently disparaged us. The author criticized Koka (and the likes of him) of the Ministry of Culture for selecting us, rumbling on: *What sort of writers are they anyway? Why have they and not some other, worthier writers been chosen for the seminar?* He claimed I was helped by my mum (she is the vice president of our national Chess Federation), but was sparingly critical of Zviad: *He is not bad, but there are others, million times better poets.* In short, he assaulted me more passionately, calling me "the author of a heartless brochure."

"We don't give a damn, do we?" Zviad wisely suggested. "We're on the plane already, while the dick's in his lousy office."

I wasn't perturbed in the least anyway and didn't need his encouragement. I immediately guessed he was uneasy about the whole thing and tried to hearten himself with the words.

Later I found out he wasn't disturbed by the article at all. The truth was, he was scared stiff of flying and, like any Georgian in a similar situation, drank himself unconscious. I was sure he'd puke all over me at landing, but he didn't. The flight was uneventful in this respect.

If I'm not mistaken, I had decided to write a diary novel then and there. I wanted to keep a record of my impressions. Of what happened and of what was about to happen. I just had to find a place for the war and Elene. Zviad already was a designated character.

What I didn't know at the time was that another Helena in my life would become the main character of my novel.

This is the diary of a month-long pursuit of Helena.

2. THE PLANE

Helena was still far away. While I was suspended somewhere in midair, she might have been driving to the Athens airport with her husband.

There was water beneath me—the Black Sea.

As a rule, the outward flights from our home airport leave early in the morning. I believe it's explained by the fact that the night sky is cheaper compared to that of the daytime, which is sufficient ground for all the vampire airlines flying to our country to passionately hate the daylight. Our flight was no exception—we were to take to the sky at four in the morning.

Zviad had insisted on getting to the airport three hours ahead of the scheduled flight. Not two, but a full three hours. I've firmly learnt from my childhood that one absolutely has to be there two hours earlier and I've got nothing against the long-standing tradition. I'm all for these two hours, but three was somewhat unexpected and, to tell the truth, a little alarming. It was when I first suspected that the man was an epitome of classic Georgian male fretfulness, which meant spending the entire month fighting his pet worries. Could these three hours be an indication of something much more sinister to come?

I have to admit I also tend to be gripped with a kind of pre-departure hysteria. I sometimes think I might lose my way in a huge airport or, worse, that I might be mistaken for a wanted terrorist, unable to convince the airport authorities with my broken English that *I'm someone else.*

I detest those seconds when my passport is checked by foreign officers (I don't fear my countrymen). I abhor the minute I have to stand behind the glass awaiting the paradise pass from a green-uniformed alien.

At times like these, I try to look as gentle as possible, my expression saying: *Such a pity you don't know me. I mean no harm. I'm as law-abiding as you are.*

I guess the Europeans don't suspect such complexes exist. One has to come from the former Soviet Union or be a survivor of the '80s in order to understand these fears. The fear of making a mistake. The fear of misdemeanor. The fear of pissing in the Vienna airport toilet designed for the handicapped and being obliged to pay the fine out of the miserable amount you managed to save for your trip abroad. *Why have you urinated in the toilet for the handicapped, citizen?*

To cut it short, I also feel a little uncomfortable before departure, but the poet Z. Meipariani certainly overdid it in this respect: he phoned me five or six times, compared the info on his ticket with that on mine, repeating over and over again that his brother-in-law was going to drive us to the airport. Finally, hearing I was planning to take a nap before the flight, he made a heartrending confession: he hadn't slept for days and had lost any wish to go on living. He was sixteen when he'd last flown—his uncles had taken him to Moscow to bring back his deceased great-aunt. No wonder his memories connected with air travel were far from cheerful. It was then, in the plane toilet, that he wrote his first serious poem. "It was a strange feeling," he told me. "We were up there, in the air, with my great-aunt in a bag."

Zviad started drinking in the airport, couldn't find his passport in his pocket when needed, kind of crashed into an energetic, hypocritically smiling doll-like air hostess and then, already in his seat, rammed his knees into the seat in front. "That's it, he's going to piss everyone off," I thought with a sinking heart, regretting

I had accepted the invitation to join the Literature Express. I couldn't help thinking Zviad was only a tiny link in the chain of misfortunes.

Customarily, I'm a bit depressed in the morning, so no wonder 4:00 A.M. isn't my brightest hour. The war two months ago, Elene dumping me, sleep-deprived passengers, inflatable life jackets and an utterly unrealistic survival procedure demonstrated by the air attendant, along with puking packets and drunken Zviad, depressed me to the extent that I seemed to be seized by the characteristic anxiety of all Georgian males—the fear of novelty.

"I'm suffocating," I remember thinking as I positioned my forehead in the direct line of the weak fresh air current coming from above.

I wasn't sure why I was going, why I had to be torn away from my comfortable routine for a whole month, why I was there so early in the morning among all these strangers—a bunch of aggressive psychopaths.

Yes, I felt bad, pretty bad, but at least one thing was crystal clear—sleep was the only escape route from drunken Zviad and hypocritically smiling air hostess. Falling asleep was the way out. For self-preservation.

"Zaza, are we airborne?" Zviad turned his puffy red face toward me.

"Not yet," I replied.

My guess was he couldn't bear to look through the window.

"We humans are so miserable," he muttered with the desperation of King Lear and sunk into his personal phobias: with his eyes closed, he began producing funny spurting noises with his lips and nodding his head in the manner of a coquettish jazz lover. A foreigner with dyed hair sitting next to him (unquestionably a foreigner because of his unnaturally popped out eyes and a tense smile) gave me a horrified look. He had no explanation for Zviad's behavior.

In short, we were all terrified: I of the unknown future, the foreigner of Zviad, and Zviad of flying. My poor colleague was unaware he'd already become someone else's horror. Was it completely inconceivable that this suspicious muttering was an indication of a far more sinister danger looming ahead of us? Could it be nothing more than a prayer? But it's no secret how petrified the well-organized Anglo-Saxons are of praying during flights. So what if the plane just left a Christian land—an audible prayer is invariably dangerous!

And what images might have flashed through the foreigner's mind: a dark-haired man (poet Z. Meipariani) jumping from his seat as soon as the plane straightened, stabbing the air hostess (exactly at the moment when she was offering apple juice with an annoying hissing *S* sound: "With iccce?") and then the plane heading toward an Arab country. Or, possibly, to the Christian Copts in Africa.

He was glancing at Zviad with deep concern. I thought he was about to send his wife a farewell phone message, as prescribed: *We're hijacked. Love you. Wish I'd told you more often.*

"Zviad." I nudged the nodding poet.

"What?" He opened his eyes.

"Are you praying?"

"No. Why?"

"What are you doing then?"

"Nothing. I really need to pee."

"That man thinks you're a terrorist. Please, stop it."

"Who?" He sat up.

"Him." I indicated the passenger next to him. The man smiled back at us with his glass eyes.

"What's it I'm doing?" Zviad smiled back at him.

"Nodding and spurting."

"I'm writing a poem," he laughed. "No guts for terrorism!"

He unbuckled his seat belt and rose.

"You can't leave your seat yet." I grabbed his arm.

The foreigner was visibly scared of even looking at him. He stared at the seat in front and turned into a stone passenger.

"I'm going to burst if I don't take a pee," Zviad said and nearly trampled the poor man, practically pressing his bum into his face and stepping over his knees. Then he wobbled toward the toilet.

I'm rather selfish. Elene ran from my egotism and not from me. But that's another story. "I don't give a damn what he does," I thought, looking up at the panel with the crossed cigarette and mobile phone and red-lit seat belt signs.

The thick-legged air hostess reached Zviad before he got into the toilet. In the meantime I put fingernail-sized rubber plugs into my ears, telling myself I was alone. There was no Zviad.

It didn't take much to put him back into his seat. A couple of strict words uttered by the thick-legged hostess did the job. I'm pretty sure he didn't protest only because he wasn't on a Georgian company flight, otherwise he'd certainly haggle with each and every passenger and possibly smoke in the toilet as well.

"I shouldn't have drunk," he said as he took his seat.

I pretended I was asleep. I wasn't in the least interested what he had to do and what he shouldn't have done. Content with the results of the policy of ignoring him, I fell asleep.

However, I was soon woken up by a jolt. "Just turbulence," I reassured myself and looked at the miserable chap. He was asleep with his mouth agape. He might have pissed himself for all I knew. The foreigner with the dyed hair seemed to be still immobilized by a wicked witch. It smelled of food on the plane. I rested my head on the porthole and peered down. We were flying over the Black Sea.

Before I dozed off again I remember thinking I needed to write something about the sea. Can you recall many Georgian writers depicting the sea, producing marine stories, novels, plays, or poems?

There was a two-hour literary void underneath.

As often happens at the moments of complete idleness, I began thinking of a new plot. I wanted to come up with a marine plot, but to my great annoyance, I ended up with one single image out of all the possible ones related to the Black Sea. I might have nodded off as I pictured a middle-aged seaside village woman going into the water in her light dress. I've often witnessed such a weird moralistic tradition: the village women tend to bathe in their light summer frocks, always stay close to the beach, hold their naked grandsons tight, happily splashing and loudly giggling in the shallows . . .

I clearly remember getting angry with myself for such an idiosyncrasy: the sea is so vast, while I got stuck with these women.

3. LISBON

There we were, the poet Z. Meipariani and myself, at the airport exit, looking for someone holding up signs with our names. Hundreds of people arrived, plenty of those waiting with the signs in their hands, but no one with our names around. All unfamiliar names.

Those passengers who had arrived with us found themselves (or their names) quite easily, while Zviad and I stood there, at the exit, lost and seemingly stranded.

I already knew my next step: I had Heinz's phone number, also someone named Iliko's (I was told he was a Georgian student living in Germany, supposed to be a kind of a guide for the two of us). I meant to phone them if worse came to worst.

"Have we been dumped?" Zviad asks a rhetorical question. His tone reveals he's not particularly worried because he's got me.

"The Germans would never do that," I say. "Out of the question. Have we muddled up?"

"Arrived somewhere different, Zaza?" Having calmed down, Zviad feels like joking.

In the meantime I register a comical and at the same time (if looked deeper down) sad reality: that the words one of the tanned young men wearing well-polished shoes has on a piece of paper are actually our, Zviad's and my, names, and not those of some obscure household items:

Mr. Xaxa, Mr. Jviadh, welcome to Lisboa!

Yeah, you have no idea how insulting it can be to walk up to a

Portuguese man in well-polished shoes and tell him you are that Xaxa, that he's been standing there awaiting something like Xaxa and Jviadh.

"Don't they have a Z?" Zviad asks me in astonishment while I shake the young man's hand and give him an insincere smile (actually hating him).

"Hi, I'm Xaxa."

"Zdrastvuite," Zviad greets him in Russian, revealing the simple fact that he doesn't speak English.

The bus we were led to fully reflected the post-Soviet conflicts of the '90s: the Armenian writers, Anait, an elderly woman, and Mr. Artur Zeituntsyan occupied the front seats; Mr. Eldar Aliev from Azerbaijan (I'd have been utterly surprised if he had a different surname) sat midway, while the Chechen poet Raul Aldamov occupied a raised seat at the very back. The Russians climbed after us, greeting everyone with a *Hello* with a heavy Russian accent. One was younger (later called the Little Russian), wearing glasses and a beard, the other was red-faced and older (consequently, the Big Russian). The latter had a thermos in his hand.

The Armenians endowed us with parental smiles and adopted a pleasantly reserved attitude, conversing in an unhurried manner. I couldn't figure out their relationship: were they a husband and wife, partners, or just colleagues? Both showed signs of dignified aging, but one couldn't say they were old. I decided the woman belonged to an elite category of Armenians—she had a silvery scarf wrapped like a turban on her head and a pair of tight jeans across her fleshy thighs.

The aroma of Europe reached me as soon as we left the airport. One of my acquaintances had told me Portugal was the backwater of Europe, which I immediately and foolishly accepted. With an air of wizened sophistication, I had even shared this knowledge with Zviad, who wasn't burdened with rich traveling experience.

No sign of a backwater though—it was paradise on earth! It's us who live at the back of beyond. Once I accompanied Elene to Tkibuli on a business trip. I went for fun and found myself in a real hell! The parched hills were covered with windowless, burnt-out apartment blocks. People inhabited only the ground floors of these ten-story buildings. The impression was that the high-rise structures were put up in the pre-Ice Age. I wouldn't be surprised to come across dinosaur eggs in one of the abandoned flats. Chiatura, another town, was even worse—the place looked as if an atomic bomb was dropped on it a couple of weeks ago. Rusty trolleybuses seemed to be suspended in the air. In the past, there were cable cars connecting the town with the surrounding mountains. Now torn cables were hanging down everywhere, some stretched as far as the half-demolished houses on top of the hills. Trees and bushes protruded like antlers from the rooftops of the Stalin-era factories, or rather what was left of them. Looked like the continuation of the ground. Occasionally, what I thought to be solid ground turned out to be a half-buried, rust-eaten skeleton of a truck or a trolleybus—something transformed into a sickly landscape, a pathological extension of nature.

Portugal was magnificent. Even the shining highway which I could see from the window of our ethno-conflicting bus.

The soft-spoken Armenians were obviously stuck with the not particularly talkative or enthusiastic co-passengers that we embodied. We were both extremely sleepy, hardly managing to utter a word or two. Zviad's and my souls seemed to have been stranded in yesterday's Tbilisi.

Later it transpired that the Azeri Eldar Aliev was the most famous writer among those from the Caucasus. Even Zviad had read one of his crime novels. Detective Kraus (or someone similar) was created by our Azeri colleague, the author of over thirty novels. The thought that this man dressed like an MP came up with crime stories amazed me. He looked like a Communist

Party senior I'd seen in my childhood. He was smartly dressed and treated women with exaggerated respect.

In truth, any decent European would have committed suicide if obliged to take a ride on our bus. The air itself was vibrant as the most politically incorrect tension was rising high.

It's awful how irritating we find someone without even knowing them. You have no idea the kind of books they write, what features they possess, whether they're generous or baleful. But if you happen to be, say, an Armenian and the other person an Azeri, you're automatically expected to hate him. I had no clue about the personal traits of the Russians on the bus, but I found them abhorrent. The bomb-dropping people. Weren't they killing Elene and me just a month ago?

In short, if not for our respective countries, the climate in our bus would have been as agreeable as that in the bus carrying the Scandinavians.

We met Iliko, the Georgian student, in the hotel lobby. Other Iliko-like students welcomed the rest of our group. I had visualized an emaciated lad combining his studies with part-time odd jobs. I was right in the latter two, but my guess was a far shot when it came to his age and appearance—Iliko was a worn-out, rather heavy bachelor with thinning hair. He was wearing a threadbare jacket, the type you expect an eccentric sci-fi film character to sport, no doubt bought at one of those legendary sales.

Iliko and Zviad instantly disliked each other. I, on the other hand, immediately took to this strange, all-knowing man. I like being advised on everyday practical matters. And I hate being mobilized. That's why I'd fallen for Elene. She was in charge, she made the decisions. That's how it worked for us.

I can't say Iliko reminded me of her, but he was very good at ordering people around. Zviad, it seemed, was annoyed by exactly those features that I found appealing.

"You'll be given the keys now," he snapped after a brief

introduction-welcome. "The registration point is over there. You need to get registered and then go up to your rooms. There's a meal at three o'clock. They gave us some shit for breakfast, but come down anyway. It's good to be seen and you can grab something."

He was irritable but attempted to joke. It was his manner of speaking.

"If that's how they feed us in Portugal, I dread to imagine what it's going to be like in Poland," he laughed and led us toward the registration tables set up at the lifts.

In one of the corners of the hotel lobby there was a registration point set up for the Lit-Express passengers. A smiling but severe young woman shoved medium-sized bags and barked information at us (she was German speaking angry English):

"You can find our itinerary and maps in your bags, also the participant photo catalogue, money and your room keys. We have to assemble in the hall at five this afternoon and get to know each other."

Her name was Irmeli. She had blond hair and round glasses.

Iliko spoke to her in fluent German and even made her laugh. In the lift he told us:

"She's a kind girl, but quite neurotic. Know her from Berlin. She had a crush on this Turk tea trader." Then he sighed ruefully. "I haven't had sex for eight months. It might be worth considering her ..."

Zviad and I were allocated rooms on the ninth floor; Iliko was on the eleventh. Zviad's windows overlooked old Lisbon; mine, the new part.

Soon Iliko knocked on my door.

"Have you got slippers in your room?" he asked.

I had a look around and indeed, I found a pair of soft slippers under the clothes hangers.

"The rogues! I don't have them. You might have a bathrobe

there, as well," he said, peeping into the bathroom but finding nothing to his interest.

"They must have given them to the writers, no?" He sulkily looked down at my hotel slippers.

"You can have them if you wish," I said. "I've brought my own."

"Can I?" His eyes brightened up.

"I never leave Tbilisi without them."

"Yeah, these are real good," he said, stuffing them into the pocket of his checkered jacket. "They aren't meant to be for one-off use, you know," he explained. "You can use them for a time, so why leave them behind, right?"

"Oh," he turned in the doorway, "have a rest before the meal in two hours."

As soon as I closed the door behind Iliko, Zviad called me.

"How do I phone Tbilisi?"

I thought I was surrounded by maniacs. Controlling my disgust, I patiently dictated every digit to be dialed for the call.

The meal mentioned by Iliko was laid out in the hotel breakfast hall.

Iliko introduced us to Heinz and Rudy:

"These are our bosses."

Heinz was a withered man of indeterminate age. Rudy was a tall centaur with four earrings in his left ear.

Laughing, Heinz reminded me of his mistake as he shook my hand:

"Mrs. Zaza!"

I laughed loudly at his joke and was joined by others.

"They say the Caucasians don't easily forgive such mistakes," he went on with a smile. "I told Rudy I made a fatal mistake and will be killed for it. But he calmed me down, saying you're a writer and will let it go."

We all laugh even louder at this. Rudy is frightening, laughing like a robot: his eyes are empty, his mouth closed, while the sound comes directly from his lungs. Heinz becomes serious again.

"Have you met your colleagues?" he asks, immediately answering his own question: "Some of them haven't arrived yet. We're expecting more tomorrow."

"It's good you're alive," Rudy contributes to the conversation. "There was a lot of talk about your war."

That's exactly how he puts it: *your war.*

"Yeah, when the Russians bombed you, we were very worried," Heinz agrees. "It was awful," he says, shaking his head in commiseration.

"We plan to take it out on the Russians here," I say laughing.

Heinz laughs too, but Rudy looks tense. He feels I'm joking but doesn't fully trust me. Who knows what I'm capable of?

"It's quite peaceful now, isn't it?" Heinz asks.

"What peace are you talking about?" Iliko winces. "They're bringing their army into Abkhazia and South Ossetia! Do you know where Ossetia is? Right in the heart of Georgia. Akhalgori . . . it's a town."

"I know Gori," Heinz volunteers. "It's Stalin's birthplace."

"No, no." Iliko becomes agitated. "Gori is different. It was also shelled, but Akhalgori is a bit higher," and he begins drawing an imaginary map in the air. "No Ossetians live there, only Georgians . . . But now the Russians have taken the town, which means they've occupied the whole region. Do you understand? Now, Tbilisi, the capital, is only a forty-minute drive from there. So, if they want, they can be in Tbilisi in forty minutes. They can easily crush us in a mere forty minutes."

"How dreadful," Heinz sighs, but he's worried only for the sake of being civil—his gaze darts to other guests. On the other hand, Rudy listens to Iliko very attentively, with an angry expression. However, I'm not sure if he's angry with the Russians, the Georgians or his Chancellor.

"We're practically conquered," Iliko laughs for no apparent reason.

"I believe it's George Bush's fault," Rudy concludes.

"What does Bush have to do with it?" Iliko sounds surprised. "It was Putin who bombed us, not Bush! Let's leave it to the Iraqis to swear at Bush. It's Putin who's killing us," he laughs again.

"Enough of politics!" Heinz stretches his arms like a TV host. "Shall we leave politics behind and only discuss literature on the train?" He turns to me, "You didn't tell me if you've met your colleagues."

"I have." I point at Zviad. "Back in Tbilisi," I chuckle.

"Are you laughing at me, man?" Zviad looks confused. He finds it hard to believe I'm capable of betraying him and siding with the people speaking a foreign language.

My joke is appreciated by Rudy with the sound:

"Ha."

That's his laugh.

"Enjoy yourselves," Heinz commands, and moves away. Rudy follows him like a slave.

"Are they lovers?" I ask Iliko.

"Rudy's new," he explains. "I used to know the previous one."

"See what's going on here?" I point out to Zviad.

"Are they my kids or what? I don't give a damn!" he explodes.

"Let's have a look at the food they're offering." Iliko moves toward the long table.

Looking rather miserable, the Armenians stand aloof, helping themselves to some meat dish. The Russians have already changed into sandals. The Big Russian is wearing a pair of green shorts, showing his white legs (just like grandma's)—withered and hairless. No sign of the Chechen and the Azeri. A heron-like man (the Belgian poet) seems the most gluttonous: stretching his long neck, he inspects all the sandwiches on all plates, then eats some with an expression of disgust and great doubt.

I had no wish to meet anyone. I even regretted I had to spend a whole month looking at these faces. Exhausted by lack of sleep, I mechanically stuffed an assortment of colorful food into my mouth.

"Hello, Georgian!" I was surprised to hear Armenian Zeituntsyan address me in my native tongue. With my mouth full, I didn't reply, just nodded in the noblest way I could manage. Iliko was talking to a elderly lean woman, while Zviad was putting tiny salmon sandwiches into a napkin. I thought it was an ideal moment to sneak out, so as soon as I drained my glass of orange juice, I edged toward the exit. On the way I smiled at Heinz and Rudy and even showed a thumbs-up sign. That's how I rated the supper.

Now it's hard to remember where I'd seen Helena for the first time: at the elevators or at the hall door. Where was it exactly that my month-long journey acquired meaning?

. . .

2 October. Lisbon.

I succeeded in having it my way. We're in Lisbon.

He thinks I'm still a child. It drives me mad. Would it be better— me in Athens, him over here? "Do as you please. I don't mind." Keeps repeating for the last seven years . . . But still sulks when I do as I please. We kind of talked in Athens. "I'm old, blah-blah-blah . . ." The concert at the Herodion. Mozart. Symphony sol major. Mahler Chamber Orchestra. Hardly managed a page and a half. Don't even remember what I wrote. We smoked. Maček drank in the airport. He's "punishing" me. Says: "You've been flirting with Eugene. But that's only natural." And he means a gay chap! I say, "You're not sure what you want. I know what I want: I'm with you and that's it." He sent some money to his eldest son. Cracked jokes: "You're fit to be his wife, not mine." It's been like this for the last month. He's been pretty muddled since he talked with Mum. "I promised your mum I wouldn't stand in your way." Screw you both! We arrived in Lisbon yesterday. It's the third seminar this year I'm accompanying him on. We're to be on a train for 30 days. I'm not sure whether it was a good idea to come with him. Am I stubborn? He easily leaves me on my own. Believes he's controlling it as well. "It's better for you. You're just obsessed." I refuse to believe he's so conceited. He had a drink and became jealous of Eugene. He's real when he drinks. How wonderful it was in Nancy! The day after tomorrow we'll be in Madrid. All sorts of people here. But the same, in a way. I have a feeling they're the same we saw in Nancy and Constantinople: notepads, shorts, glasses, pipes, beards . . . (even women!). The boss is German. With a round bum. But gay. They're all gay! That's why he feels safe for me to be on my own. I shouldn't have brought the black dress. All women are dressed like hikers here. Maček pretends he doesn't care.

I'm too lazy to write this.

4. THE TRAIN

"Helena." I take pleasure in writing her name in Latin letters. I recall the first seconds, minutes and days spent with her. Writing her name reminds me of my first impressions of Helena.

Helena. A stranger. So attractive. I never thought Latin letters could excite me so much.

Helena reminds me of her slightly rounded belly, the line from the belly button to her chest, the taste of her lips, the unnaturally shiny breasts, the nipples hardening at a touch, her black hair coming down her back, her knee at her mouth and the way she bit it when I entered her.

When I entered her.

How strikingly unsexual my mother tongue is! What the hell is this "when I enter her"? The Georgian language can't stand a sexual act. If you decide to describe an intercourse in my language, it becomes either unbearably high-flown or amazingly aggressive. Nothing in between. *When I enter her* or *when I fuck her.* You have to choose either one or another, but I like neither. The former is uninteresting and dead, the latter loveless and irate. There's no sex in Georgian—only a hint at it. But I refuse to hint at what I want to describe. I prefer to be straightforward about my feelings and emotions. I'd love to say how Helena bit her own knee when we had sex. But I lose all interest for the episode because of the words that come to my mind. Where's passion when one has to write: *we had sex?*

Well, yes, there's yet another possibility, for instance: *while we screwed.* Sounds like swearing at the person you love. However,

32

there's a medical term as well: *coitus*. But that's neither medicine nor sex—it's just daft. And all the while, I'd like everyone to fall for Helena as she bit her own knee in the act . . . I'd hate to spoil a lovely episode with the grotesque by adopting the pretentious sex terminology fossilized in my native tongue.

As I writer I'm not happy with the Latin writing of "Helena." "Helena" is a human choice, not that of a writer. Barbarisms annoy me greatly—only tasteless writers revert to writing their sweethearts' names using the Latin alphabet. That's my conviction, for some obscure reason. But still, something's going on inside me when I write H E L E N A. Her name written in Georgian only reminds me of how we parted and not the passion we had for each other. Helena in the Georgian script depresses me. Saddens me. I realize I let something precious slip through my fingers.

It's true I can't recall where I first saw her (near the elevators or at the hall entrance?), but I'll always remember what she was wearing. Later, when I described her clothes in detail, she was visibly impressed and that's not my imagination. I didn't want to make a mistake, so I concentrated hard and came up with an exact description of her clothes she had on that day. The previous Elene (sorry, Elene, for mentioning you in this way) found such things fascinating. Women never dress "casually"—they always consider the context, so they invariably remember what they were wearing for this or that occasion and why. Everything is carefully and consciously chosen, the problem is interpreting the meaning. When I told the previous Elene she was wearing green jogging shoes at the time we met, her solemn reply was she hadn't cared for me and wished to express exactly that. Do you get it? I'll never buy such crap! She just wanted to look like a girl fed up with male attention. That was the message sent and that's how I was to interpret her green jogging shoes.

Helena looked like a film star. She floated into the lobby like a movie ghost . . . She was holding hands with her husband, dragging him along as if he were a stubborn child.

What do I remember?

Her white dress, her white teeth, her cheek bones, her black eyes and a glittering silver chain hanging down her neck and resting on her tanned chest.

I failed to notice at the time, but later her burgundy lips, the ideal oval of her fox-like face, and a slightly narrow chin became extremely important.

Helena didn't look at me then.

I don't seem to exist when it comes to foreign women. They just don't see me and that's a fact. I'm a mere foreign specter living my own life—well outside their sexual and aesthetic interests.

I did look at her, thought her attractive, and forgot about her then and there.

In an hour I was in my hotel bed, trying to go to sleep and praying Zviad wouldn't come knocking on my door ("Wanna drink, pal?"). Apparently, I was heard in the heavens, as that day I was spared the unwanted company. I was safe.

The whole next day, however, we spent roaming the hilly streets of Lisbon.

"In the eighteenth century the entire city was razed to the ground by an earthquake," Iliko told us. "But I'm not interested in the royal Lisbon. The real city is out there, behind those houses. Yesterday I even came across street football."

Iliko headed for small taverns without intending to spend money in them, though.

"Let's not sit here, let's just have a look," he suggested. "Think of the pittance we've been given." He turned on the organizers. "Are we supposed to starve or what? All Germans I know are misers."

Zviad was carrying two small bags he'd bought for his children. He'd got two mini-bear bags made in China at one of the street stalls.

"You could have bought them in Tbilisi," Iliko reasoned with him.

It was a sensible comment. For the entire month Zviad kept buying things he could have easily found in Tbilisi markets. He definitely had a knack of finding dismal shops and stalls, which became clear for me in Lisbon. As opposed to Iliko, it didn't annoy me in the least.

"Why on earth is he wasting his money?" he raved. "If he bothered to walk a little further, he'd find better stuff! One should leave him among the black marketers, then he'd be really happy. He's got no business among writers! The likes of him feel miserable here."

"We're visiting other cities, you know. Don't spend all you've got here. We won't be given any more," he warned Zviad like a strict teacher.

I'm not sure if Zviad was miserable in Europe. All I know is we felt terrified when we were taken to our train. No, it wasn't the train itself that was scary—we were daunted by the number of writers and poets! We'd only seen a tenth at the supper the previous evening. Many more had arrived and what's more, they were all drunk. My heart sank. I hated the idea of meeting them, remembering their names and seeing them day in day out. How I hated being with new people!

I remember sharing my fear with Iliko.

"Don't worry," he calmed me in his typical way, "they hate you too."

The Estonian poet looked most ominous: a shaved head, a goatee, a leather suit and plenty of metal hanging down his neck. More importantly, he was alarmingly fat and disturbingly wobbly.

"I hope we're not in the same compartment." I gave Iliko a frightened smile.

Neither was I thrilled with the train—it's our touristic trait: we Georgians aren't easily impressed at first sight. I had expected a modern, shark-like steel structure but was staring at a colorfully painted steam train. The carriages were painted in yellow and brown with LITERATURE-EXPRESS written all over them—horizontally, vertically and in circles.

We soon found out that only we, the Georgians, felt dejected. Others were laughing, talking loudly, shouting, drinking and meeting each other in an enthusiastic way. Heinz was at one of the carriages, talking to reporters. One of them had an enormous camera on his shoulder, while an aging sound boy shoved a bushy microphone at him. Later I saw this footage on the Net and when I glimpsed Helena in the background, my heart missed a beat, then quickened as I watched the five-minute long coverage at least ten times.

The Georgians are so miserable! We expect danger from all sides, so we tend to frown in advance. That's the way we defend ourselves. The problem with Zviad and myself is easily explained: both are the products of our native Tbilisi, scared stiff of strangers, eyeing them with suspicion and utter distrust. But what was wrong with Iliko? He behaved exactly like us at the time. But, thank God, not for long. One of the trip organizers, blond Milena, came running and gave Iliko our carriage and seat numbers.

Iliko is a true womanizer. He goes for any female, regardless of her looks. And of course, her character isn't even worth mentioning. He doesn't believe in long-term relationships so he shows no interest in finding out what women really want or need. He only cares about the easily approachable ones, which saves him effort in taking them to bed.

You can't imagine how he transformed when Milena appeared. He joked with her, laughed raucously and even brushed her freckled arm with his hand.

That day I spotted fair hair in Milena's armpit. Quite long at that. Later I discovered more long hair on her white thighs.

"I like it," Iliko said. "She's nature's daughter. No need to shave!"

I was prepared to argue but at that minute Heinz sounded an old-fashioned silver bell and let out a loud, neurotic laugh.

"We're due out!" Iliko yelled.

Some of the passengers got their cameras out and took pictures of Heinz ringing the bell.

So very original: *Heinz ringing the bell. So cute!*

We found our carriage number six and made it to our seats, a bit sweaty though. There were no compartments, which meant we were saved from sharing one with the weird Estonian. We couldn't see other ex-Soviets. We were among unfamiliar people, smiling at them without saying anything.

"How long is it to Madrid?" I asked Iliko.

"We're supposed to spend a month on the train, so how do hours matter?" came his philosophical answer.

Soon we moved out of the station. The train produced a howl-like signal for departure. We all laughed. Had we been alone, we definitely wouldn't have, but being uncertain what to do, we laughed. In that way, firstly, we reacted to the howling sound and, secondly, we expressed affability toward each other: *Isn't it wonderful that our journey has started?*

Next I witnessed a comical show: in an instant everyone turned into writers.

All stereotypes came to life simultaneously.

They all drew out writing pads, turned on their laptops, spread papers across the tables, held pencils in their mouths and stared out at the changing landscape with silent admiration. The little man with a goatee sitting across from me took out a newspaper with his own photo on the front page, put it on his knees and started reading. He was Paulo Tesheira, a Portuguese writer-journalist, a silent photographer, who watched his colleagues with his small, sly eyes—just like a secret agent.

A French grandma in jeans (Mme Roget) was jotting down her thoughts in her ancient notepad; a bearded young man with long ringlets (Vitas from Lithuania) was hitting the keyboard of his laptop, while the Czech speaking the elfin language (Iliko's description of his German) was writing in a lined notebook. The writing bug had bitten everyone on the Lit Express. These people tremendously enjoyed playing the role of a writer—their zest for literature was mind-boggling! Could it be that this kind of behavior was natural and it was me being inadequate? Me with a confused-ironic-stunned expression? Should I have also pulled out a notepad, taken a minute to think and transferred my impressions and emotions onto the paper, just like everyone else? Yes, I was absolutely sure they were recording their impressions of that very minute. They felt comfortable—like genuine writers, poets, or whatever. Felt great, in short, attempting to record this wonderful moment of romantic-professional-spiritual comfort. Right there, before my eyes, an enormous heap of pulp-fiction was created. Literary surrogate in huge amounts—texts not worth a penny! No one on the face of the earth could have convinced me that at the time—on the train just out of the station—anyone had anything fascinating or valuable to say. They were nothing but cons! I had a feeling that the entire space was filled with their artificial, one-off plots . . . I'd have gladly joined them as a chemist or a laryngologist—anyone but a writer. Their literary passion put me off my profession in a matter of few seconds.

Nudging me, Iliko poured a bucket of icy water over me by saying:

"Now you see why they're doing so well?"

"Why?" I asked in surprise.

"Because they work!"

"You don't say so!" I laughed. He was inane.

I'm not sure if it was my reaction that irritated him but suddenly he attacked Georgian writers and Georgian literature in general. He was so vehement that Zviad and I exchanged stunned glances, as if just sworn at.

"What's going on in Georgian literature anyway?" he began. "I haven't read anything Georgian in twenty years."

What could we say in reply? His question was asked in a tone that instantly informed us our answer had no importance whatsoever.

"You're a closed nation," he announced. "The entirety of Georgian literature is one big provincial crap! First it was the rural problems, then all these drug addicts and the shit of the '90s! Are you copying from each other or what? And this disgusting egocentrism! I haven't read a single Georgian book where I'm able to forget the author. I'm reading this shit and I'm haunted by the fucking author, with his ghastly stubble and empty pocket, reeking of cigarette smoke."

"Do you know any other word apart from *shit*?" Zviad laughed, but his face was already flushed.

I didn't utter a word. I agreed with Iliko on practically every point.

"The poetry is tasteless!" He raised his voice, annoyed by Zviad's remark. "Provincial, pathetic and tedious, sheer epigonism! Who needs such claptrap? Who's gonna be interested in this shit?"

"Do you consider the entirety of Georgian poetry tastelessly provincial?" Zviad asked with childish naïveté.

"I do, all of it!"

"Including Rustaveli? Good for you!" Zviad laughed but actually was pretty upset.

"Theirs is a dynamic process, but what's going on in Georgia? An illusion that something's happening . . . In reality, nothing at all. Everything's dead, isn't it?" Iliko turned to me.

"Are you by any chance writing at your leisure?" Zviad asked him, furtively glancing at me. "You seem suspiciously knowledgeable. And you don't sound as if you last read a Georgian book twenty years ago."

"Who says the Georgians have got books?" It didn't sound ironic anymore. Hatred and sarcasm came gushing from Iliko now. "If they're real books, why aren't they sold here? Why do they refuse to read your books about your junkies here?"

"Very little is being written," I interfered at this point. "You can't compare us to the Germans and the French. In our country five people read books while two write them."

"And those two are either about themselves or junkies!"

"There are other themes. You're behind the times."

"The same old shit, I bet!"

I didn't think it was worth arguing with him. I was too lazy for that. Besides, he was partially right. Also, Zviad's guess had to be correct: he sounded like an angry writer, not a frustrated reader. There are some who fear publication, or rather fear the failure of their publication. He must have been working on something, a text he kept editing, tearing up, returning to it and as time went by he got more and more convinced he was far from completion. That's the reason he was permanently irritable: he took literature with such a lot of responsibility while the likes of us, half-assed writers, had the audacity to publish our literary garbage.

"Experimenting isn't helping either," Iliko preached. "I used to believe experiments were necessary, but I don't think so, not anymore . . . Because everything turns into an experiment in Georgia. You just can't get past experimenting . . ."

"Wait a second," I interrupted him. "Look at these people. Are they better off? They write the same kind of shit as we do. When was the last time you read a good book?"

"I haven't read anything in five years."

"Didn't you say twenty?" Zviad asked.

"Twenty years of not reading Georgian stuff, five years of the rest," he answered with a deadly serious expression.

Because you're too cheap to spend money on books, I thought to myself, but said nothing.

"Ah," Zviad sighed, "I'll have a smoke." He rose to his feet.

"Where?" Iliko sounded alarmed. "Don't smoke in the toilet. It's not allowed."

"Why would I? I'll find a smoking corner. There has to be one." Zviad sounded insulted.

"I'm not sure about that," Iliko said severely. "You'll have to give up smoking."

"Writing too, ha?" Zviad chuckled and looked at me. He always looked my way whenever he made a joke. "I'll find one." He moved away.

"Is he your friend?" Iliko asked me.

"Want to criticize him?" I laughed.

"Do you like his poems?"

"They aren't bad."

"Can I find them on the Net? Has the bugger published anything?"

"He isn't a bugger. He's got an army of fans."

"Of ugly girls."

"But sexy."

"No way," Iliko grimaced. "I've never heard of an enthusiastic reader being a beautiful girl in Georgia. A reader should be sexy enough for a screw."

He's a maniac, I thought and liked him even more. I had no more doubts he was a secret writer. Only a true writer could fantasize about sleeping with a beautiful reader. It wasn't typically a reader's fantasy.

"But that's not the main point." He looked drained now. As was his habit, he soon changed into a despondent chap. "I still prefer the new ones to the old. The bugger, I'm certain, writes in a more interesting way than those of the '70s."

"He's not a bugger!" I protested.

"Doesn't matter. He's better than the old ones, isn't he?"

"I don't know," I shrugged. "I don't really care."

Suddenly I was too weary of the banalities I was hearing. As if ejected from my seat by an invisible force, I sprang to my feet, frightening Iliko as I did so.

"Are you off for a cig?"

"Nope. For a piss. I don't smoke."

Having walked through two carriages, I concluded that the most zealous and active writers occupied our carriage. Others were clearly more reserved compared to our co-travelers.

Helena was in the eighth carriage. She was wearing white again (pants and a T-shirt) and was scribbling (!) in her little book.

As soon as I saw her I remembered I liked her the previous evening.

Helena also looked at me and though I hadn't done anything wrong (we had just looked at each other, no harm done, right?), I instinctively threw a furtive glance at the man sitting next to her.

Helena wasn't wearing a bra. Her T-shirt bulged revealingly. Did the man notice that I had noticed?

It was odd. Foreign women normally ignore me, but this one looked at me.

I don't remember what I did. I believe I smiled at her and walked past. Nothing else that time.

5. MADRID

This is a city of squares and kissing couples. I've never seen so many young people kissing each other. Wherever you look, you see passionately kissing couples.

One lad with a crew cut stuck in my memory particularly vividly. He didn't give his poor girl a chance to breathe. I was sitting in a cafe in front of our hotel and wasn't in the least keen on watching them, but I couldn't help looking at them. It was absolutely impossible not to notice what was going on. Generally speaking, I'll never get accustomed to ignoring people kissing in public. I know perfectly well I have to get used to not reacting, I have to learn not to show surprise and take it calmly, but I still can't help staring and feeling irritation: Doesn't our presence get in their way? Don't they find us redundant? I've always doubted (and will still do) the sincerity of publicly kissing people. Okay, I understand it when the young people just fallen for each other can't curb their feelings—they are drawn to each other like magnets. But what do long-standing couples find enjoyable in socializing their passion? Or do they only get horny by exhibitionistic kissing? If left alone, they might not even as much as look at each other.

The crew cut and his girlfriend definitely were old-timers. They weren't swept by love fervor: their kissing was more like a sport, very similar to what porn actors do. The lad was leaning against the wall, pressing the girl closely and holding her buttocks in a tight grip. They seemed to be intent on setting a new world record—ten minutes of nonstop kissing with closed eyes.

Despite my irritation, I believe it was while watching their exertion I thought it'd be good to have someone, to have a chance of kissing that girl in white . . .

When we arrived in Madrid, Iliko passed on Heinz's new order:

"Tomorrow you're all going to be taken to read in public. Have you brought your writing? You can choose a fragment."

"Am I supposed to read in Georgian?" I asked in surprise.

"Yeah. Everyone's doing their own language."

"They won't be able to understand a single word!"

"I don't give a damn!"

"I prefer the poets to read aloud. I hate that."

"The poets are also expected to read, don't worry."

"I don't care if they do." I can be extremely stubborn at times. "Let's pretend you haven't told me anything."

"It's offensive. No one will understand if you skip it." He sounded angry. At that minute I must have irritated him immensely: he couldn't stand irresponsibly egocentric Georgians. I was being just one of them at the time.

"What's there to worry about, it's just reading aloud, isn't it?" Zviad told me.

As opposed to me, he was ecstatic to be given a chance to demonstrate his talent. I had heard he was exceptionally skillful at reciting his own poetry. On the whole, I like hearing poetry read by its authors. Good ones are really very impressive. At the same time, I absolutely hate actors reading literary excerpts.

To cut a long story short, that night I fell asleep having decided I wasn't going to read anything, but, as expected, I was uneasy at it all. You might choose not to believe it but I was scared of Heinz. Definitely scared, which pretty much describes how I felt about him. Somehow he managed to turn us into unresisting slaves and did it with a wise subtlety. I caught myself at it and noticed others as well: For some obscure reason we all tried to please and flatter him. Without even realizing why we felt the need to do so. Could it be that he had given us money? Normally people feel grateful and sympathize with those who give them money. Or could it be that, like a true German, Heinz was an expert in manipulating human minds by applying various psychological methods? I'm still not sure whether it was hypnosis or something else, but we all tried—to a varying degree—to deserve a warm smile or a kind glance from him.

As soon as we woke up the next morning, we headed for the Prado, though Iliko refused to accompany us.

"I hate museums," he said. "I prefer live people."

He was lying. I was absolutely certain he had spent days and days in Berlin museums . . . Young, penniless, and inquisitive.

Curiously enough, only we—the Azeri detective writer, the Armenians, the Russians, and one Bulgarian—went to the Prado. There was no sign of the "western camp" in the museum.

I was wearing beach flip-flops because I felt more comfortable and less like a tourist. The Russians resembled clowns in their multicolored hats and with huge cameras. The Big Russian was in his customary sandals.

I could sense Zviad's uneasiness at my flip-flops. He looked at me several times and eventually said something I didn't expect from him:

"You're childish." That was his appraisal of my eccentricity.

The Little Russian followed the example of some Japanese tourists and took a snapshot of Bosch's *Hell*. The museum attendant shouted at the top of his voice that it was forbidden to take pictures. Strangely, no one forbade the Japanese.

"The Russians are disliked everywhere," Zviad concluded.

The Azeri writer of detective books treated me to a sandwich and juice. With bits of food clinging to his teeth (just like mine, I guess), he asked in a fatherly tone:

"Are you a poet?"

It must be disquieting to be obliged to give a positive answer if you are one. Isn't it comical to say, *Yes, I am a poet?* It's much more modest to say, *I write stories.*

"We are colleagues then!" he rejoiced.

"Indeed, we are."

"I gather I'll listen to you today," he smiled at me.

He was going to listen but would he be able to understand? Did he think I planned to read in English, Russian or Azerbaijani? Or did he know Georgian?

"I don't think I will be reading," I winced. "I don't like reading to a lot of people."

"Don't you?" Eldar was surprised. "Such a pity."

"Yes." Then I added, more to convince myself, "I don't suppose I'll be reading."

Contrary to my principles, at seven that evening I was in the hall, waiting for my turn to read out loud to the assembled colleagues.

I don't know what forced me to walk into that hall or what made me change my mind that evening. Was it my slavish compliance with Heinz, the sense of tactfulness, the fear of being exposed as an unruly participant or the conceit—a powerful drive behind any ambition? *You're a writer too and should be among your colleagues. So what if only Zviad and Iliko are going to understand you? The main thing is for the organizers to see you there, so that they know they haven't wasted their efforts and expenses on you.*

Or was it simpler and more dignified? Could it be that I wanted to see the girl I bumped into in Lisbon and then saw in the eighth carriage?

Whatever the reasons, I found myself in the literary Babylon. The writers read their pieces in their native languages, blushed, waved their arms, fidgeted and howled, but, alas, failed to make us understand. God knows how much we craved to be heard, how much we wished our work to be appreciated by the listeners! True, we only understood our own languages, but was it possible that the audience could exercise their intuition, audio or some supernatural sensors in order to realize we were reciting extraordinary texts?

There he was, an Albanian, giving an emotional, singsong recital of his poem or whatever it was. I'm pretty sure had I known Albanian, I'd have enjoyed some of it. But all I heard at the time was a flow of harsh, unpleasant sounds gushing in a strange Italo-Slavonic accent. No doubt, my recital would leave the same impression on the listeners—my mother tongue was bound to sound unsavory, a mere cacophony of guttural noises. An introduction in English might have helped though: *Please listen carefully as the Lord will judge you in this language. My native tongue is the language of the doomsday.* Had I been bolder, I'd bring forth the infallible authority of Ioanne-Zosime . . .

Throughout, Heinz's face showed sheer delight. He was listening without understanding a word! And all the while, with visibly throbbing veins, the writers exerted themselves, sweating, flailing their arms, tensing their muscles in an attempt to prove their talent and uniqueness.

Suddenly it dawned on me that Heinz and Rudy were nothing but conmen. They had planned that reading orgy just to proudly claim later that: "We created the conditions where all writers got to know each other. The evening was extremely interesting and significant for everyone involved." What was interesting? The way we howled and bawled but remained deaf and dumb?

All in all, I was able to follow the Russians, Eldar Aliev from Azerbaijan (as he wrote his books in Russian), a Dane who read his poem in English and a lovable grandpa from Belgium (who I initially mistook for an Englishman). However, this Bernard Shaw-like, white-bearded elderly man spoke English with such an accent that I missed most of his poetic-philosophical essay.

Had I lived in medieval Europe and been an inquisitor chasing heretics, I'd have definitely introduced the following torture: I'd make heretics listen to a text in an unknown language to them until they confessed, pleading guilty of liaising with the Devil. Having sat through our international literary evening, I had no doubt the method could be highly effective in owning up to all possible or impossible sins. How would it feel if you were a decent German heretic with the sound knowledge of German and Latin, a little Ancient Greek as well, but were made to listen to the Koran in Arabic? You'd confess to anything, wouldn't you?

It might have been the sound of my native language that cheered me up or else Zviad's poem was really good, but the fact is I was wide awake, starting to like this man. Suddenly I realized Zviad Meipariani wasn't an insignificant poet and got terribly angry with myself—why did I persevere in hating him and on what grounds? Zviad sounded like a deacon reading a prayer. He attempted to cue the audience to the rhythm of his poem, to keep them on the same wavelength and by all evidence he succeeded: as opposed to others, his efforts weren't futile. Everyone listened. No irritating noises, no rustling or whispering. Zviad managed to grab their attention in full. In the meantime, I was swept by the most sentimental banalities: there he is, a poet from a country inhumanly bombed, his grief genuine and acute. What country is that? Oh, Georgia? Yeah, Russia dropped bombs on them a couple of months ago . . . Now it's crystal clear why his poem is like a lament. But do we feel sorrow, do we feel like crying? Of course we do, he succeeded in making us cry . . .

O, divine naïveté! What tears, what sorrow! My foot! Who was there to remember the bombs? But aren't we exactly like that? What do I care what's going on, say, in Pakistan? We are just another Pakistan for them.

Zviad was even awarded with some clapping. Flushed and content, he stepped down from the dais. Beads of sweat glittered above his upper lip.

"You're really good," I told him.

"I know," he smiled happily.

Then it was my turn.

The walk between my seat and the dais seemed endless. I had my short stories in my back pocket (a small book, not even a hundred pages). My hands were shaking as if I had Parkinson's disease. Dreadful! I willed them not to, but they kept shaking as if of their own volition. Still trembling, I found the story *The Red Forest*, greeted the audience in English, adding that I wasn't particularly good at reading aloud, so my story wasn't necessarily that bad. I attempted a joke, but no one laughed. Only Heinz was smiling. I guess that was part of his genial disposition toward the whole event. As usual, I was caught off balance by my own voice distorted by the microphone. Why on earth does our own voice sound completely different from the inside? I wonder if anthropologists have any explanation. Many years ago, the birthday party of one of my classmates was filmed and then the tape circulated among all the kids' families. I still remember my shock at hearing my voice . . . I refused to believe those high-pitched, alien sounds were produced by me. This strange-sounding, unfamiliar—but definitely my own—timbre still baffles me. I'm not sure if it was just to quell my uneasiness or from sheer shyness, but I began to read barely louder than a whisper. All I wanted was to go through one single paragraph and return to my seat having done my duty. I soon heard the rustle of the bored and the weary (the noise I had made myself not long ago when others stood at the microphone). So I sped up, murdering the long paragraph complete with complex sentences with great dignity and immense hatred.

That girl, Helena, was sitting in the front row. When I looked up from the page I was reading, she was the one I saw. Strangely enough, I failed to notice her on my way to the dais. I can't say she was listening with close attention, but she was watching me with unmistakable interest. I even began to question if she understood

Georgian. Sitting with her legs crossed and frowning at me, she had her hands crossed in her lap, looking with a mixture of fear and concentration. That minute she was like a small animal—dark eyes, longish nose and sharp chin.

It was impossible not to notice her legs. I did notice them. What I didn't know was whether she had a tan or it was her natural olive skin. Her right thigh was divided by a long line at the perfect, absolutely ideal place. I called it the sex-muscle.

Since I arrived, it was the third time I came across Helena's dark eyes. Until then, before climbing down from the dais, I'd thought she was attractive, nothing more. I hadn't gone further, even in my fantasies. Everything changed that evening. I believe that was the moment I got seriously interested in her.

I clearly recall shoving my book into the back pocket of my trousers, coming down from the dais and smiling at Helena. She didn't take her eyes off me—I actually believe she even turned her head to follow me as I went past. No smile though. I was confused. You smile at a foreigner and don't get one in reply? Such things never happen in Europe.

. . .

5 October. Madrid.

I bought a pink caterpillar for Iako. 8 euros. An ice-cream seller Barbie and a blue shirt for Piso and Antoshka. 12 euro and 4.80. A lighter for Zaur—3 euros. I saw a pair of shoes for Ekuna, but thought 35 was too expensive. I'll find something else. Besides, they had a silver line at the sole, so she mightn't even liked them. And yeah, I got myself a gray waistcoat—15 euros. Had it on at the reading this evening. And a reproduction of Bosch's Hell—1 euro. All in all, I've spent 54. Our per diem is nearly 600 euros. Yesterday's 50 have to be taken off too. I need to spend more carefully. These guys look down on street stalls. Zaza's cool, a real man. The other one's a prick. Dresses like a clown. Lectured us on literature the other day. Today I shut his fucking mouth with my "Dead Hours"! I read in my old style, with my endings. There's a woman from Croatia here. She shook my hand saying I was really good. In general, the level's pretty high. Some serious poets. I liked the Russian and a Spaniard, Miguel. He broke the rhyme, like a cardiogram. I thought it was cool. They let us read only one poem or else I'd have read "The Rooster's Prayer" as well. I supported Miguel with "Super! Super!" Now we're buddies. He gave me an album with his poems and his wife's photos—she's naked. No bra, no panties. She was standing right there and he introduced her to me. She definitely looks better in the photos. Apparently they're old. Now her hair looks different too. We spoke with our hands. He'd say "Robert Burns," for instance, and I'd go "Oh!" He blew kisses, so did I. We communicated with names, so to speak. Probed each other's tastes. I managed to make myself understood. Then Zaza and I walked through the streets. I am impressed with Madrid! We went to the Prado (I bought Piso's Barbie somewhere there). Zaza's pretty reserved. Looks like he needs a woman's company. He pointed out every kissing couple he came across. I haven't yet found a key to him. He keeps to himself, but watches you closely. I'm surprised his mother, a woman with balls, can have such a tactful and quiet son. He can't stand Iliko and sticks to me. Like a younger brother. If interested in something, it's only me he asks. I tell him it's my first time in Europe, can't he find someone more experienced? Two years ago everyone supported Menabde with his short stories, but the prize was given to Zaza's book. I'd also thought Menabde deserved it. When I got acquainted with him, I changed my mind. He hasn't taken after his mum, nothing in common. Kindhearted and somewhat pitiable. He's young but already has got gray streaks in his hair. Iliko is absolutely disgusting, always getting at the boy. He dares not try it with me. Must be afraid. Apparently, he's in Tsertsvadze's group. Said he used to write denouncements on others for the Party. I'll tell Tsertsvadze about his reputation in the European Union. Eventually, Zaza's going to kick his ass. He's getting on our nerves and it'll be stopped when we're fed up. I've been carrying "Evrinoma's Dance" with me for a whole week, but haven't written more than three lines. Poetry has fewer chances here compared to prose. And it's only natural. How are you gonna translate "The Rooster's Prayer" into English? And they haven't got [dg] and [kh] sounds if I'm not mistaken. If I manage to adopt the correct schedule, I'll be able to write. I'm sitting in my hotel room, at the window, looking out at the night city, trying to capture my impressions of the moment and putting my emotions on paper. I wish my lovely Khatuna Tkemaladze were here with me!

We're off to Paris tomorrow.

6. UNDER MAČEK

We were leaving for Paris the next day. It was one in the morning. I got bored in my room and decided to go down into the lobby. If the bar was closed, I could just sit around. I wasn't keen on going outside. I don't like the night Tbilisi, so why would I like Madrid at night? The scary '90s of my native city put me off the nights spent outside. I feel much safer in lobbies.

"Excuse me, could you help me? I can't wake him up."

It was her again (fourth time) I ran into. This time at the elevators.

She spoke English with an accent. Initially I thought she was Spanish. She was visibly nervous, her lips pale.

Why me?

I didn't even understand what she wanted, who it was she couldn't wake up.

"Yes, sure," I replied, a little uncertain, waiting for her next move.

"Thank you," Helena said.

Her husband lay sprawled in one of the spacious red armchairs which added to the coziness of the lobby and which I meant to recline in. As soon as I saw him, I realized he was stone drunk. The reception clerk was standing nearby.

So, she's appealed not only to me, I thought.

"We have to heave him up," Helena addressed us in desperation, but immediately smiled to make the task sound easier. "I'm so sorry to bother you . . . He's my husband. Very drunk."

I knew I had to say something. If I found a nice Georgian girl in a similar situation, I'd definitely say, *No problem, you don't have to apologize.* Or something even shorter: *That's okay.* But because I was in Europe, I had to come up with something only a European would have said. Something like:

"Shall we call a doctor?"

"No, no," Helena sounded taken aback. "He's just had too much to drink. It happens."

I could have asked, *Are you sure?* as they do in American films, but I didn't. I already liked her and was about to show off. And under the circumstances, a mere *Are you sure?* would sound absolutely impotent.

An elderly couple walked briskly into the lobby at that very moment and the clerk hastily left us.

"Excuse me," he dropped as he headed to tend to the couple, who didn't so much as glance in our direction.

Helena bit her lip. She wasn't happy at the prospect of losing a helping hand.

"Don't worry," I said. "We can do it."

I was beginning to show off.

Initially, I didn't have a clue where to start though. There he was, a complete stranger, two heads taller than me, slouching and not even thinking of rising to his feet. I didn't have the slightest idea how to haul this massive body: should I grab him by his hands and pull or should I try to get my head under his shoulder and heave him onto my back? I did both. I pulled him to a more or less upright position, put his right arm around my shoulder, slipped my right arm under his back and attempted to yank him. Helena copied all my movements like a diligent student: she bent, put her husband's left arm across her shoulder and heaved with all her might. To no avail. He was closer to me, so it was handier for me to pull him to his feet. All of a sudden I found myself too close to a stranger's face. I even saw red pimples on his unshaved neck. I smelled wine too—he breathed spirit right into my nostrils. Little bubbles formed on his lips as he muttered. I'd never seen a head that size—we must have looked like David and Goliath. However, one thing I can say for him: when I tugged him, he didn't resist (which must be the main difference between a European and a Georgian drunk man). Helena also succeeded in raising her husband's iron-weight left side and even managed to call out to the reception clerk, who had finished with the elderly couple by then. To his credit, he came running to help drag Maček (that was Helena's husband's name) to the lifts. At that point he excused himself, explaining he couldn't leave the lobby, and sprinted to his desk.

Being in the lift proved to be the hardest part of the job. Maček leaned heavily on me, his arm only lightly resting on his wife's shoulder. My legs were shaking and I couldn't help dreading he was about to puke all over me. Helena kept apologizing every other second, driving me mad with her phony courtesy. I'd never said so many *Not at all*'s in my life. I believe I even said it once in Georgian.

I don't remember if I was able to take in Helena's beauty at that time. As the drunk giant was squashing my head and shoulders, I would have been of de Sade's pathological character if I managed to sensually appraise her under those heavy conditions, get roused and show off all at once.

But I was already badly affected by Helena: I was looking at her, being flooded with the contrastingly harmonious emotions of sadness, rage, and thrill. There was no need to think about her burgundy, now gray, lips, sharp chin, long neck, kissable ribs, hollow belly, small round breasts under her T-shirt . . . What was truly frustrating was the realization of the inevitable failure, not the task of hauling blotto Maček.

The dude had a gorgeous wife.

When the lift door opened, I heaved a sigh of relief, smiled at Helena and set to unloading Maček. I guessed I was expected to take him to the room and put him on the bed.

Hope she's going to take his trousers and socks off herself, I thought looking at her. Before parting we had to exchange a couple of words. I just couldn't turn and leave, could I?

"I'm really very sorry. Thanks a lot," she said for the hundredth time and stretched her hand for a shake.

I wanted to say he'd "sleep it off," but failed to find a corresponding English phrase. Moreover, I didn't want to make a mistake, which would put us in a more awkward situation. Everyone knows how hard it is to talk to beautiful girls one isn't familiar with. One has to be absolutely precise.

I still recall my personal experience of three years ago.

I fell for a girl I met at the seaside. She had two tiny wings tattooed on her shoulders. In the beginning it looked as if everything was fine, she seemed to respond in the same way. Then suddenly, as if I were jinxed, whatever I said or did turned out wrong. Mistakes or slipups led to more mistakes. It was only later that I realized the cause of my failure—it was our lexical incompatibility. Though we both spoke the same language, we used different words. It taught me a valuable lesson: you can't speak standard, literary Georgian to a girl. The more refined your language is, the more she is going to distance herself. I can say more: you definitely shouldn't use any commas in the phone messages sent to her! If you type a message inserting a comma, a colon or a semicolon, consider yourself suspicious to her. An exclamation and a question mark will debase you in her eyes, while an ellipsis is going to bury you forever. If a lad uses an exclamation mark and finishes his message with an ellipsis, a girl will first think he's strange, to put it mildly. But if he persists in applying fatally correct grammar, he is deemed hopeless. She might forgive once or twice, but she will certainly ignore your third message. You will end up with the punctuation marks but alone, without the girl of your dreams! Speaking of messages—they should be made of simple, three- or four-word long sentences, preferably chaotic, commonplace and, above all, without any punctuation. It would be ideal to completely discard anything complex, going for short nouns only. She'll work out the meaning herself. But don't forget to use plenty of smileys and such. Whatever you do, forget about ellipses, commas, colons and other punctuation marks! Proper punctuation and correct spelling kills the flow of love. The same can be said about your speech: success lies with a limited vocabulary. You just have to be economical and exact. You can be artificial, but be careful not to sound unnatural. An eighteen-year-old girl has no patience for a twenty-eight-year-old lad speaking literary, standard Georgian. Full stop. She is going to appreciate your rich vocabulary when she's been twice married and fed up with both husbands.

However, it wasn't only my vocabulary that ruined me. I made other grave mistakes. It's another well-known fact that you have to be ready to make concessions if you wish to maintain your relationship with a girl. I mean all sorts—aesthetic, social, and even moral compromises. You have to pretend you're rather superficial, otherwise you're going to lose your appeal. I used to say I liked the music which I actually hated but she enjoyed; I used to go places with her where I definitely didn't want to be and approved of things that I thought idiotic in my heart of hearts. In short, all was fine at first—I discarded my principles, only craving her eighteen-year-old body . . . But then I began making mistakes. Too many slipups. Once she was in a commercial. I was watching TV and there she was, my girl. I was pleasantly surprised as I hadn't known about it. So I picked up the phone and sent her a message then and there (I still remember the exact wording): "Saw u on TV u were cool." An ordinary, neutral text— and no punctuation! Why couldn't I be content with it? But no, I couldn't, being as stubborn (Elene, can you hear me?) as I am. I just need to be original! So I send another message: "Recognized your voice." And what did I get in reply? An utter defeat. "It wasn't mine. I was dubbed." And three smiling suns. Do you get it? I was punished for my lie: her voice, my foot! Nobody was speaking in that commercial. What could I write after that? Definitely not, "Oh, really? You don't say so!" I sent four smiling suns and deeply ashamed, disappeared from her life.

One day (just this one and no more about that girl) we went to a cafe with her two stupid friends. Needless to say, I had told myself (bearing in mind the above mentioned principles) that I would contribute to the conversation only if absolutely necessary. You have to keep quiet if you're hunting an eighteen-year-old. Keep quiet, emanating moderate severity and mystique. As I said, they begin appreciating talkative types only after they're twenty-five.

So, I was determined to keep my mouth shut. I sat there, listening to their inane patter. Surprisingly, they were discussing politics—yes, they were young and stupid, but argued with great enthusiasm. And suddenly, as if the heavens mocked me, one of them mentioned the political talk show of the previous night. At the end of her unintelligent and vague rendition of the show she proudly said: "It was fun." Unfortunately, I had also watched it. I don't know what came over me, but I completely forgot about my sensible strategy and attacked one of the guest speakers with deep disgust: "A real Georgian scoundrel!" Wish I hadn't said *real* at least. Before even finishing the phrase, I knew irreparable damage was done. The girls blushed, while the one I was after smiled somewhat tensely, gave me a reproachful look and said through her clenched teeth (first time I got the literal meaning of the idiom): "Ghia's great. He's Anano's dad." You've guessed right— Ghia was the politician, while Anano was the best friend of my wing-tattooed girl. So much for my sensible strategy. Not surprisingly, the girls eyed me with unhidden loathing and we left the cafe in about five minutes. Our socializing was a complete failure. True, I apologized later by sending several messages (without punctuation), but received nothing in reply. I thought she'd sulk like a child or give me an ethical lecture in line with her best teenage intolerance, but nothing happened. You normally lecture and reason with someone you care for, don't you? Someone you're deeply interested in and wish to change for the better. But she didn't care. She must have deleted me from her life the moment she left the cafe that day. I'm pretty sure she calmed her offended friend by saying: "Forget about him, he's an idiot." And the other one, insulted as she was, would have replied: "I don't give a damn, cross my heart." Such would have been their verdict—unruffled, short and sweet.

I had to avoid similar slipups with Helena. That's why I was so laconic.

I shook her hand, setting myself the task of translating "sleep it off" into English. My brain was working fast.

We were standing at the bed, shaking hands like presidents while Maček lay face up, rasping.

In the end, I opted for a simpler sentence:

"If you need, please call me. I'm in room 402. Please don't hesitate."

Then added with a smile:

"My name is Zaza."

"I'm Helena," she smiled back.

That was when I heard her name. I had no idea she was called Helena. *The second Elene in my life.* How terrible when you can't get away from Elenes.

The thought came later. That minute I was just pleasantly surprised, nothing else. Of course I could have said my ex-girlfriend was also called Elene, but you can't say everything that comes to your mind. I learnt my lesson three years ago when I was courting the girl with wings on her shoulders.

A sudden realization that I was looking for an excuse to linger frightened me. I wanted to stay with her, and the discovery was alarming. If I lingered, I'd start making mistakes, so I bid a hasty good-bye and left.

I'm scared of beautiful women . . .

7. PARIS

We were spending the night on the train. We were due to arrive in Paris in the morning.

Iliko's heart sank:

"Should we spend all night on those seats? If I don't get a good night's sleep, I'm no use the next day."

There were no berths resting against the compartment walls on our train. That's the reason Iliko was agitated. But he needn't have been. Another train was waiting for us in the station—much more comfortable, with berths and all.

That was the only instance when we didn't travel by our yellow-brown Literature Express.

Iliko's mood changed instantly:

"I like this much better! Wish it were ours for the entire trip."

Then he opened his bag and brought out a nice fluffy bathrobe. I had seen a similar one in my hotel room.

"This one can easily cost around forty euros," he said. "One missing gown won't ruin Juan Carlos!"

"Have you nicked it?" Zviad sounded incredulous.

"It's common practice," he answered. "When we were in Basel about five years ago, Heinz himself took five towels from the hotel. Pink, very good quality. I regret not having done the same." Then he added severely, "I'm sleeping on the berth below, because the upper one makes me dizzy."

He can suit himself, I thought to myself. *There's plenty of room.*

"We're likely to get the fourth passenger," he muttered with a kind of sadistic pleasure. "The Germans can't stand wasted places."

All three of us instinctively looked at the fourth, vacant place. Zviad's and my spirits dropped visibly: we knew that the fourth passenger, a total stranger, would certainly strain us. That's how we feel—the Georgians become tense among strangers.

"Hope it's not going to be that Estonian in his leather pants," I laughed. It was another self-preservation instinct—laughing to quell anxiety.

"If it's the Russians, let's beat them up," Zviad said, climbing on the upper berth.

"One Russian, not two!" Iliko corrected him. "It can only be one. There are four berths, so they can't bring in an extra one."

"They can," Zviad's voice came from above. "They sleep together."

It wasn't funny but I laughed so as not to offend him.

"If they let me sleep with Irmell, you won't hear me till we get to Berlin," Iliko said, yawning.

"You like her a lot, don't you?" I asked.

"I like them white, all white with a glowing red clitoris," he replied very solemnly.

Now it was Zviad's turn to roar with laughter, but more out of embarrassment.

Iliko chortled. He was in the mood to talk:

"They love masturbating and I enjoy watching them at it. Irmell is one of them. She's got watery eyes and pink fingertips. Her bum is rather small, but that's okay. The main thing is it shouldn't be flat or wrinkled at the end. I can't stand lined asses!"

"Let's find some whores in Paris," Zviad suggested.

"I hate whores. If there's no chance of orgasm for her, I lose interest," Iliko grimaced. Then he turned to Zviad, "I'll take you to the Bois de Boulogne to screw a couple of transvestites. They're the most expensive. If you're a poet, you should try that too."

"No, thanks, though!" he laughed.

"There's another broad here," Iliko went on. My heart missed a beat fearing he might mention Helena and start her anatomical description, just like he did with the pink-fingertipped Irmell.

But Iliko spoke about someone else:

"Milena. Doesn't wear panties. I know."

"Who's she?"

"She arrived yesterday. I talked to her before we got on the train. A necrophile's dream."

Indeed she was—skinny and pallid, with dark circles under her eyes. I couldn't figure out what he liked about her. I thought he wasn't such a maniac after all. He was just fooling us.

So I asked:

"Why do you like that cadaver?"

"That's what I like about her. She's hot inside. You can't even guess how many times she's coming. She's a multiple-orgasm type."

I didn't mean to argue. I stretched on the lower berth knowing I couldn't help thinking about Helena. I was bound to imagine having sex with her. So far thinking about her didn't hurt. I even believed I could easily get her out of my mind if I chose to.

Iliko's fears proved groundless—we didn't get the fourth passenger.

Only Miguel opened our compartment door, said "Oh," which was meant to express surprise, I assumed, and disappeared.

"Lock it," I told Iliko.

"They'll make us open it anyway," he replied sadly.

Then he addressed me with an unexpected question:

"Have you got your book here? Can I have it? I'll look through and if it puts me to sleep, it's a good one."

"I can't stand someone reading my book in my presence."

"Go on, it's a literature seminar, isn't it? You've got to get accustomed."

I wasn't lying. I can't stand being there if someone's holding my book. Once I even quarreled with my mum. We were watching TV when I saw she had my book of short stories in her hand. I demanded she read it when I wasn't around. At times like these I can't concentrate on anything else except the reader's reaction. Watching them closely, I attempt to interpret the impressions expressed on their faces, which is pretty depressing and humiliating. Probably it's my inexperience. On the other hand, I didn't want Iliko to thrive on my complexes, so I didn't persist, pulled my book from my bag and handed it to him with a smile:

"You can start reading when I'm asleep."

With an expression of deep disgust, he leafed though my book and grunted:

"The quality of publishing is questionable—one wouldn't know if it's a book or a writing pad."

Then he propped up his pillow and looked at the table of contents.

Which one is he going to read first? I wondered. There were only ten stories—the oldest and the weakest were at the end. Iliko started with the first one.

What would a reader like him find interesting in my stories? What could I have written that would amaze an eccentric like him? I had never counted on Iliko-types for appreciation and this was the first time I began to contemplate my readers.

My book seemed unbearably small in the hands of this world citizen, multicultural tramp, eternal student-intellectual and unlucky pervert. My book didn't provide enough room for the Iliko-type cosmopolitan to freely maneuver.

My mum likes my stories, but not only isn't she a world citizen, she's not even a reader, strictly speaking. She reads them because I'm her son and she loves me. She heard about Zviad and his poetry only before our departure. She accompanied me while I was getting my visa and often heard me mention his name.

Actually, Zviad is considered to be quite well-known among Georgian readers. But there are only about five thousand of those left. Most died in this or that war. Not much of an audience.

As if to annoy me, Iliko's face was devoid of any expression. His head resting on his arm, he was pulling at his earlobe.

He was reading the first story, about a shooting gallery. A man is a sharpshooter and gets a lot of toys as prizes. He's a former KGB and suffers from a severe neurosis. I think it's a funny story, but Iliko didn't laugh . . .

Iliko, my own countryman, doesn't find it funny, so why would Heinz or Rudy?

Some time ago my stories escaped the confinement of my study, passed through the small corridor and the hall, went out of the building, out into the street, then another street and seeped into the houses of the Georgian language speakers. Along with a hundred thousand similar literary amphibians, they must be still hitting the walls . . .

We are the writers of Georgian flats.

If I were younger, I'd write a story about stories that, just like our pets, feel safe and comfortable only in familiar places. I'd call it *Domestic Stories*. How secure my stories were in Mum's and Elene's hands! Purring contently, my book didn't need more air or room. But with Iliko, it felt disheveled and weary, especially when it was compared to a writing pad.

At least he could have smiled, just to be civil or make some approving noises, but no! A terrible chap . . .

Feeling upset, I picked up the book I had started reading in a toilet in Lisbon.

"It has made me hungry!" Iliko muttered under his breath and tossed my book. It landed on the little table between our berths.

Zero reaction, only *made him hungry*!

I didn't respond, attempting to concentrate on the novel, but couldn't get beyond the first sentences. If my memory doesn't fail me, it was something like this: "The baby cut from my body was standing on the rail tracks. A small, transparent body . . . And it wasn't my hallucination."

How I hate Georgian feminist novels!

I wonder if the opening phrases of my stories revolt my readers in the same way. Judging from Iliko's reaction, they do. He put the book down without uttering a single encouraging word.

He didn't like it, I thought.

I don't remember if Iliko and Zviad had anything to eat. I didn't. I fell asleep sulking. Neither did I occupy my mind with the thoughts about Helena. My professional ambitions pushed my sexual fantasies aside.

. . .

Hello Heinz,

I apologize for not replying yesterday. I haven't got my computer with me and the 'business center' of our hotel was occupied by some of our colleagues.

In short, I hope you will accept my apology:))).

To be frank, your request somewhat surprised me. I believe you could get an idea about the Georgian group on your own, without my help. But if you wish to hear my impressions directly from me, I will gladly take up, if temporarily, the function of a Stasi secret agent (don't forget that Beria, the creator of KGB, was my countryman:)))!). Also, you might be paying me specifically for this very job, so I have no moral right to refuse:))). You're the boss (as always! ref.: Antwerp, 2004 and Zwickau, 2006:))!) I'm obliged to comply. I can only speculate on the reasons you need such "information." Is it that you don't have time to get to know them better in person and need my prompts? Are you interested if they've got the potential and appeal necessary for writers? Are you interested if they're content with the trip? Are you interested if they've set up contacts with other writers? Are you interested if they're considered to be successful in their home country? Are you interested what sort of people they are? I don't know precisely what "information" you expect from me, so I'm going to provide short answers to the above:

1) To my mind, it's too early to refer to them as professionals. Both are in the process of becoming writers. Zviad is an easily translatable poet. He somehow reminds me of our mutual acquaintance (ref. Berlin, 2002), poet Max Krzhizhanowsky: the themes of death, prayer and whores. Zaza writes short stories. He makes lots of grammatical and stylistic mistakes in his Georgian, but a competent translator can easily brush up his language. His plots are original. You would like his story "Speak through the Umbilical Cord". If you get interested, I won't object to translating it myself. You know about my availability.

2) I have already assessed them as writers (see Question 1), so I'll move to the third.

3) They are quite happy to be here, though find it hard to adapt. It's a common problem for all Georgians. They prefer sticking to each other, being wary of strangers. However, these phobias subside after an initial stage. Hopefully, they will start socializing in a little while. They like it here. They went on long walks in Lisbon and Madrid. They visited the Prado in Madrid.

4) The Spanish and Croatian writers easily broke the ice with Zviad. Zaza still shuns contacts. He hasn't gone beyond greeting his colleagues.

5) Back home, they aren't known to the wide public. They are more or less popular in a relatively small circle of readers. As he told me, Zviad has eleven (!) poetry collections published, Zaza—only one: short stories (winner of the 2007 Geo-Universal Bank prize in literature).

And finally, something about their psychological types:

6) Zviad reminds me of Rudyard Kipling's famous character (comp. Maugli or [again] the poet Max Kzhizhaniwsky, a recent arrival from the socialist Poland). It's his first time in Europe and he attempts to hide his uneasiness with [self-preservation] aggressiveness. He needs a little "love and care." He's bound to become quite at home soon. You're perfectly well aware what poets need: some praise. He's waiting to be praised. I don't spoil him in this respect:))). You know I'm "sadistic," not believing in compromises. I've got my own methods of taming the likes of him. The Georgians (about 100 people!!!) consider him talented. He's not retrograde. I haven't seen him reading even once. Like most poets, he's pretty ignorant (as you know, I don't hold high esteem of the living writers). He's got a wife and two kids.

Zaza is smart and thoughtful, a little fearful though. Not very sociable and rather ironic. I feel he's torn by an inner conflict with the seminar idea. He was astonished when everyone began writing on the Lisbon-Madrid train. Just like Zviad, he doesn't write in my presence. That's another typically Georgian disease. They can't work on a journey. Any trip sends them into a deep "shock." However, finding common grounds seems easier with Zaza than with Zviad. Zaza is certainly more progressive. He is single, no kids. His mother is quite a well-known chess player.

Both, Zaza and Zviad, are heterosexual.

What else can I communicate? I'm not sure I correctly understood your request about supplying you with the information about my group. But also, I've done no harm either as my "prompts" have enabled you to get to know your guests better. Now you'll find it easier to connect with them.

Always at your service in future trips,

Your friend,
Ilia K.

. . .

We arrived in Paris at dawn. It was cold and windy.

It was my third visit to the city. The first time I was so thrilled by it that I wasn't bothered by not having money. The second time was slightly more annoying. Elene lost her earrings, we changed trains twice (because of strikes), I had an upset stomach because of a disgusting sandwich and above all, we spent our money—not that we had plenty—senselessly and too fast. So I wasn't that ecstatic with Paris. It was Zviad's first time. When he got off the train, he was beaming. He didn't even notice the cold, I believe.

It's terrible when you have to wait for a hundred other people, expect to be told where to go and when. That was the most unnerving part of our journey: getting off the train, waiting for orders and getting to the hotel. We couldn't go our separate ways, obviously, so we had to stay together, hang around till everyone assembled and, after Heinz's or Rudy's yells and shouts, energetically tread toward the waiting coaches.

Apparently, no one had managed to get proper sleep on the train. Everyone, including the invariably brisk Lithuanian, looked ashen. I felt like I was catching a cold. The Armenians seemed to be the most pitiable: they were standing at a dustbin, shivering and sneezing quietly, with their mouths shut. Their synchronized sneezing sounded like a well-rehearsed concert piece.

Only Heinz, Rudy, Irmell and Milena radiated enviable vigor.

Meanwhile, I was watching Iliko, feeling increasingly guilty about my thoughts of the night before. I nearly started to hate him for not praising my stories. At a glance, I'm not conceited in the least, but as Elene told me once, I leave the impression of a modest and quiet type, while in reality it was a cover-up of a den of vice. She thought I was baleful, spiteful, and overambitious.

A den of vice. Just like that.

Finally we were ready to move, but failed to reach our coaches—in the middle of the square there was a makeshift stage where people with white-painted faces were waving pieces of paper and shouting something.

"These actors are reading your texts," Iliko told us.

Heinz happily jumped onto the stage. Clearly, it was his idea—Paris met us with our texts. He meant it to be a pleasant surprise. Some clapped. The wind was so strong we couldn't hear anything. Though the actors tried their utmost, their efforts were lost: the microphone was clanging loudly, the Armenians kept sneezing and I was shivering.

"They're reading your poem now," Iliko looked at Zviad.

"Are they?" he rejoiced like a child.

Iliko stood grinning. We didn't feel like joking.

"No way . . ." Zviad sounded offended.

"I heard with my own two ears 'The Ditches of Vardzia,'" Iliko persisted.

Now Zviad definitely looked angry:

"I haven't written anything of the kind!"

Most of all I hate such surprises: spontaneous and original at first glance. Especially if you don't know how long they're going to be.

The Big Russian had been drinking on the train, judging from his puffed eyes and tousled bushy eyebrows. The Little one wasn't a better sight: his beard was tangled and his gaze was lifeless. He had rolled up his evening trouser legs to his knees and was wearing old white sneakers.

With her teeth clattering from cold, old Mme Roget was standing next to me. She was so lovable—with her boyish hair-cut. She had the habit of smiling at you whenever you happened to meet her eyes. She did the same now:

"Too cold," she said in English and smiled.

"Heinz isn't," I smiled in reply. Then we froze. I didn't know what to say, neither did she. It always happens to me when I'm with foreigners. God knows how many times I've been like that—with a frozen smile on my face!

"Zaza," I heard from behind.

It was Helena. She was with her husband.

"I'm very heavy, aren't I?" he stretched out his hand.

I didn't say anything, fearing I'd come up with some stupid remark. I just smiled and shook his hand.

"If not for Zaza, I'd have left you in the lobby," Helena told him.

Za-*Za*. She stressed the second syllable. I can still hear her voice.

"I'm sorry," Maček said, smiling.

He seemed kind and intelligent. Nothing like the man I saw two days ago. He was much older than Helena. Fit to be her father rather than her husband.

"You're excused," I said.

Good thing Heinz called us, because I didn't know what to do next. He saved me from another frozen embarrassment.

The performance was a total flop. The rain had joined the wind and Heinz was pointing to the waiting coaches.

"Ooo-la-la," the French woman laughed and dashed to the coach.

"See you later," Maček winked at me.

Though we were all dripping wet, I thought Helena looked particularly drenched: raindrops were trickling down her thin nose (as if she was melting) and her eyes became nearly transparent.

"Why did he apologize?" Iliko asked me as we got on the coach.

"He made a confession to me," I answered, "on Heinz's orders."

"Yeah." He appreciated my joke. "The train can only carry the innocent."

We were just passing the Eiffel Tower. The wind was so strong I thought it would sway. But it was as firm as ever—neither swaying nor breaking in half.

"I don't believe it's real," Zviad muttered. "I think I'm looking at a copy."

I felt happier in my room. I could see rainy Paris from my elongated window, which reminded me of the French films I'd watched in my childhood. The rules of the cinematographic romanticism prescribed that Helena and I had to fall in love in Paris, but life was much harsher: Zviad was bound to be my partner.

I didn't want to call home using the hotel room phone. This kind of apprehension is just another relic of the Soviet times— "Don't ever use the room phone, it's excessively expensive!" But it was raining so hard, I was reluctant to go out to buy a phone card. I had left my mobile in Georgia and was extremely proud of the decision. If I still had Elene, it'd make sense, but why would I send messages to Mum and Dad every day? Neither did I particularly miss Reziko (my teenage heirloom) or his wife Nutsa (my classmate, incidentally), not to mention my colleagues and workmates. Most often I thought of Elene, but somehow weirdly, lifelessly, unemotionally . . .

So, I had no real need for a mobile but I had to phone Mum— since my departure I'd talked to her only once. And I hadn't detected any burst of enthusiasm at my call . . . Her mind was completely occupied by the Russian tanks and the protest rallies across Georgia.

My mum is full of life, the Vice President of the Chess Federation. She's twice bought my idle dad a car. He is well liked, sings beautifully and occasionally plays tennis. Tries to stay young. In truth, he's nothing. Old and superficial, like most of his buddies. They're all former ministers, without exception. The last Communist elite. Dad was always the same: enjoyed singing Russian ballads with a slight tremolo and, if he had a glass or two too many, he'd even drop an artistic tear. Mum is his second wife. She was charmed by his table-side ballads and married him.

Later, she grew into an intelligent woman. I refuse to believe that Mum of today would marry Dad of today.

Dad stopped talking to me in spring and is still sulking at me. Even the war couldn't reconcile us. He phoned only once, the day Tbilisi was bombed, to ask if my TV was receiving Russian channels. But when he heard it wasn't (apparently, there was some kind of directive from *above* because Russian channels were switched off for the general public, fearing that their informational programs had the same effect as their bombs), he grumbled they weren't saying anything (he meant the Georgian national channels) and hung up. As for sulking, it all started when I wrote a story about him . . . A table laid out for a feast. Aging men are enjoying themselves. They're still showing off, pretending they're still young—gold chains with huge crosses around their necks and sizeable signet rings on their fingers. But the wine they're drinking appears to be poisoned and they all turn into monsters. They start devouring each other: arms, thighs and ears. I had used Dad as a prototype for the toastmaster—the reason he easily identified himself with the story character—singing the same songs and talking like him. At the end the monster-Dad bites the nose off his buddy's face, eats him and then regurgitates him as a mushy half-dead creature . . .

It was a nightmarish version of a typical Georgian feast. Dad didn't suspect anything as he'd never shown any interest in my stories and wouldn't have read this one either if not for Mum. She had a good laugh and thought he'd find it funny too. Actually, he hit the roof. Phoned to tell me I was becoming bigheaded. Judging from his tone, I suddenly realized my own dad was going to use the street-language and methods of settling the dispute. I was furious. This good-for-nothing dandy living off my mum was going to preach ethics? I admit: I insulted him. He swore at me, to which I threatened to throw him out of the window. The minute I hung up, tears came down my cheeks (good I didn't cry while talking to him). Then Mum called to chide. I didn't utter a word in self-defense. I meant to phone back that very evening to apologize, but I couldn't curb myself. My dignity was badly hurt and I couldn't help it. The next day it was even harder to swallow my pride, so it got worse and worse.

Wasn't it he who had to make the first move? Mum would have definitely phoned first. Or was that phone call at the time of the shelling meant to be his step toward reconciliation? I don't know. I don't know my dad.

Mum was in. She must have been watching TV as I could hear its sound in the background.

"What's going on?" I asked.

"Oh, this and that. At four they're blocking the Baratashvili Bridge. And how are you?"

"What do you mean blocking?" I was baffled.

"There's a protest rally at four this afternoon. Aren't you watching TV?"

Tbilisi is swept with rallies. Mum is immersed in politics, finding my apathy toward the current events absolutely inexplicable. She believed the bridge story should have reached Paris.

The Baratashvili Bridge is connecting the President's residence with the rest of the city. The rally organizers intend to stop the traffic as a sign of protest while Mum watches TV, beyond herself with worry . . .

"All my friends are going to be there," she tells me, "but I can't go."

The spirit of opposition has deeply permeated Mum's Chess Federation. The chess players, especially women, can't stand the existing president (they loved the first one, now referred to as "the ousted"). Inwardly, Mum shares the oppositional sentiments but is scared—she is afraid the government will cut the Federation funds if she joins an opposition rally. Or even worse, stop subsidizing it altogether. If you ask me, the subsidy should be stopped regardless of whether they join rallies or not—they haven't won a single championship in the last thirty years. I first beat Mum in chess when I was thirteen, so what kind of professionals are they? True, years back, they used to be like gladiators, but look at them now! Their main office reeks of soup because they cook it right there, along with innumerable cups of cheap coffee they brew. Their offices look like their flats—fridges, clothes, icons, crosses, the Patriarch's photos and old Soviet tournament medals.

"What do you care? Go if you want," I tell her. I'm sure she won't, but I want to tease her.

"Do you like it there?" she asks.

"Yeah, it's great."

"Any proposals?"

That's my real mum, businesslike and caring. She wants my trip to bring tangible results, wants me to be awarded with something. She sees me as a kind of sportsman—I absolutely need to get a prize, medal or at least a certificate of participation. Preferably something saying: "The Georgian writer-wrestler in free-style pinned his Russian counterpart to the ground, winning for his home country the millionth gold medal smeared with the blood of the Russian athlete."

"None," I answer.

"So, the trip is pointless," she says.

"What sort of proposals do you expect?" I become irritated. "I'm not auditioning for a film, you know."

"I mean, you could've given the book to someone to read."

"In Georgian?"

As if she doesn't know. A heartless, rhetorical question in essence, asked by a person gripped with her chess pieces, slavish friends, an eccentric husband, given and not-given salaries, and TV live coverage of the current events. It's only fair to say that she was genuinely happy when others praised her son and awarded him with a literary prize for his stories. And yet, she considers me shallow. She is confident my choice of a writer's career was deeply wrong. For her, the value of what I write remains dubious. Had I been a poet, she might have understood me better. Sometimes I believe she feels sorry for me . . . She's going to stop pitying me when her son's stories become part of the national school curriculum.

Heaven knows I can't stand school writers!

Mum's voice was drowned out by the TV and we bid each other a sad good-bye.

I thought it was good I wasn't back home.

I looked through the window. It was still raining hard.

I switched on the TV and watched the French for some time. The anchors talked about everything except Georgia. It was consoling: no shelling, no bombing, no small-scale protest rallies.

I must have fallen asleep. Iliko's knocking woke me up. He brought back my book.

"The one about a baby talking from the inside is good," he said. Nothing else. He had liked the story of a talking fetus.

I smiled at him. Hadn't expected even that much.

"Lots of typos," he said severely. "And, by the way, there are no five-story cottages."

"Have I written that?"

"You have. Page 102."

How I dread readers like him!

"You're entering a completely different phase tomorrow," he told me. "You're taking part in the planned public discussions. There are going to be some publishers. You might even grab a couple of agents."

"Where?" I shuddered.

"No idea. You'll be taken to the venue."

"Is it a must?"

"No, just significant. You need to make them like you. You're going to speak English. You can manage that much."

I nodded. I'm not sure whether it was because I was newly woken up or something else, but I was certainly as docile as a diligent schoolboy.

"What language is he going to speak?" he asked about Zviad. "Does he know Russian? It'll be translated."

"I don't know," I shrugged.

"He knows nothing," he grimaced. "As ignorant as any poet."

I didn't occupy my mind with what I was going to talk about the next day at the open discussion. Neither was I nervous. I didn't prepare any speech. For some reason, I didn't believe Iliko's information about the publishers. Heinz and a couple of literary critics were all I expected to see in the reading hall. I thought it'd be a mere formality. As it turned out, the whole event was pretty serious: the hall was full. They showed about fifteen or twenty of us to the dais and gave up headphones to listen to the translation. I was red in the face and rather confused, feeling as if I were doing something really shameful.

The moderator was asking incredibly tricky questions. The discussion started and proceeded without me following it and I don't think it was due to the quality of the translation. I can't blame the interpreter—the themes were just too remote from me. I dreaded my turn, fully aware that the moderator would put a question while I'd talk about something quite different.

As far as I understood, my colleagues were talking about their texts. They seemed intent on grabbing the offered opportunity to advertise themselves. At times their manner of doing it was too direct and brash. I don't suppose their callousness was the explanation. They appeared to be quite naturally and comfortably discussing any topic from the viewpoint of their own texts. Until then I had believed that was only permissible for the geniuses and widely recognized writers. In my country this kind of categorical, opinionated self-expression of hardly known writers would be met with general disapproval. Back home we've got other conventions: an unknown man of letters claims he is too far from what true literature is and doesn't consider himself a writer yet (better chance not to be immediately loathed by the public). On the other hand, a relatively well-known writer is mostly reticent and looks gloomy (because he empathizes with the nation). And if he says anything, it's mainly in a roundabout, superficially philosophical style, something like an elaborate toast. At the same time, it is essential that he eulogizes Mother Nature (*mother* being a key word) and the ancient, wise, martyred Georgian nation. If he fails to do so, firstly, he will violate the eternally trendy tradition of the classical rhetoric and, secondly, he will be looked down by that very nation. Here, in Paris, everything was the other way round: the writers tried hard to be original, unpredictable and exasperatingly extravagant—they were talking about their novels, stories, plays, and screenplays without a hint of embarrassment.

Apparently, I had to adopt the same manner. I had to drop all modesty, using every single minute given to me to stress the originality of my stories. But how can you suddenly become original if you aren't? Especially in five minutes. Or what is that precious grain you're going to dig up from your writings that can turn you into a superstar in the eyes of these thick-skinned literary agents?

It was akin to hell for me.

Whether it was my mum's voice ("Any proposals?") or that of another, more ambitious person, I clearly heard in my ears: *Sell yourself! Sell your stories!*

But how? Where do I start?

I shouldn't talk about myself. That was the first and the easiest decision. The selling point was *Georgia* itself, not my stories. If I kept talking about the problems my country was facing at the time, I had more chances to interest the listeners with my personality. The Georgian events were bound to be more original and attractive than my literary experiments. As luck would have it, the Big Russian was also participating in the discussion, so I firmly settled on the Russian-Georgian war as the focal point of my talk.

Eventually, it was my turn. The moderator asked me a question that sounded too general and vague (I only caught *Géorgie*).

Someone handed me the microphone and next minute all eyes were on me. I felt my pulse quicken, but I managed to brace myself and said, hardly audibly:

"Good evening."

As expected, the microphone changed my voice pitch shockingly. I blushed to the tips of my ears. I thought I might joke: "My mum expects specific offers from you. You all have mums, but I can only talk about my mum's personal expectations." Needless to say, I didn't try anything like this. I saw Helena. Or rather, first I caught sight of her husband's white hat and only then did I see her. So, there they were. It was the second time I was on the dais and she was in the audience. I couldn't afford a failure. I had to start getting her attention. Now, from the dais. Only Helena could inspire me and only in a provocative way.

That's why I took my courage in both hands and said loudly:

"I apologize for not being able to talk about literature. Russian tanks have occupied my country and I intend to use this opportunity to tell you how Russian bombs destroyed Georgia."

While speaking, I was apparently waving my hand with the microphone, which meant that only shreds of my phrases reached the listeners.

"Please, stop waving and keep the microphone at your mouth," the Portuguese writer Tasheira, sitting on my left, told me. "They can't hear you."

I immediately complied.

"Please, start again," the moderator asked me.

And I complied with him too, repeating my earlier speech word for word.

The audience, and it wasn't my wishful thinking, fell quiet.

"Can we leave politics out of it?" the moderator said, smiling. The Big Russian raised his bushy eyebrows and was listening very attentively. Curious to find out what I was up to. But I looked in Helena's direction—I sincerely wished to draw her attention . . . I couldn't rely on my stories for that.

She might sleep with you tonight if you don't screw up, I thought, clutching the microphone with both hands (which were trembling shamelessly) and went on even louder:

"This isn't politics. It's about people's lives . . . The Russians have killed our peaceful population . . . Their tanks are still there, in Georgian villages. I believe it's immoral to call this a political issue . . . Why are we afraid of Russians? Why can't we talk openly about their crimes?"

"Monsieur Zaza, Monsieur Zaza," the moderator interrupted me. My name sounded like *Tsatsa* in his speech. "Do you believe Mr. Varlamov is dangerous?"

I came up with the answer quite quickly:

"No," I waved the microphone. "I meant the Russian politicians and not people in general. What has Mr. Varlamov to do with it? It was the politicians who sent tanks to Georgia, not the writers."

"That's very significant," the moderator uttered seriously, "but let's talk about your beautiful country and its problems later. We've got many countries here and if everyone starts discussing politics, there won't be room for literature."

"My conviction is that human life is more important than politics and literature."

I wanted to say something else, but ended up with that phrase, trite as it might sound. To my surprise, the Croatian writer sitting on my right agreed with me:

"Literature is uninteresting without a human focus. People have perished in Georgia."

"No," the moderator persisted. "I promise to find time later to talk about politics. But not today. No politics today."

He's gay and likes Varlamov, I thought. I hoped the listeners would side with me, but no one spoke. The hall was watching silently. In the meanwhile, I glanced toward Helena but saw only Maček. Helena's seat was empty.

Passing the microphone to Danuta Prochorovič, the Croatian lady, I felt terribly insulted and humiliated.

"No, no, please," the moderator addressed me. "Keep talking, but can you get back to our topic of discussion?"

"I've finished," I said.

"Are you sure?" he smiled at me.

"I am."

Yes, I resented being interrupted. I felt miserable because Helena's seat was empty. I had no wish to talk about the war and moral issues. Would I be seen as a traitor in Georgia?

I know I wasn't particularly tactful—it's not admissible in European discussions and debates—but I just couldn't stay in my seat. I had worried too much and felt exhausted. My joints ached from nervous tension.

I had been making all *those grand plans*, while Helena found me quite bland! As simple as that.

I have no idea who spoke after me or what they spoke about, as I was too preoccupied with my own hysterical reaction. The only thing I clearly remember is the phrase said by the elderly Czech writer: "My father, ladies and gentlemen, was a clown." However, I have no recollection of how the phrase was connected to his speech and how it fitted our discussion. It was really rather difficult to guess what language he spoke. Iliko had very appropriately labeled him "the speaker of the elfin language." It was also obvious Czech wasn't his native language. Occasionally he reverted to English and German, but his manner of pronouncing these familiar, easily recognizable words was rather unpleasant. Exactly like elves and gnomes speak in fairy tales: *trock, crakh, croct.* But still, he was an extremely gentle and kind man. Incidentally, right after the discussion he approached me and said in the tone of a noble but exhausted aging elf:

"Ich liebe zer Gruzia."

On the way out of the hall, Maček also supported me:

"You shouldn't have stopped. You could've been sterner. I guess you stopped to avoid a scandal. But it was good, I liked it."

I nearly asked him why Helena had left if it was so good.

"That Russian's face was pretty distorted. Never expected anything like that," he laughed.

"I didn't mean to hurt him. I just wanted to talk about the war, nothing else," I tried to justify myself.

"Did you notice how the chap defended him? Like an over-protective mother." He meant the moderator. "When the Russians are criticized, it's the French who overreact. All my life I've been trying to explain the phenomenon but no success yet."

"The Germans seem to like the Russians more," I said.

"No. The Germans are suffering from a bunch of complexes. No one can be sure what they're harboring down deep in their hearts."

Our conversation was too general and somewhat superficial. Both of us felt it. I thanked Maček for his support and headed for Iliko. He was at a long table scrutinizing the plastic cups laid out, debating whether the liquid inside was worth drinking.

"Wait, I haven't told you the main thing," Maček stopped me. "Have you written anything about this war? I'd like to translate it."

"About the Russian-Georgian war?" I was genuinely surprised.

"Yeah, but I don't mean an article. I'm interested in fiction."

"I think I've got something," I lied. "I mainly write about wars."

"No, no, not World War II. I mean your war."

"Yes, I know," I laughed. "It's just that we've had four wars in the last twenty years in Georgia. And I've numbered my stories according to them."

"And you survived all four?"

"The first one was in the downtown, when only the adjacent houses were burned down. I lived in the suburbs at the time. The fourth one scared me stiff though . . ."

"Have you got any translations?"

"Yeah, several."

Actually, only two. One story was translated by an American scholar of the Georgian language, the other one by a Georgian student. The third one about the dropping bombs wasn't even written.

"Can I have them?"

"Sure."

I had no idea Maček was a translator.

"I'm not a professional translator. (*Aha, he wasn't!*) I'm a literary critic. But I've got an outline of an extremely important project: the history of the Caucasian wars through writers' eyes."

"Including Shamil and the Russians?"

"Who?"

"Shamil . . . Imam Shamil."

I couldn't believe he didn't know about him.

"No, no. Only the 20th century. The post-Soviet period." (*So he knew after all.*)

"That's great," I felt relieved.

"It's a huge project. If we like your stories, they'll be published in our book."

I was about to say, "Please, tell my mum yourself. We can call her immediately."

"Okay," was all I said.

"Can I have your email?" He stretched out his hand, palm up, and drew a marker from his pocket with the other hand.

"Shall I write on your palm?" I asked in amazement.

"Go ahead. I haven't got paper."

Helena must have liked him for such a witty and lighthearted attitude.

There was nothing left for me but to write my email on his open palm. Then we walked out together into the street.

Helena was sitting on the curb. Her lips were black from drinking red wine.

She had a short dress on, which was hardly covering her legs, the way she was sitting. The worst part was she didn't keep them close together, so the minute I stepped on the pavement, I couldn't take my eyes off her shiny thighs and even peeped beyond them, a little higher. Into the hidden depth. Sheer instinct. Completely unconscious.

Finally I met her eyes.

I believe she guessed the direction of my stare.

And—I can take an oath—she smiled back.

. . .

11 October, Paris

I am continuing the second part of my memoirs.

. . . I'm in Paris now. The Germans have gathered writers from across Europe and are taking us to various cities by train. Last time I crossed Europe in a similar way was in 1961. My poor dad had a tour with the Bratislava circus. By the way, today, I mentioned him at the literary discussion. These days I've been dreaming of him and just couldn't help it. And the weather keeps changing all the time. Dreaming of the deceased prognosticates bad weather, doesn't it?

Irena and I used to visit Paris at least once a year. Then there was a pause between 1968 and 1987. The borders were closed, so we spent our summers with the Dubceks. In the '90s the borders were opened again, but by then Irena had lost all interest in travel. I don't know many who at the age of 58 find the courage to divorce. I did. I left my wife, daughter, granddaughter, and son-in-law! Clowning around runs in my blood, doesn't it? Compared to women, we men get older more slowly, but die early. That's why I prefer spending the remaining years as I please. I'm not one of those senile egotists—I'm not afraid of living on my own and taking care of myself.

The writers here are mostly pretty green. If I'm not mistaken the Belgian poet and I are the eldest. We stick together—not intentionally, just happens so. I'm not particularly keen on spending time with him though. Firstly, he smells of medicine and, secondly, I don't feel old inside—I'm no less mischievous than these lads. If not for my gray hair and wrinkles, I'd show some of these "men" what it means to be one. The Belgian and I seem to be the only straights. The rest mostly wear leather trousers, which is the gay fashion, I believe.

Today I read an extract from my Memoirs. *The one about how Dad lost his red nose in the Moscow Circus. Sadly, very few got the idea behind the metaphor. Danuta Prochorovič, the Croat writer, praised my language. The language of the text as well as the spoken one. She said my German was original and beautiful. I was pleasantly surprised . . . I haven't spoken German since the War. I didn't suspect I'd remember anything from pan Wražek's lessons! Jesus, how long ago that was! Poor chap, his bones must be gone by now.*

I feel fine here, though it gets a bit boring in the evenings. I find the train more enjoyable. Hotel rooms are awful, but there's nowhere we can "hide" on the train, so we are obliged to communicate with each other.

The Belgian has affected me adversely: I suspect I also smell of medicine. That's the reason I've cut on some. I've stopped taking anti-cholesterol, digoxin and godasal. Still take the one for keeping my blood pressure low. I don't believe a single medicine is going to make me smell like hospital. As it is, people shun us, the old, so I'd hate to give them yet another pretext. We're punished from above . . . Wasn't I running away from pan Ludvik in the same way? The old man craved to talk to us, but we felt bored. He must have had such a lot to tell. He was there in Sarajevo when Archduke Ferdinand was killed by that student. In other words, he was there to witness the start of World War I.

I wonder if my colleagues would feel sorry if I were to die on the train. I'm curious about their reaction. But I prefer the Belgian to die and not me, as I'd like to be an onlooker.

Foolish things I'm writing . . .

I'm in my room, not knowing what to do. All channels are French, which means I don't understand a single word. If I were 15 years younger, I'd certainly flirt with the Croat Danuta Prochorovič.

Enough fooling around. I'm getting back to the memoirs:

"In 1951 we moved from Prague to Karlovy Vary. Dad was suffering from kidney failure and needed a systematic medical treatment. I was planning to study physics and mathematics at university. I had no time for romance, but fate decided otherwise. The Novaks had a daughter—Irena. I saw her first in the Karlovy Vary central public baths. She was helping her father, pan Novak, get out of the pool. Little did I know that years later these fragile shoulders would take on the burden of my "exotic" family . . ."

8. THE PARISIAN DEAD

In the morning they took some of us to the Père-Lachaise, the old cemetery of Paris. Iliko woke me up saying:

"There's a coach taking people to see their dead. Want to go?"

I did. He stayed behind. Just informed me, adding he'd visited it.

"How many times am I supposed to grieve them?"

I went alone. Neither did Zviad join me. He was saving himself for the discussion as it was his turn to sit the test. On the good side, Helena was on the coach, talking to the Azeri Aliev. She had a red raincoat and a blue beret on. Before taking a seat I threw a furtive glance at her legs. As expected, she wasn't wearing much under her raincoat. She must have been extremely proud of her shapely legs.

As soon as I sat down, a Chechen writer turned to me (he was sitting right in front of me). He looked unnaturally well-disposed.

"I listened to you yesterday," he said, smiling. Until then we'd never spoken. "How old are you?"

It was an unexpected question.

"Me?" I sounded unsure. "Twenty-eight."

"You should've been more active. Could've made the Russian mad and won."

So that was what he enjoyed.

"It's not his fault that his superiors are no good," I said.

"Yeah," he said laughing, and turned away. It seemed rather abrupt as I thought he'd ask more questions. I wasn't sure what the meaning of that "Yeah" was.

The Père-Lachaise is the city of the dead dating back to the nineteenth century. The graves look like old palaces. The whole cemetery is divided into sectors and streets and numbered, which means each of the dead has got an individual address.

We were handed the cemetery maps at the entrance.

I had a quick look at the names:

Delacroix

La Fontaine

Molière

Morrison

Wilde

Chopin

And many others, well-known and relatively unknown. Or well-known once upon a time and then completely forgotten.

Oscar Wilde's grave is covered with kiss marks. The fans love kissing their idol's grave. A heap of letters hides Chopin's grave. They write love letters to him. Jim Morrison's grave is strewn with used syringes. The devoted music fans come here for a jab and leave their syringes instead of flowers.

"I wouldn't have buried him here," the detective novel author Eldar Aliev told me. "It's an insult to the other deceased."

I smiled but said nothing.

"I'd open a separate cemetery for the celebrity drug addicts," he added.

"Used to masturbate too," I said for some obscure reason.

"No, just pretended," he laughed.

I laughed too.

He was an interesting man. At one point he told us he was so popular in his native Azerbaijan, he was obliged to move around with a bodyguard. Good he had enough common sense not to bring one along. I even doubted whether he was the true author of the novels he claimed he'd written. Iliko was likewise skeptical, saying he probably kept a whole staff writing for him. He only supplied his name. However, on another occasion he revealed a rather strange fact about himself:

"When I write, I always undress to my trunks. I have to be naked at my computer."

Only a genuine writer can say such a thing. An ex-party bureaucrat would never dream of admitting such personal details.

We strolled among the graves, looking out for those we considered worth paying respect to. Everyone was consulting their maps.

The red raincoat and blue beret were within my sight at all times.

Helena was sometimes ahead of me, sometimes behind, but never by my side. Mainly I had to be content with Aliev's company.

Then we halted on a small square—the streets of the dead converged at that point. We decided, or rather they decided, that we should wander on our own and meet at the entrance in an hour.

I immediately resolved to follow Helena.

I had no specific plan, just blindly obeyed my instinct without a trace of doubt or fear. I liked her and thought I was doing no harm. Maček became quite friendly with me, even intended to translate my stories. I didn't have anyone, no strings attached. Helena was lovely—great bum, but I wasn't up to anything (What was there to be up to?). My career was more important than that bottom—Maček's translation was going to make me famous in Europe.

That's why I boldly followed her. I'm irresponsible, no initiative whatsoever—come what may, I thought.

And all the while I knew perfectly well *nothing was going to happen*. Nothing to worry about. The red raincoat kept showing among the marble palaces, here and there. Helena was making her way between sad stone angels and weeping muses. Everything was gray except her raincoat.

For me it felt like being inside the old Soviet film *Dariko*. It's black and white. Only the Bolsheviks' flag is red. Glowing red in a monochrome old film.

Helena stopped at one of the graves.

I unhurriedly approached her. We looked at each other.

It wasn't accidental I was reminded of an old film—we were standing at the grave of Charles Chaplin. But not the actor-director. Just a namesake. Died in the nineteenth century. One couldn't help feeling sorry for him—he lived, strived, was buried in the Père-Lachaise only to be mistaken for someone else.

I was about to share my thought with her, but Helena turned her back on me and walked toward a chapel-like monument.

I didn't know what to do: follow her or walk away. Finally I decided to follow her. I hated the thought of facing a defeat at such an early stage of the hunt.

She stopped at the sepulcher, turned abruptly and walked back toward me.

Her stride was so brisk that it confused me. I found it hard to believe she was coming back to me. A nasty premonition settled in my heart.

She didn't look me in the eyes, her gaze focusing at a lower point.

"I don't like that you're watching me," she said.

I remember my utter disbelief. I hadn't expected either those words or that tone from her.

"Watching you?" I asked.

"Yes. And you're looking at me. In a strange way. I don't like it at all. I meant to tell you yesterday, after your speech, but then I thought I was imagining things."

"Are you serious or is it a joke?" I managed to say.

"Dead serious, Zaza," she said, looking down at the ground again, never meeting my eyes.

Those were terrible minutes.

It was my fault again, my mistakes, my blunders . . . It was a nightmare. Was she paranoid? That very minute I even thought her ugly.

"I'm sorry," I muttered.

"Please don't apologize. Just stop staring at me. It's unbearable. Right now I saw you following me, which stressed me out. I don't like it. The other night you really helped me and I'm deeply grateful . . . Sorry."

She's crazy. I suddenly realized she was crazy and took pity on her. I toyed with the idea of annoying her even more by saying: "Helen, you're the most beautiful, the sexiest woman I've ever seen and that's why I'm staring at you," and then disappear behind the graves just like the Phantom of the Opera. In reality, I apologized again and retraced my steps to the unknown Chaplin's grave. I must have been a pitiable sight—a deeply humiliated idiot.

Not as bad as it might seem. It finished even before it started. That'll keep me calm.

What helped me most at the time was my infinite optimism—I had to leave the whole thing behind, otherwise, if I kept brooding over, it could drive me to moodiness, glumness and even to depression. Then I'd start hating everything and run back home. I hadn't been so miserable and debased since my childhood. As if all insulting techniques were used all at once—a face slap, a kick in the ass, a spit in the face, a bucket of icy water, and mockery . . .

I felt as if I had received a sound beating.

"It was fantastic!" Aliev greeted me as I got on the coach. "Our graves are very different, devoid of any spirituality. The graves look like garages, but here they're so refined! Such architecture, such style! Is it the same with you?"

A conversation could do the trick, as sitting silently would inevitably lead my thoughts to Helena. So I gave an elaborately imaginative description of a Georgian boy buried in honey. A rich father built a rocket-like monument to his dead son, filled a glass sarcophagus with honey and put him inside as, apparently (neither consommé, nor sour sauce, nor any other cooking ingredient) only honey could preserve a body from decomposing. Incidentally, this culinary necropolis is on the side of our highway, making it impossible to miss it.

"Yes, we've got something similar," Aliev said, "when the dead are placed in cooked rice."

The world provides an endless list of themes to write about. I'm pretty sure the honey-dead story would sell extremely well on the European literary market. Worth giving it another thought. However, Aliev and I didn't deliberate, just took our seats and waited for the coach to take us back to the hotel.

In a short while Helena got on too.

I looked though the window. I wanted to stress I didn't care at all and that I stopped staring. As if deliberately, she chose a seat across from me, on the left. The window presented me with her excellent reflection. I believe she was looking at me. I tried hard not to glance at her, but then, unable to resist the temptation, I looked around, as if out of sheer boredom.

Incredibly, she smiled at me.

She's making fun of me, I thought.

What was there for me to do? I couldn't pretend not noticing and smiled back. As I said I'm weak.

Helena immediately regained her attractiveness. I liked her again, my hopes returned, together with the sense of anxiety. How reassuring the state of hopelessness was . . .

That day I would have reflected on Helena's words and her puzzling smile if I hadn't witnessed Zviad's crashing failure.

The fact that he had been drinking became obvious as soon

as I walked into the discussion hall. I'm not sure whether it was his drunkenness or nervousness, but he talked such nonsense that even ever-smiling, robotically polite Heinz felt rather annoyed.

I still don't understand why he chose to speak Russian during the discussion. It would have been better if he didn't utter a word at all. His language was a mixture of the Russian used in the times of Ivan the Terrible and of medieval Romanian (I doubt there is such a hybrid). Later, Iliko reprimanded Rudy for not supplying a Georgian interpreter, to which the latter apologized, saying Zviad was expected to speak English.

"We couldn't imagine that following the Russian-Georgian conflict a Georgian poet would choose Russian for the discussion."

I didn't expect Rudy to come up with such a politically incorrect remark.

The interpreter kept asking poor Zviad to repeat:

"Please, say it again, I can't hear you."

And he repeated—flushed and sweaty, in his wild Russian. He waved his arms and shouted, trying to tell about the August war with sounds and noises, using everything but words to depict the disaster. Forgetting even the simplest words, he kept mentioning the classical Georgian writers, absolutely irrelevantly:

"Rustaveli . . . Vazha Pshavela . . . Galaktion . . ."

He failed to communicate anything, but most of all it was his anguish that deserved sympathy. He didn't manage to get a word into the discussion. He would start, then stop, wave his arms and say in Russian: "No, no, sorry."

"Celan . . . I have . . . Paul Celan," he kept repeating. He seemed intent on letting them know he's translated Celan's poems.

The final part was particularly sad: instead of answering the presenter's question, he rose to his feet and addressed the audience with a wide grin:

"Let me read my poems to you."

The presenter (as maniacally pedantic as my moderator had been) vigorously protested his initiative and asked him to take his seat.

Zviad's face turned alarmingly red. He looked in our direction asking for help. He was beyond himself with desperation as if waiting to be shot. I felt so embarrassed I averted my gaze. Iliko, on the contrary, stared at him with some sadistic delight. He seemed to draw pleasure from watching a Georgian poet in such a pitiable condition.

I think it was the Lithuanian poet who shouted from his seat:

"Let him read his poems! It isn't a scholarly conference, is it?"

I can only imagine Zviad's thrill at these words had they been spoken in Russian. But as the Lithuanian addressed the presenter in English, Zviad didn't even realize he had at least one supporter in the hall. However, no one sided with the Lithuanian. No one cared for his poems, so Zviad went back to his seat, looking utterly dejected.

I didn't wait for the discussion to end. I couldn't bear watching the torture of my countryman.

After a three-hour stroll I returned to the hotel. I thought I'd see how Zviad was, calm him as best I could. You never know with poets—he might have felt suicidal.

How naïve I am . . .

They were drinking in his room—the Lithuanian, Raul Aldamov, the Chechen, and Zviad.

"Raul is a Muslim, but he's my buddy. He's drinking with us," Zviad explained.

His eyes were bloodshot. I feared he was ready for a downward slide.

"Vitas and I read each other our poems. He's cool," he winked at me and smiled at Vitas.

I decided to leave but thought it uncivil to run away so soon.

Zviad was in slippers and had already succeeded in turning the cozy room into a pigsty. He was showing a weirdly aggressive hospitality toward his guests. For instance, he told Raul they had to compete in naming poets and the one to lose was to be re-baptized.

Initially we didn't understand what he meant.

"It means that if I lose, I'll become a Muslim, but if you lose, you'll be baptized as a Christian," he explained to Raul.

Luckily, Raul definitely had a sense of humor. He laughed while I tensed even more. Zviad persisted:

"Frightened, aren't you? Then let's start enumerating what Allah did and what my God did. Let's find out who's mightier, once and for all!"

"I'm an atheist," Vitas, the gentle giant, said. "My Granny is my god—she fought on the Nazi side. Hated Stalin."

"Oh, please, Vitas, don't set on him," Zviad protested dramatically.

"Does he admire Stalin?" Vitas turned to me with a smile.

"Only as a poet," I replied.

"No, man, he's crap as a poet," Zviad reacted to my reply. "He tried imitating Ilia Chavchavadze," and began to recite Stalin's poem, "*The rose bud, pals, gently opened . . .*"

"There is no 'pals', it's his improvement," I said in an attempt to joke.

"Did Dudaev write poetry?" Zviad persisted with Raul. "All our kings, presidents and even MPs did."

My guess was he was headed for a row, simply asking for it. He wanted to be beaten either by the Chechen or by the Lithuanian. He felt lousy. Wholeheartedly hating the discussion presenter, he was about to set his demons loose. He was drunk and just had to spurt the accumulated venom! If nobody beat him, he'd go pick up a fight with Iliko. He'd brawl and insult the unsuspecting chap. I was pretty sure of the scenario.

"Tell me this, Raul," he turned on the Chechen again, "do you sincerely believe that by killing a Christian you'll end up in Paradise? Can you explain it?"

"Nonsense," I interfered.

"Wait, man," he stopped me. "Let's have some clarity, once and for all."

"It's the Crusaders who invented that myth, out of spite," Raul smiled. "A black PR."

"Who?" Zviad's eyebrows shot up. "We helped the Crusaders in the twelfth century or maybe the thirteenth? Correct me, Zaza, if I'm wrong," he appealed to me with his bloodshot eyes.

"I'm not interested," I said, resolving to leave.

"Yeah, but they say if a Muslim kills a Christian, he's going to get an army of heavenly broads. Isn't that right? Bang! Kill a Crusader and get yourself an eternal blow job . . . Sheer bliss . . ."

While he was saying this he unconsciously grabbed his balls and scratched his groin.

"Can't stand virgins," Vitas grimaced.

"You want to discuss theological issues in the heart of such a progressive Europe?" Raul chuckled.

All my worries were groundless as he was a very civilized Caucasian. It was the southerner Zviad who seemed a savage. Actually, he wasn't ill-disposed toward Raul, neither was he disrespectful toward his faith (his wildness didn't go that far). He just wanted to punch where he believed was the most painful. Had there been a German in Raul's place, Zviad would certainly say something like *Heil Hitler!* Just to annoy and embarrass him. Or he'd condemn pederasty in the presence of some poor gay chap. He could easily disapprove of some tradition in the face of a pathologically self-respecting Japanese with a suicidal streak.

When I rose to leave, Zviad drunkenly grabbed my arm but his grip was rather feeble.

"Don't go . . . Stay, we can talk," he asked.

Clearly, I didn't intend to stay.

"I'm leaving too," Raul said, and followed me.

"You're still the same Soviets, no fear of God!" Zviad shouted at our backs.

"He's a good guy," the Chechen told me as we stepped into the corridor.

"Yeah, but difficult when drunk."

"You have seen nothing of bad drinking," he said with a smile.

I didn't like the phrase in the least, neither his smile nor, above all, his tone . . . There was something stereotypically Chechen in his manner.

We said our good-byes at the lift.

Zviad's drunkenness and his room reminded me of Georgia. I remembered that I lived among pretty aggressive people, so the present lull was temporary. To think I had second thoughts about coming here! I was reluctant to move and fearful of change. But now I shuddered at the idea of going back home. Zviad reminded me of my acquaintances and family engrossed in their problems, of our TV barking about our fortunes and misfortunes and of the belligerently cheerful people terrified of the war and stupefied with the all-embracing idiocy of nationalism . . .

Sometimes I wonder who I write for. Why should my abracadabra be significant for these people? And Zviad, who is he writing for? Who are his readers? His colleagues, possibly, and a couple of philologist-journalist-art-critic girls. And these will remain loyal to him until they get married and start having babies.

We do have older writers as well, those labeled "the living classical authorities." They lost the status of official dissidents as soon as the Soviet Georgia disappeared from the world map. Naturally, they turned baleful, directing their hatred at the green lads such as Zviad (thank God they don't know me), because they believe the likes of him have stolen their success.

It's only fair to say that, just like us, the respectable writers have also started using "ass," "you asshole," and "screw you" in their writing (they still avoid "pricks" and "dicks" but eventually will come to them as well). They believe they can restore their lost fame and glory by reverting to such cheap indecencies. Most of all I pity this kind. One can weep while reading their miserable exertions.

Yeah, Zviad definitely is an excellent poet but no one knows him . . . What lengths he'd gone to be noticed! In his younger days he even planned a showdown together with a handful of other antisocial poets like himself: with chamber pots of steaming excrement they walked into the old building of the Writers' Union and began reciting their poems in this poetic stink. It was meant to be taken as a protest: You are shit and our poems are going to reveal your true identity.

No wonder they were beaten then and there—Zviad together with his genius buddies. They were given no chance to read their poems. The attackers were the writers. Mainly middle-aged. Provincial wannabes, schemers and plotters, claiming to be writers only to be members of the Union—the dead Soviet dinosaur.

The scandal received TV coverage.

"How dare they take excrement into the Writers' Union?" my mum seethed.

"They're shit and shit is all they deserve!" I tried to defend a totally unknown poet.

In truth, I neither liked the chamber pots nor their poems. It was the Union I despised, so I sided with complete strangers. The sad reality was that people in general didn't care for either the literary fate of the judo-writers' union or that of the chamber pot carriers.

It's such a curse to be born a Georgian writer! No one cares but you keep writing, dejected by the don't-give-a-damn attitude of your fellow countrymen.

I believe being a poet is slightly better than being a prose writer. If you're a poet, you can lock yourself in a hotel room, have a drink or two, sting a person or two, and then can even manage a couple of baleful lines.

But what is there for me to do? I've given up drinking and can't write poetry.

9. BRUSSELS

We left for Brussels in the morning. Nobody could boast of high spirits. Our mood was hopelessly ruined by bad weather. It had been raining nonstop. The green fields so well remembered from the French films were now waterlogged gray. The moment we moved out of the station, they resumed writing. Every head was bent over notepads and laptops. When it's pelting outside and you're traveling by train, it seems a crime not to be a writer. So what if the organizers didn't provide a better train for our tour? You should be happy with what you've got at any one time: here's the rain, a piece of paper, and a perfect literary context. What else is there to do but write? At least something like philosophical sketches or analytical essays.

By the way, I also felt like writing (first time since I left home), but the literary frenzy of my colleagues pushed me toward sympathizing with the natural sciences people . . . I just couldn't write under the circumstances.

Disheveled Zviad was sitting facing me.

"Did I make a fool of myself last night? I don't remember a damn thing," he asked—a classic Georgian question.

"You did." I didn't spare him. "You swore at the Chechen."

"Did I?" He went pale.

"Nearly."

"Why would I do that?"

"You decided to re-baptize him."

"Why didn't you stop me?"

"You were stronger."

"Did I apologize?"

"He wasn't insulted."

"Suppose he picks on me from now on . . ."

"I can't say . . ."

"That session really got to me. The French kicked my ass."

"Why? I liked you," I lied.

Zviad waved me off for pulling his leg. He remembered everything perfectly well.

"Did the Lithuanian beat you up by any chance?" I asked.

"Vitas?" he sounded surprised. "Why would he? Was I rude to him too?"

"You swore at all blond people in general."

"No kidding?"

"In your heart, but he'd know, wouldn't he?"

"I ought to be locked up," he muttered, but I detected pride rather than regret in his tone. "I should apologize to him. And the Chechen as well. Their hearts are in the right place. Unlike those zombies."

At that point Iliko joined us.

"I'm nauseated." he sat down, groaning. "Their breakfasts are awful. If only we'd get to Germany, then I'll be fine."

Zviad remained silent. When Iliko was around, he tried not to talk a lot.

In a short while Irmel popped into our compartment. She had pink pimples on her forehead, but Iliko still found her attractive, I noticed.

"Salut!" he greeted her joyously.

Irmel dropped into an empty seat, handed out small envelopes to us and fired away in good English, with a German accent though:

"You've got to participate in a competition." She laughed very loudly for some reason, nearly hysterically. "As you well know, we're going to have a gala evening in Berlin, so we're asking you once again to write short texts about the tour and hand them in before we arrive there. It can be your impressions . . . Pieces of prose or poetry, as you wish. We would like this journey to be reflected in literature and your texts will be published as a book. Some of them will be read out in Berlin."

Irmel resembled a tired robot. Apparently, she had to go all along the train, repeating those words to every single one on it. Only Heinz was capable of designing such a devious punishment. "I'd rather you talk to everyone in person," I imagined him saying. "I don't want our request to sound too formal. We have to be friendlier because we need to gain the writers' trust."

Okay, poor tired automaton, we trust you, Irmel! We know how that literary usurper-politician Heinz tortures you and our hearts bleed. And I suspect Iliko even fancies you.

"And finally, a piece of excellent news," she beamed at us. "The best among the competition texts, which will certainly be chosen by a special panel, will be published in the magazine *Simplicissimus*. In this way we've got a serious intrigue."

"What's this?" Iliko looked down at the envelopes.

"It's a detailed version of what I've told you."

Iliko nodded like a diligent schoolboy:

"Okay."

Irmel laughed again—this time as a signal she was leaving—and rose to her feet.

Each of us smiled back at her in our own individual ways: Zviad docilely, I hypocritically, and Iliko lustfully.

"What did she say?" Zviad looked at me.

I recounted her words.

"Is it a good magazine?" he asked.

"In mothballs," Iliko answered instead of me. "As soon as your poems are published, you're acknowledged by the entire German-speaking world!"

"But what about the English-speaking part?" Zviad attempted to joke.

"They come later."

Then he yelled at us:

"Get off your asses and start writing. I might push you into the wide ocean!"

I can't say about the ocean, but we soon arrived in Brussels. As usual, we took ages waiting for each other, dragged our tired feet onto the coaches and spent a depressingly long time in reaching the hotel—nearly the same as it took to get from Paris to Brussels. We had to stop every other second at traffic lights and wait full five minutes for the green light. We moved at a snail speed, which drove us absolutely mad. Some swore, others slept. Aliev, for instance, pulled his cap well down over his eyes, just like taxi drivers do, and snored resolutely.

"His sleep betrayed him," Zviad whispered to me, "showed his true face."

Those of us who stayed awake were feeling sweaty, dirty, and utterly depressed.

Our hotel was on a street which made me think we were in Damascus. We found ourselves in Brussels Arabia. The manager was dressed exactly like the late Yasser Arafat and only heavily veiled women were walking in the streets. Even the water was of the color you would expect to see in Cairo or Damascus when you turn the tap. Yellowish brown. However, I didn't despair as I quickly recalled the Soviet popular wisdom: "Let it flow and in a little while the water's going to be clear." How many times have I witnessed bog liquid turning into genuine water in my own bathroom!

The city made itself memorable by three things: the Arabs, a beautiful square, and a pleasant conversation with Helena.

I've already mentioned the Arabs and women in burqas. As for the square, Zviad made me take at least twenty pictures there. He wanted to be seen here and there and everywhere in his faded, creased jeans.

Then he halted at the golden Pissing Boy, which turned out to be the city symbol, and happily informed me:

"I'm going to have a photo exhibition in Tbilisi: *The Apotheosis of Tourist Stupidity.*"

I parted with him at the boy with a never-emptying bladder.

"I don't want to get lost," he whined.

I explained in great detail how he could return to the hotel and went on to buy CDs. I had promised to get two operas for my aunt's tenor husband.

In the little book I kept for jotting down interesting phrases, the plots of my future stories and many other bits and pieces that might come in handy while writing, he had written himself: "Go to a large shop called FNAC (easy to find everywhere), get to the classical music department and buy me Verdi's opera *Un Ballo in Mashcera* and Leoncavallo's *Pagliacci*, pronounced [paliachi] performed by Beniamino Gigli." He's crazy about Gigli, but his own voice is pretty awful—donkey-rooster-like. Only fit to sing our traditional songs, I think.

FNAC was really easy to find. The building resembled the department store in Tbilisi. An escalator took me up to the airtight classical music hall, filled with the muffled sounds of piano and violin.

A lad with a shaved head was standing at the counter. I headed for him with my book in my hand. He immediately guessed where he had to look for the operas, came from behind the counter and went toward the shelves laden with countless CDs. His movement was amazingly light, his step surprisingly soft, just like a ballerina's. His pants were pushed down, revealing the line between his buttocks.

"Verdi's over here!" I heard a familiar voice.

It was Helena. She was behind a mountain of discs piled in the middle of the hall.

"Helena!" I cried and went to her. I didn't know if I was

supposed to kiss her or not, in other words, was I still sulking at her?

Dozens of boxes had the same inscription: VERDI, VERDI, VERDI.

"What are you looking for?"

"His operas," I pointed at the name on the boxes.

"Yeah, I heard the name . . ."

"It's not for me. My aunt's husband is a tenor," I thought it necessary to explain because, as always, I didn't have the faintest idea what to talk about.

She had a disc in her hand, which helped me, if only temporarily.

"And you?" I asked.

"Shostakovich, Quartet No. 8," she replied.

"Great . . ."

What else could I say? I failed to think of anything better. But I had enough time to think: *She's an intellectual, easy to chat up.* Much more difficult to deal with the dumb ones when it comes to sex.

All of a sudden, Helena touched my sleeve and said with a smile:

"The other day I was so foolish . . . I regret it very much . . ."

I expected nothing of the sort.

"When?" I played daft.

"That day, at the Père-Lachaise . . . I felt pretty down and you just happened to be there . . . Besides, I really freaked out. You followed me like a cop . . . Sorry I hurt your feelings . . ."

"Isn't it amazing that you've been apologizing since the day I met you?"

I scored a bull's-eye. I'd never been so wittily precise. Her laugher drove me crazy. I hadn't heard her laugh this way: her cheeks lined and her dimples disappeared. It sounded like a deep sigh or something, not a laugh at all.

"You must think I'm mad," she said.

"No," I felt braver. Retreating was akin to utter defeat at the moment. "It's you who should think I'm an ass. Believe it or not, but I followed you instinctively. No conscious thought, trust me."

"And you were looking at my legs," she smiled.

I could hardly believe my ears. She was saying amazing things!

"That's instinct too," I said.

"My phobias are sheer instincts too," she echoed.

I thought I might voice one of the Georgian toasts: "It's your fault I can't keep my eyes off you! Don't be so beautiful and I'll stop staring." Obviously, I said nothing of the sort.

"I've been scared of men's eyes since my childhood," she said.

"I'm sorry." Now it was my turn to apologize. I was genuinely worried—what did she detect in my gaze?

"Stop apologizing," she cried, laughing.

"The things you keep saying don't leave me a choice," I laughed too. A weird, neighing sound came together with my laughter. Indicating embarrassment, I guess.

"Ah," she waved me off. "It's me saying stupid things, which is so awkward . . . 'Don't look at me, why are you looking at me' . . . As if I'm paranoid."

I wasn't imagining: she was nervous.

I thought I'd smile at her again, but about-to-lose-his-pants lad helped me—he came back in a flurry with two largish boxes in his hand.

"*Un Ballo in Maschera, Pagliacci,*" he smiled coldly. Apparently, air attendants and shop assistants had similarly artificial smiles. That's what I guessed at the FNAC.

"Okay then, see you at the hotel," Helena said.

"Or on the train," I added.

Somehow I wanted all my remarks to be extremely witty.

Helena turned to the disc heap. I bought the CDs and left. The violin and piano stayed confined to the glass hall. Another kind of music was heard elsewhere in the shop.

She's flirting with me, I thought as I came out into the street.

I was facing a dilemma: if I kept flirting with her, it was highly improbable that Maček, her husband, would translate my stories. Consequently, I couldn't take back to Mum "specific offers" and literary-Olympic medals and prizes.

Now, in hindsight, I could still joke about all that . . .

I couldn't write though. I can recall it quite clearly. I hate writing as it is and, from my observation, I find it practically impossible to even sit down to it when I'm abroad. And getting down to it is essential for the process. As you might know, if you don't physically sit down and close the door, nothing is going to come of it. But how was I supposed to sit down when we were driven like a herd from city to city? I wasn't their type—the automatons that could write in all conditions. I started to think of them as acrobat writers.

As soon as I got the hotel I set my mind on Heinz's task. Since my arrival, I failed to find any strength to write. I did have (and still have) several potential stories I could put to paper, but was just unable to concentrate on them. If you're already in the process, everything seems easy (at least the contact with the writing paper), but once you're out of practice, all looks unmanageably difficult. The plots you had in your head lose their attraction and significance, and life itself becomes monotonous and uninteresting.

Considering all this, I took Heinz's proposal (passed on to us through Irmel) as a well-timed sign and, equipped with a pen and writing pad, I settled in the toilet, which was the only place in the hotel one could feel relatively at ease. The room was so small and uncomfortable that one could only use the TV set for a table. I guess I should have been grateful the Arab didn't make us sleep on the carpet.

Writing for Heinz certainly had another benefit: I could kill time. It was pretty important as I really didn't know how to entertain myself. I had read all the books I had brought with me, while the TV programs I watched were designed for the inhabitants of other planets. Definitely not for me.

Even before I went into the bathroom, I knew what I had to write. I was to describe the night a bomb was dropped on Tbilisi. I had to tell how my girlfriend and I woke up and waited for the end clutching our passports. As if we would have been denied entry into paradise without them.

But every time I was about to write the first sentence, I saw Helena in my mind's eye . . .

I couldn't figure out if she was really so absentminded or just mental. First she rebuked me at the cemetery for following her, then gave me that strange smile on the coach and today apologized in the disc shop.

Basically, was I supposed to look at her or not to look at her? I was utterly lost.

Because of these thoughts I was unable to write even a single sentence in the Brussels bathroom. To be precise, I started to but couldn't go on.

The word *bomb* was the only one that stuck in my mind. I already knew I'd use it in my opening sentence. I even wrote: "The Russians dropped bombs on us in August." But I didn't like it and stopped. I didn't care for either bombs or our passports. I was thinking about Helena.

. . .

15 October, Brussels.

Another competition . . .
How I hate competitions . . .

They'll award us in Berlin. The winner will be published in Simplicissimus.

Shall I write or forget about it?

If I do, what about?

Options:

Political,

Subjective,

Objective—non-political—documentary (say, the description of our train?).

Or can I eventually get down to writing the story of my exile?

The title versions:

Why was I banned from Croatia?

Why are the Croats disliked in Croatia?

How the eleventh century Church schism affected Croatia: Catholicism and exiled Danuta Prochorovič.

Does one put on weight in exile?

What would hurt the Croats' feelings and what would hurt me?

Two home countries: Croatia and Serbia. One home: Germany.

An Orthodox Catholic of the twenty-first century.

Why can't I stand competitions?

Why is it me who deserves the prize?

Hateful Serbia + One Croat.

Should I send these titles as an entry?

If I get down to it, I can write it in three days. I'll start on Friday and finish on Monday. I have to (if I get started).

I'm in Brussels. Have attended four seminars. My turn is in Germany. I praise everyone. Happy as children. How pathetic male writers are! We women are hyenas. That's why our colleagues don't sympathize with us. I praised the Czech Theodore Kubelik (story of his clown father), the Georgian Tsviad (don't remember his surname . . . for his poem and for the war), the Estonian Urmas Ods (story "Antelope"), the Romanian Stephan Enesku (a fragment from his novel) and the Swede Rolf Eklund (a poem).

The appearance: -5/-4/sometimes 3 and sometimes 0. Eklund's bum is more or less okay. The Czech must be at least 100. Good he's not accompanied by his nurse. Tsviad is dark, invariably unshaven, with a pimpled forehead. The Estonian—a fat old punk. Romantic aspect: 0000000000000!!!

Good-looking: the Serb man (the Serbs again!), German Rudy (gay, unfortunately), the Portuguese Tasheira (but short), and Slovenian Tadeusz (super bottom!).

First place: Rudy, but (I'm repeating myself) gay. Oops!

Have eaten (15 minutes ago for breakfast): eggs, fried sausage, salami, cheese, a cherry tart, and fruit salad.

Checked the weight: 105 kg. In the morning! What's it going to be in the evening?

I'm going out. Have to meet Mari Roget and the Turk Sybel. I'm leaving my credit cards in the room. Only taking my purse. They say mugging is usual in this quarter.

Yesterday finished Hilde's book. First 40 pages pretty dynamic, the rest—dawdling.

I was told the Hungarian, Bulgarian and Belarusian were published in The New Yorker. *Someone's got it. I'm curious.*

Today I'm going to choose some poor young writer for my praise. The young ones need it so much.

Enough is enough. I'm starting a diet in Frankfurt. I'm embarrassing my readers.

God, I'm too lazy to write . . . Especially for the competition!

10. FRANKFURT

I didn't write a single line in Brussels. Neither sitting in the bathroom nor Irmel's promised prize helped. I just couldn't gather my thoughts. Everything I wrote seemed superficial, vague, and commonplace.

Another crushing defeat of a Georgian writer in Europe . . .

We left for Germany at seven in the morning, planning to be in Frankfurt by midday. Straight from the station, we were taken to the Buchmesse, or the international book market, where Heinz and Rudy were to introduce us to journalists and publishers. As expected, Iliko moaned a lot about it:

"Couldn't we have slept a bit longer? Why don't they take you and leave us alone?"

His "us" meant other Iliko-type guide-interpreters designated to accompany the writers.

However, as soon as it transpired that we were to be greeted by the Nobel Prize winner Ajia Akunadal, he immediately cut protestations:

"I'm just curious what he says," he told us. "He's written a good book . . . with tigers in it."

We lacked sleep. Our eyes and faces were puffy. The Croat Danuta looked particularly miserable—this lovable, obese, highly excitable lady.

"I like sleeping," she admitted. "I've hated getting up early since I remember myself. There are nations that can't stand mornings, those that only come to life at night—just like vampires . . . I'm not a very typical Croat in this respect. The

Croatians are morning people. I should've been born in Italy . . . What kind are you?"

Momentarily I was lost for an answer.

"I believe we're midday people," I replied. "Georgia wakes up at around noon."

"I see," she listened gravely. I thought she'd laugh, but it was I who laughed at my own joke. Apparently, the Croats didn't feel like laughing in the mornings.

Hardly had our train left the station when Valeri Pushkov, nicknamed the Little Russian, came to our compartment.

It was the first time since the beginning of our tour that he spoke to us. He left the impression of being extremely upright and deeply indignant. It was the Kremlin policy that drove him to us.

"I had no idea you haven't got Russian visas," he told us. "It's absolutely despicable that you're not allowed into my country!"

"The war," Iliko said, putting a lot of significance into the word.

"Yes, but what do you have to do with it? It wasn't you personally who fought!"

It had already been three years since Russia started denying the Georgians entry visas (the punishment devised by their authorities). Our colleague should have heard about it.

"We're deaf and dumb." He sat between Zviad and Iliko. He was wearing his permanent sandals and cocoa socks. "We knew nothing! Found out accidentally . . . Kolya is appalled too. I'm going to write a letter today. All writers must sign it! I'll place it on the Internet."

We said nothing. Back home, in Tbilisi, we had been told we weren't accompanying others into Russia, so why would we react now?

"What are you doing about it? We're going and you're staying behind?" he asked compassionately.

"We'll wait for you in Warszawa!" Iliko thundered cheerfully. Once again, he put a lot of meaning into that single "Warszawa": his loathing for loitering, displeasure at being woken up at seven, hatred for the chauvinist politicians, the inaccessibility of Irmel's physiological essence and god knows what more. Basically, everything he considered worth raving about. His Polish pronunciation of Warsaw was deliberately chosen to express his contempt for the world.

"Can't they do anything?" The Little Russian must have meant the organizers. "They're pretty powerful if they choose to be. Their initiative carries serious weight and they can't get three visas? If only they'd written to us . . . We'd have raised our voices."

"You'd all be arrested," Zviad said softly, with a smile, timidly.

"That'd be excellent!" the Russian laughed. "But it's not that bad, you know. We're the force they have to consider in any case."

"No, you'd be all arrested!" Iliko repeated Zviad's words. It was the first time their opinions coincided.

Possibly that was the reason Zviad was encouraged:

"You've got dictatorship!" he said directly to the Russian.

"It's worse than hell," Pushkov said, plunging into such self-pity that it reminded me of Dostoyevsky's dispirited characters: decent but desolate Russians, unstintingly preaching their misfortunes.

"They're sick," he went on, "only thinking about demonstrating how big their dick is to the Americans. And while these two are comparing their dicks, we're drowning in shit. But you've got your own madmen, don't you? An American can screw your ass without you even noticing it."

He must have reverted to such strong vocabulary in order to gain our trust. Within seconds he managed to pour out an amount of obscenities that made the air seem heavy and greasy. Eventually, he once again promised to write the protest letter, swore bitterly and with deliberation, and shook only Zviad's hand for some reason.

"A classic verbal sublimation of a typical Russian intellectual," Danuta concluded. She had inadvertently overheard our conversation. And she understood Russian.

"The Serbs made us learn Russian at school," she told us. "However, your Stalin wholeheartedly despised our Tito. Even harbored an assassination plan. But Tito's revenge was teaching schoolchildren Russian and not Stalin's native Georgian."

"Not only Tito—he likewise hated Georgia," Iliko disagreed with her. "His mother was a whore, his father a drunkard who beat him regularly. Why would he like Georgia?"

"His mum did everything she could for him and her whoring isn't proved!" Zviad protested. "He was an awful child."

"Just like Rosemary's," Danuta chuckled.

We laughed at her remark and she gave us the smile of a happy grandma.

"You Georgians are so cute—always stick together and laugh a lot," she said in pidgin Russian.

Frankly speaking, it was she who was cute—truly like a granny—but not because of her age, but thanks to her weight and red cheeks. I had only seen such attractively portly ladies in old Soviet fairy-tale films. But who could have said we were cute? Iliko's sleepless eyes had made him look like Great Mao and his hair hadn't been washed for a week, I suspected. Zviad was irrationally frowning at the Belgian landscape whizzing beyond the window. As for me, I could hardly keep my eyes open for lack of sleep, exuding boredom and melancholy. However, she was right about us sticking together—like a trio of apprehensive provincials. It wasn't love or friendship that kept Zviad, Iliko, and me together. We seemed to be glued to each other by some unhealthy national instinct. We were obliged to *adjust* to each other. Actually, with time, I was beginning to get weary of both.

And after Danuta's words I wanted to leave this entity more than ever.

The minute the realization crossed my mind, I sprang to my feet.

"Hungry?" Iliko asked me.

"I'm taking a walk," I answered and headed for the door leading to the seventh carriage. I wouldn't have gone anywhere if not my urge to find Helena. If not for her, I wouldn't have budged, would have closed my eyes and fooled everyone, except myself, that I was sleeping.

As a rule, we traveled in the sixth carriage, she—in the eighth. There was the seventh carriage wedged between us—full of puffy-faced, irritable, sleepless, or dozing off writers.

First I saw Maček sitting with his feet on the front seat. Holding a plastic cup which she occasionally sipped from, Helena was actually sitting next to those feet. She was talking quite loudly and energetically to her husband in a language unknown to me. She stopped the moment she spotted me, smiled and waved.

"Zaza," she told her husband.

Maček was sitting with his back to me. Apparently, he silently asked his wife whom she meant. Then he turned and noisily greeted me:

"Hey, why didn't you send your stories?"

I couldn't have said I was unable to make a choice between his translation of my stories and his wife, could I?

Finally, I opted for the truth:

"I haven't got a computer."

"Oh, it's such a huge problem," I detected mockery in his voice. "Don't tell Heinz, just in case."

There was nothing I could say. So I smiled at him.

"I've got one," he went on soberly. "A business meeting in your or my room is okay with you?"

I wasn't sure whether he was joking again or not, but I agreed:

"No problem."

"Want a fag?" Helena asked unexpectedly.

Initially I thought she was asking her husband, but no, she was looking at me. It was somewhat rude of her, as if she didn't wish Maček to talk anymore. Or was I imagining?

I must have taken ages to react, so she simply ordered:

"Let's go."

Maček and I exchanged smiles—at that minute he looked like an eccentric retiree. Helena walked past me, heading for the toilet.

Completely inanely, just like a senile Party leader at the Soviet parade, I raised my hand saluting Maček, grinned widely and followed his wife.

"How can you be bothered?" he muttered and sipped from the cup left behind by Helena.

For some reason I was certain we were going to smoke in the toilet (the women in my life mainly smoke in there), but I was wrong. Helena chose the space between the carriages, deftly pulled down the thick-glassed window and, pleased with her own dexterity or something else, laughed happily.

"We're going to have a fag and feel much better," she said.

Have a fag . . .

How could we if I'd given up smoking? Did I have to compromise again? I'd given up three years earlier and smoking now would take me back to pre-Elene epoch.

I was unfaithful to Elene, now I had to give up my principles . . .

I recall Maka, the girl from Skype, asking me if I was married. Had I been truthful, I'm sure, no harm would have been done—she would have been loyal to her decision. But I freaked out. I feared the truth would prevent me from getting to Maka's non-virtual tits. I feared those tits would remain in the virtual reality forever if I didn't deny Elene. So, I immediately denied her by saying: "No, no wife!" That time I struck lucky as the Skype striptease was followed by quite a corporeal one. Neither had a rooster crowed thrice. And then I talked in my sleep.

On the train that day, however, neither did Helena ask about my wife nor did I feel guilty of betraying anyone. I just hated the thought of another compromise. I didn't give a damn for Skype Maka, but strangely enough, I couldn't bear lying to Helena.

So, I simply told the truth:

"I don't smoke. I just followed you."

She shrugged her shoulders and pulled a packet of cigarettes and a lighter from her pocket (I clearly remember she had a thin gray cardigan and jeans on).

"What?" she smiled at me.

I didn't understand her question.

This time it was my turn to shrug. I shook my head.

"Awful that I smoke, right?" She lit her cigarette.

"Your voice will become hoarse," I answered.

Smoking had burned my aunt's vocal chords. And before I said it aloud, I pictured her: with yellow fingernails and a husky voice of a jailbird. It was her fault that her poor husband failed to turn into a great tenor. He sang while she smoked and the other way round. Complete failure any way you look at it. I believe we're dealing with a subconscious protest: my aunt hates his profession and fights his main instrument—his voice—with her toxic fumes.

"You don't smoke because of your dad?" Helena asked.

"No, why?" I didn't know what my dad had to do with it.

"Isn't he a tenor?"

Aha, she had remembered.

"No, it's my uncle, but he doesn't care if I smoke. And I don't care whether he sings well or not. I think he offered me my first fag . . . I was three when he gave me one and then took me to a brothel. It's our tradition."

"Taking a three-year-old to a brothel is your tradition?" She nearly choked.

"Yes, it's an ancient tradition. A whore has to put a silver ring on a boy's penis. The ring is bought by the family for the occasion. If you don't do it, you're not taken for a man."

"Aren't you Orthodox Christians?"

She looked so ingenuous I felt guilty.

"On the whole, yes. But our Orthodoxy is older than Christianity."

"You're pulling my leg," she smiled.

I didn't feel like fooling around, so I smiled back.

"You've been lying through your teeth, right?" she asked.

"No. My uncle is a tenor."

"Aha."

"Yeah."

We nodded to each other. Our last remarks helped fill a potentially embarrassing pause.

"Okay," she said and flicked her cigarette ash onto the packet top. I thought it was solely the habit of Georgian smokers. I even told her:

"I had no idea such flicking was also a habit in Poland."

"I'm Greek," she corrected me with a diligent schoolgirl's expression.

"Hundred percent?"

"What do you mean?"

"Your parents . . ."

"Mum's German. If she were Greek, my bum would've been heavier." Laughing, she raised on her toes, stuck out her bottom and slapped it.

She's so lovely, was what crossed my mind.

"Which means you're Orthodox too." It wasn't an ideal phrase to bridge the conversation gap but, unfortunately, I couldn't think of anything better.

"I really don't know. My dad's father had a restaurant on Rhodes, where my mum used to spend her summer holidays and that's how they fell in love. You see?"

I thought she didn't understand my question but I agreed:

"Yeah. It's very romantic."

"The island yes, but not holiday sex. I'm the result of a holiday sex," she laughed again.

She's a girl with problems, I thought. *Has gone through some bad times, but hasn't lost her sense of humor.*

I wondered what I was the result of.

What was happening in Georgia at the time I was conceived?

These two I said aloud.

Helena looked at me with interest:

"I don't know."

"A revolution erupted in our neighboring Iran, the Russians went into Afghanistan and my mum and dad were on a holiday in Dagomis."

"Cool." Helena was impressed.

"Yeah, I'm pretty proud of the history of my conception!"

I thought I'd said everything. Nothing more came to my mind. I could have only invited her to dance . . .

In films they've discovered a wonderful way out of similarly embarrassing situations: the train brakes abruptly, while a man and a woman fall into each other's arms. Suddenly I felt an urge to kiss her. I had lived like a saint for the last two weeks, which might have explained it. I was truly scared because if I followed my instincts blindly, I'd inevitably make some fatal mistakes. What I needed at the time was to be rational . . . rational and honest.

Some of my thoughts must have been too obvious as Helena returned to the safe topic of cigarettes:

"Maček only smokes when he's writing. Helps him stay more focused."

"Yeah, there are some who find it useful," I agreed and immediately regretted saying *some*. I shouldn't have included Maček among others.

"Do you write?" I asked.

"I dance."

Oh, my! I got frightened.

"No, no," she smiled, "I was joking. I teach at school. And write, just a little." She showed how much with her thumb and index finger.

Hope it's not prose, I thought. God knows how prose women-writers scare me! Every single one I've met looks like a transvestite. I much prefer women poets if it comes to choice.

"Do you write novels?" I asked.

"No, not novels," she laughed. "Only reviews."

Oh, such a relief, I thought. *I just love girls writing reviews.*

"I go, I listen and then either praise or criticize," she said.

"Are you a music critic?" I showed surprise.

"My mum plays the clarinet . . . You know a clarinet, don't you?" She tried showing what it looked like with her hands. "I'm a musician too, but rather untalented . . . I can listen though and understand music pretty well."

"All kinds of music?"

"All kinds of what?" She didn't get my question.

"I mean do you write about all kinds of music?"

"Oh, no," she dragged at her cigarette. "Only classical."

"Great. There's a man who's been steadily putting me off classical music since my childhood . . ."

"Your uncle," she laughed.

"Exactly," I chuckled.

"Can't stand singers," she flinched.

Her skin creased funnily between her nose and her eyebrows.

At that point the Bulgarian writer Borisov invaded our tiny space, smiled meaningfully and went into the toilet designed for the handicapped (the carriage had two: one for the physically handicapped and the other for those suffering from literary ambitions).

Helena dropped her cigarette butt into a litter box fixed to the window frame (first time I'd seen a litter box hanging midair) and laughed.

"So much for a smoke," she said.

I guessed it meant going back to our places.

"I suggest we stick to the tradition: you go, I follow," I said with a smile.

"It's already a tradition, is it?" she smiled too.

I nodded and, I believe, it was for the first time that I used a purely Georgian, traditional showing-off technique: I offered her *my melancholy.*

"Are you okay?" She sounded worried.

Apparently I had overdone . . .

"I'm fine, fine," I reassured her.

My expression must have changed so abruptly that she felt alarmed. I couldn't have told her I was just showing off, could I?

I saw her to her seat and Maček, who greeted us as if he hadn't seen us for ages.

"We're settled on the texts, aren't we?" he asked.

"Sure," I answered and glanced at Helena—I had to indicate a good-bye by raising my hand or winking (definitely both eyes, as winking only one would clearly be rude and highly suggestive). However, I failed to do either because Helena put a thick magazine on her knees and began leafing through it. I was positive about my impression: she changed. Seemed sterner and tenser. At least she was completely different when she smoked. I remember wondering if Maček was aware of her metamorphosis, because if a husband missed such telltale signs, there was something very, very wrong. For some reason, her sudden transformation cheered me up more than our recent conversation. At exactly that moment I began to suspect there were problems in their family . . .

. . .

17 October, Brussels—Frankfurt

I'm on the train, trying to peruse "Headway". Got as far as E. Learnt words including "equipment." Yesterday memorized 20 words.

I'm hot.

Valeri's running up and down the train worrying about the Georgians. We've denied them entry visas.

I'm sick and tired of this crap! Why is he so obsessed or why aren't they given visas? He sulks at me for not getting involved. Spent all of yesterday on the Internet, sending letters to Chikalo and Seryozha urging them to stand up for it. Fucking revolutionary! I tell him to screw them all—the Kremlin, Tbilisi, Ossetia and Abkhazia. Forget about them!

I've got an impression Valeri's more worried than the Georgians. Nearly hysterical. Has been like that since Vera.

We had a discussion in Paris and one of them mentioned the war. I wondered what he had to say about it. Wanted Valeri to hear it too. The moderator wouldn't allow him to speak—the lad was in an idiotic position. I take pity on the Georgians. They live in a nightmare: their presidents are either psychopaths or impotents, unsure what they want, can't stand foreigners in their tiny Christian khanate.

Valeri says all the TV coverage of the August war was Kremlin propaganda. Why the hell does it matter? If they can't stand the Abkhaz and the Ossetians, what propaganda does it need?

Valeri frets while I don't give a damn—to hell with them all!

What was happening today?

I was thinking about the text I'm supposed to have ready for Heinz's Berlin competition ("Man-eater," "Zhenya's Dream," "Fire in Medvedkovo"—not sure yet).

Yeah, bought myself a pair of gray corduroys in Brussels. A huge reduction: initially cost 125 euros but I got them for 70. Hate buying things for myself. Such a waste of money. Looked for a jacket for Vadim. Sveta got me on the mobile. Had a kind of row. Said she shouldn't phone as I'd call her with a cheap card. I didn't like how she sounded, she didn't like my voice. Hung up. Don't want them to waste money. Will call her from Frankfurt.

I miss both girls . . . When the journey lasts for more than two weeks, it stops being pleasant. Becomes tedious. We get tired easily, very easily . . .

What's wrong with me? Am I writing a diary?

Everyone does. Me too. Being idle is boring. This train has an advantage: one wants to write. Even if foolish things.

P.S. There are two of us—Valeri and me—from Russia, not three. Raul Aldamov is on his own. Should I protest? We condemn, condemn, condemn!

. . .

As soon as we crossed into Germany, I became a witness to yet another transformation: cynical Iliko changed into a dynamic, tactful, and caring gentleman. He must have felt at home there and acted like a considerate and well-mannered host.

"It's a lovely city," he told us as we arrived in Frankfurt, "but in summer. Whoever comes here in late autumn or winter hates the place, because it's rainy, cold, and all streets and parks lose color. You have to come in May or June to appreciate its beauty and fall in love with the city. During the war the allies razed Frankfurt to the ground. Everything you see was restored later. Their Goethe was born only three streets from here. Such large-scale fairs are held several times a year, including book and car fairs. They also have a taste for good food. I'll show you an excellent sausage place. And don't order two dishes, don't be greedy. It's Germany you know, the portions are huge and the plates are so large you can lie on them. Nothing like Paris where we were obliged to starve on their diet. There's a big street here, excellent for shopping, so Zviad can get things for his family. Also, the underground is the easiest—designed by rational people. It takes you either downtown or to the Buchmesse. Everyone thinks it's a large city, while in reality it's quite small. My estimate is it's not larger than Kutaisi. But their airport is really huge. In the city center there's the Euro Monument. Zviad can go, lay flowers, and pray for his wallet."

But how could praying help poor Zviad? He'd spent all his money with black street vendors.

From the station we were taken directly to the book fair. Straight from the city we found ourselves in another one—the book city where one had to take a special bus or an extremely long escalator in order to get from one pavilion to another.

The fair was closing that day. People swarmed like ants and it was unbearably hot. Like cattle, we were driven into a pretty small hall called Blaue Sofa (popular writers usually preach from its blue armchairs), were met by an applause (nobody knows for which achievement), our photos were taken and then we were placed at the feet of Ajia Akunadal, the Nobel Laureate. Mr. Akunadal was wrapped in a cloth that looked like the late Indira Gandhi's sari (but he was a man, if I'm not mistaken). He had long yellow fingernails and a shiny, hairless head. His beard was very much like those favored by the Al-Qaeda guerillas. Indeed, he looked like an unwashed alien. On the other hand, neither did we resemble supermodels—exhausted, sleep-deprived, untidy, wan, and disheveled. Only the inseparable quartet was sleek and bouncy: Heinz, Rudy, Irmel, and Milena. Only they caught the Nobel Laureate's every word with interest bordering on reverence. If I understood correctly, Ajia Akunadal talked about the Holocaust and the Nazi camps, turning his new book (called *The Birth of Apology* or something similar) in his lilac-brown hands and, finally, addressed us with the rhetoric of the UN General Secretary.

I hadn't read his books, neither did I have an idea about his origin, so I asked Danuta standing next to me:

"Where is he from?"

Danuta shrugged her shoulders:

"I believe he's German."

"He's German?" I was amazed.

I heard a piercing "Shh!" from behind. It was Rudy, hushing us.

"We've got no chance," I told Iliko later. "If one wants to be recognized as a writer, one has to turn into a strange creature like this alien."

"Why, he's got a good book . . . about tigers," he disagreed.

Well-known writers stared at us from enormous photos fixed to the counters, stands and walls. They seemed ironic, asking the one hundred obscure writers of the Literature Express: "What are you doing here? Who let you in?" I stood there as if in front of the icons, thinking that if I were noticed by any publisher, big or small, I'd stop wandering this side of the counter and all my problems would forever belong to the past: tanks would leave, bombs would be sucked up into the air, my prodigal dad would come back tearful, all Elene-Helenas of this world would succumb to me, and *specific offers* would pour down over my mum like a shower of gold . . .

But how was I to break through with my fifteen stories? My fifteen literary tiddlers?

I could see Zviad was similarly concerned. Staring in awe at the gigantic book counters, he was as hurt as me for not yet belonging to that community.

"Shall we look for the Georgians?" Iliko suggested.

It was a poor proposal because I knew: they would remind me

of the boring Georgian events, recount in detail every protest rally and make my throat ache from restrained fury. And all the while, I just craved to be among the cynically smiling writers looking down from the stands . . . Even with Zviad for company.

I didn't want to be squeamish. Iliko was emanating such virtue that I chose not to protest. I'm pretty sure had we been in another country and had Zviad and I offered something similar, he'd certainly be mad at us. He wouldn't wish to meet his countrymen. In this case he led us to the Georgian counter himself.

A colossal hall number 5 was allocated for the Caucasus, Russia, Turkey and Eastern Europe. The largest counter—the size of the Kremlin—belonged to Russia. The walls behind were adorned with the pictures of their bosses: their president and their prime minister.

Our counter, or rather what was left of it, was between those of Armenia and Azerbaijan. A grand cleanup was underway: the posters were being taken down from the walls, books being put into boxes and the metal frame of the not-long-ago stand was being dismantled.

We were looking at an apocalyptic scene. Among the half-dismantled structure and empty shelves there was one single drunken Georgian publisher talking to a hermaphrodite.

It had to be—this bisexual bibliophile. But the publisher didn't suspect anything as he could only see the upper part of the body: the bibliophile was on our side of the counter. The upper body was that of a typical male, while the *apocalypses* started lower: a tight leather skirt, red tights and high-heeled shoes. I could imagine the shock my drunken countryman was in for at seeing the rest of the body!

"I don't think we should go nearer," I told Iliko.

"Have they all left?" He looked at his watch. "So early? Still two hours to go before closing."

"Hi, Zviad!" The publisher spotted us.

We couldn't sneak out now. We were obliged to greet and talk.

"We screwed the Russians!" the publisher pronounced victoriously. "We sold everything . . . Crowds and crowds of people came to us and nobody paid any attention to them! I've been running around like mad for four days. I'm in charge here now and have to see all books into their boxes and then off we go to Tbilisi! But I'm going to die if I don't drink. Hate flying."

He managed to squeeze twenty stories into about five minutes and then whined:

"We've failed to sell our wine, though. We had five boxes that the Ministry had asked us to bring here. Now it's for me to dispose of them or what?"

He definitely looked stressed out, but I didn't delve into the true reason of his overexcited state.

The Armenians, Ms. Anait, and Mr. Zeituntsyan were proudly and elegantly standing at their country's counter, conversing in the gravest and most tragic manner, occasionally smiling at us.

"Have you heard any news from Tbilisi?" the publisher asked. "I've been pretty isolated, no TV in my hotel room, so I know nothing." Then he laughed bitterly, "Shall I ask for political asylum? If the Russians are going to take over Tbilisi, I might as well stay here . . ."

No wonder we left the Georgian publisher as quickly as possible. Because he knew only Zviad, it was him he called after:

"Don't abandon me here like a frigging prick!"

But Zviad didn't stay with him.

The apocalyptic scene will haunt me for a long time: the skeleton of the stand, piles of boxes, and among them a drunken Georgian and an inquisitive hermaphrodite.

Despite ourselves, we had witnessed the end of something. We caught the final episode . . .

I reckon I must have been envious of the smiling photo-writers (or I just wanted to see Helena but didn't admit to myself) because that evening I printed out the translation of my stories in the hotel Internet corner and headed for Maček's room. I had actually phoned him to ask if he had time to look at my texts and he said he was waiting for me.

He was cheerful and businesslike, as usual. I hadn't detected anything out of the ordinary.

In about five, maybe ten minutes at most, I was standing at his door. I had heard his and Helena's voices well before I came to the door, but I ignored the ominous signs. It was only later that I realized they had been quarrelling. I knocked boldly.

Maček opened the door and yelled like a football fan—happily and frighteningly:

"Zaza!"

I immediately guessed he was stone drunk. His face was red and his eyes glassy. He tapped my shoulder with his hundred-weight paw and pulled me into the room. I barely kept my balance.

"This is really important . . . It is!" he shouted into my ear.

I still don't know what he meant.

Directly in my line of vision, Helena was sitting in the middle of a wide bed, clutching a pillow. Tears were streaming down her face. Her eyes had a hazy look and I thought she was staring at something, right through me. I froze, as if time itself had stopped . . . Her weeping had pinned me to the floor.

I witnessed a scene I shouldn't have seen. Here again, I caught the *final* part of something—big or small. I found myself entangled in a completely unfamiliar marital history: a husband and wife had a quarrel, the wife had wept (those were the tears already cried out), and I was a witness.

"I'm sorry," I managed to say and headed for the door.

I recall thinking, *If Maček blocks my way, I'm going to hit him.*

But he only shouted:

"Hey, wait, it's important!"

I wonder what it was.

It was seven in the morning when he knocked on my door. He apologized, saying he was pretty unbearable when drunk, that good and evil demons had been fighting for his soul for the last fifty-two years. Then he took my stories and bid good-bye with a timid smile.

I didn't see Helena either in the morning or when we left Frankfurt. I even suspected she had abandoned the trip altogether. At least, when I got on the train my feeling was I'd never see her again.

How stupid! Did she run away from her husband and from me too? What kind of an end is this?

11. MALBORK

Everyone became horny in Malbork.

The intensity of the sexual energy that burst out in that quiet medieval Polish town astounded me. Around forty percent of my colleagues got to know each other in the biblical sense. Neither were the technical staff impassive onlookers. Iliko, for instance, didn't even have time to realize how his permanently busy Irmel was snatched away. In truth, I thought this automaton girl was frigid. I was absolutely sure she got her sexual pleasure from carrying out Heinz's orders. Irmel's body (and I suspected her soul too) was conquered by a Serb writer: a long-legged grasshopper of a man, with his hair divided in the middle Rasputin-style and invariably wearing leotard-like shorts. I hadn't heard him talk or seen him smile, but at the Malbork disco he got so drunk, he couldn't stop either talking or dancing. First he amazed us with his solo dance—with a glass in his hand, he was swaying with his eyes closed in the middle of the dance floor. Then he kissed Irmel with such passion that she nearly gave up her soul.

Not surprisingly, it was Iliko who was deeply hurt with Irmel's fall. Wasn't it him who admired her authentic, unshaved armpits, yellow-golden skin, and healthy legs? Naturally, he didn't show his pain openly, only expressed his disgust:

"She must be sick to have coitus with this grasshopper."

Another hustling German, Milena, also gave in to the majority. It can be said that both Irmel and Milena plunged into the sinful realm of the Literature Express simultaneously. At that, they did it with their characteristic professionalism as if they had received orders from Heinz to enjoy themselves, sleep with anyone they wanted, but without ignoring their duties.

Milena was snatched up by Vitas, the Lithuanian, who put his mark on her in the form of an angry red hickey and later, in our presence, grabbed her ass with both hands.

"He's screwing her," Zviad announced, having witnessed all this. A brilliant deduction.

A similar fate was shared by the middle-aged French woman, Mme Roget, the Finnish poet (an extremely nice lady, by the way), the Bosnian "giggling machine" (our nickname for the dark-haired, short woman), the Belgian grandpa (who, in his turn, was lightly raped by the Romanian youth) and probably many others—the echo of their ecstasy was absorbed by our hotel walls for keeps.

We were impressed by a long, fervent kiss between the Spanish poet and his wife, who, I suspected, had been smoking pot. She was sitting astride him, with her legs pushed outward (otherwise she wouldn't be able to press her breasts onto him), kissing him with remarkable tenderness.

Mme Roget was by far the happiest: instead of lying down to rest and sleep peacefully after an exhausting day, she didn't stop even for a moment. She danced nonstop with her Belarusian boyfriend. The lad, a poet, must have been at least twenty years her junior. He made himself memorable with his crew cut, a Mickey Mouse T-shirt tucked into his jeans, and an exotic Zenith camera dangling from his shoulder. His biceps were pretty shapely too. Good thing he didn't strangle poor Mme Roget in his embrace.

"He'll make her marry him," Zviad ventured a prediction.

We, the commentators and spectators, had grouped together, naturally and unintentionally, watching the show from the dark corners of the hall. The onlookers (or the freaks enjoying the sex show) were: the Georgians, whom nobody succumbed to or chose to lure, the Armenian Zeituntsyan, Heinz and Rudy (I believe fully content with each other in the sexual aspect), the Chechen Aldamov, the Czech "Elf," the Big and the Little Russians (faceless from excessive drinking), the Portuguese Tasheira, the Albanian "Sufferer" (an extremely appropriate nickname considering the expression of his face), the Bulgarian Borisov and one or two European Union chaps . . .

The Azeri Aliev was surprisingly efficient: with the help of the security of our rest house (I really found our hotel identical to the Soviet-type rest homes or sanatoria), he discovered the Malbork brothel and brought two whores to his room.

We certainly would have stayed in the dark if he hadn't informed us:

"If I approached one of our colleagues, we wouldn't have been able to look each other in the eyes. We wouldn't find it comfortable to travel further. You'll see how our young Milena and Vitas will be unable to fall back to routine."

Our young Milena was said in such a honey-sweet voice that I was certain he'd be ecstatic to play around with the automaton-girl.

After such an unintentional confession, he whispered to me quite amiably:

"I'd have invited you, Zaza, had you been in the hotel, but, unfortunately, I couldn't find you. You know I rather like you."

Had he said only that it'd be fine, but he winked, which alarmed me. Who could be sure about an Eastern man? Suppose he didn't mean it only in a friendly way? How was I to guess what made an aristocrat, old-timer, and conservative from Baku happy and pleased?

"Was she worth it?" I asked to neutralize his wink ("I'm likewise attracted to women, don't make a mistake.")

"Why she? Why singular?" he smiled. "There were two of them. Russians, I believe . . . But they didn't say so. It's just a hunch. Ashamed they're whoring in Poland and not in their home country."

However, prior to witnessing such a sexual outburst, we had taken a long and tiring journey from Frankfurt to Malbork. Our train had never covered such a distance—as if the trip lasted forever. We seemed to be glued to our seats, grown into our clothes, oozing greenish sweat. The most unbearable part was my inability to either sleep or stay awake. If I'm not mistaken, I went up and down the train at least three times, through all carriages, but failed to spot Helena. And all the while, Maček sat in his customary position—with his legs on the opposite seat. I couldn't ask him where he lost his wife, could I? I was sure she wasn't on the train . . . The scene I observed definitely was preceded by another, much graver one, and her not being on the train must have been the result of something I *had missed*.

I don't remember if I rued or felt deeply sorry about it, because the exhaustion had dulled my emotions, including all sentiments. I mainly thought how delighted I'd be when I got off the train and took a hot shower in the hotel. I persistently tried pushing Helena out of my head. But I was genuinely upset by the time we got to Malbork, managed to get a proper sleep, and finally concluded that Helena was nowhere to be seen.

In the dining car somewhere around German-Polish border, I came across the portly and gentle Danuta, who was reading *The New Yorker*.

"Our Borisov's story is published in here," she told me.

She was excited. As soon as she spoke, I detected it in her voice. But the most ridiculous thing was that she attempted to hide her nervousness behind unnatural giggles and fazed out smiles.

"Our Borisov?" I'm unsure why I was so surprised. *The New Yorker* seemed an unattainable height, while this man in his blue trousers and the appearance of an aging Indian movie star was so near.

"You are surprised, aren't you? Ha-ha-ha!" Danuta laughed and handed me the magazine. "I find something else surprising.

What secret is buried in his text which took him as far as *The New Yorker*?"

Actually, I was astonished to find a Croatian writer asking the same questions I had—a writer of a Georgian-Caucasian breed.

"Can I borrow it?" I asked.

"Yeah, sure, take it. I've finished reading . . . Ha-ha-ha! It's about a couple from Sofia. During World War II. That's what they liked I guess . . . The context . . . As for the story itself . . . Ho-ho-ho! A disaster."

I didn't expect Danuta to be so frank with me. On the other hand, as a writer, I was flattered to be sharing the same problems with her.

"I'll be blunt: Borisov has no talent whatsoever," she beamed at me. "But he's found the secret, got hold of something which has reached across . . . I mean across the ocean . . . Ha-ha-ha . . . Made him interesting. Oh no, it's still nowhere near true popularity—God is fair, wouldn't allow such injustice—no, sir, no way! Ha-ha! Actually, he's already more popular than you and me—has been published in *The New Yorker*, not your *Pravda* . . . Or *Pravda*'s not yours? Sorry . . . Anyway, you know what I mean, don't you? It's not Mount Olympia and too far from the Nobel Prize, but still . . . Ha-ha-ha! And I keep writing . . . for thirty years . . . How old are you?"

"Twenty-eight."

"I'm your age as a writer."

"Thanks."

"What for? You're twenty-eight and how long have you been writing?"

"Seven . . . Five."

"Seven or five?"

"Seven."

"Which means five . . . In short, you write and write and your texts are read only in clubs. You can't get away from clubs . . ."

"What clubs?"

"Literature clubs."

"We haven't got them."

"Even worse! I've been writing for twenty-eight years and can't get away from the Croats. The Croats and not Croatia! I left ten years ago . . . I was obliged to—not of my own free will! I said the Serbs and the Croats were one nation and I was instantly anathematized, you know. I mean, I've also written the history of Croatia, so Borisov isn't the only smart guy! We need to be smart, don't we? Exile is my topic."

"Yeah, but we are unlucky too," I laughed.

"That's what drives me crazy," she reverted to a whisper. "We won't get anywhere near Borisov." She laughed loudly again. "Someone cursed us, no?"

"But you are translated, aren't you?" suddenly I sounded like a reporter.

"Yes. No. Into German and French. But fragmentally. There's no book. I wish my book would be published in France! And I want it very much, damn it! Ha-ha-ha! Don't you? I want to screw the English with my book! I'm up to here," she indicated her throat. "The German Croats, the German Serbs, the Croat Croatians and the Serbian Serbs!"

"I also hate my Georgians. They can't read."

"Do you have the same problems as they've got in Korea?"

"No, we're Orthodox Christians."

"I see . . . But you don't read, do you?"

"Three thousand read, one thousand buys."

"Bravo! How many are you?"

"Four million."

"Which means three. I see . . . I've sacrificed my personal life to literature! Because I know that if you get attached to people, you can't succeed. Remember Wotan's destiny? Or don't you like Wagner? But what does it matter? The more loyal you are to literature, the more hearts you're going to break. And all these are your friends and families. Borisov must have killed his wife or offspring in order to get published in *The New Yorker*! Right, no? Ha-ha-ha! He must have made a considerable sacrifice for his achievement! I'm pretty sure Mr. Akunadal ate his son alive, or at least his cat. How else did he get the Nobel Prize? Never in his life! Apparently, we aren't brutal enough . . ."

If not for the tiring journey, she wouldn't have talked so much. Besides, she must have had more beer than she could hold. I felt bad as it was but the overagitated lady made it a hundred times worse. I still recall the Frankfurt-Malbork stretch as a nightmare. She was so wound up that, together with her cheeks, her arms were deep red, her fatty folds waggled as she prattled on, and I believe she was actually vibrating. Or else, I was dead tired (along with a splitting headache) and handled everything so painfully inadequately.

I also remember cursing myself, Danuta, and Borisov, whose success made her irrational with rage, and above all, Maček! It was primarily his fault the train had lost such a significant passenger.

The Malbork sanatorium (definitely not a hotel though we were supposed to see it as one) threw me into a deeper state of despair. It's only fair to mention that the location was fine—the "hotel" was in the middle of a wood, but I had no appreciation for the wooded area. I had problems killing time in a city, so what was there for me to do in such pastoral surroundings? Suddenly, I wanted to go back to Tbilisi. Nothing kept me in Malbork. I was there for *no one*. True, that minute I hated my home too with its repetitiveness, protest rallies, and the Russian tanks forty km away from the capital, but I couldn't stand the others either. I felt a surge of anger rising when I realized I had to forget Helena, take a walk in the woods, and then write my stories stretched on the bed (where else as there was no table in the room!). I can't stand writers writing about writing in the countryside. And, generally speaking, I can't stand writers brandishing their image of nature lovers!

As soon as we left Germany, Iliko assumed his true identity. He left his decency and other virtues in Germany, turning back into his old, cynical, and highly irritable self.

"There might be rats around," he said. "I've discovered their teeth marks on my bed. Don't leave your window open at night—you might be visited by rodents!"

When we stepped into our room (we had to share), Zviad dropped his bags on the bed (as far as I know he hadn't done anything of the sort in other hotel rooms—it must have been his way of punishing the place and himself) and uttered an extremely original phrase:

"I'm going to get drunk here."

In the meantime I was contemplating going into the woods and hanging myself on the first tree I came across.

Zviad had barely cleared his bed when Milena knocked on our door.

"There's a magnificent castle near here and we're visiting it tomorrow morning. Also, there's a disco we can go to this evening. We can relax, dance, and have fun there, okay?"

Yeah, she did have fun, while some of us sat like dudes . . .

She turned to Zviad before going out:

"Here's the translation of your poem," and handed him a piece of paper in a transparent folder. "It'll be read in the castle tomorrow."

"What translation?" I asked him when Milena left.

"Don't know. Rudy asked me to give him a poem to be translated for the reading."

"Only poets?"

"How do I know?" Zviad shrugged his shoulders.

Aha! Without any language he managed to set up autonomous-literary relations with Rudy.

That was the first Malbork finding: the discovery of independence in Zviad.

Had I stayed in a decent hotel, I'd have been reluctant to go to the disco, but experiencing the cultural life of Malbork was far more preferable than my room. Good thinking, otherwise I'd have missed the outburst of sexual energy!

For the rest of my life I'm going to remember how cheerless Mr. Zeituntsyan was when he watched the kissing and dancing couples, ruefully remarking:

"If my English were anywhere near my Russian, I'd be standing right in the center of the dance floor."

He must have been drunk or else he'd have never whined in my presence.

I noticed beads of sweat around his temple . . . I imagined how he craved to dash into the group of healthy blonde German girls and bite their brawny asses.

Obviously, he wouldn't consider Mme Anait for the purpose and failed to hit it off with the foreign lady writers. But the way he looked at them . . . I think he was the horniest among those at the disco that night. Aside from the sweat beads on his temple, his appearance didn't betray his excitement. And the way he was dressed—as if he wished to hide his vice under a gray jacket, a pair of black trousers, a black tie, and large well-brushed shoes that had seen better days. He seemed the kind of man who, ten or fifteen years earlier, would surely wear a tracksuit (definitely blue with white stripes) at a disco . . . If I remember anything from my childhood, it's pompous funerals of the Party leaders and men in such tracksuits sauntering in the sanatoria lobbies reeking invariably of borsch.

I bet he had one in his luggage.

Or did this magic tracksuit explain why he didn't dare approach a foreign woman? Was it blocking him psychologically? Suppose he dreaded she might search his bag (some men have weird phobias), discover his blue sportswear and faint?

"Who is these?" a trembling German-French-English woman would ask in her broken Russian (as only the one with some Russian would be *punished* by him) and he'd have a heart attack from embarrassment!

If I weren't pathologically lazy, I'd write a story about Mr. Zeituntsyan. The horniest and the most rigidly reserved man I know . . .

I can't claim we felt more relaxed.

Iliko, for instance, was rather direct:

"I'm going back to my room. No use hanging out here. I'll just jerk off."

"You'll do what?" Zviad asked incredulously. He was baffled by Iliko until the very end.

"Jerk off," he repeated. "Don't you see they're all coupled?"

It certainly hurt him to see Irmel being literally screwed by the grasshopper Serb. At least that's what it looked like . . .

"Had you been more proactive, we'd see who'd have to jerk off," I said sympathetically.

"She's a psychopath," he grimaced. "Know her from Berlin. She'll start weeping in the middle of it and you'll have to calm her down. Too much hassle . . ."

"Hello," Irmel suddenly called out to us. "Come on, dance!" she invited us with a gesture.

"Fuck you!" we muttered practically simultaneously. Even Zeituntsyan appreciated our reaction by smiling at us.

The most unbearably comical was the Big Russian. I'd never seen such an awkward dancer in my life. God, how he waved his arms and with what expression on his face! It must have been the Soviet-style rock 'n' roll at a Leningrad party of 1960s. His elbows posed a constant threat to those near him. His leg movements testified he was deaf to music. He failed to feel the rhythm—as if deliberately, his moves never coincided with the music. He must have danced to another song in his head, and he definitely looked like a Soviet cartoon character—a dancing savage.

Above all, it was done in order to attract the attention of Mme Zulphia, the proud and silent Macedonian. She was supposed to succumb to his crazy leg movements, desperate nudges, and phosphorescent body hair (as usual, he was wearing shorts).

The Big Russian was looking at his Macedonian colleague as if he were going to wrestle with her. But Zulphia was elsewhere . . . She was completely concentrated on herself: eyes closed and lips pursed. She was dancing with an amazing diligence and dignity and, I guess, enjoying it utterly. It was a dance of solitude, but a dignified one. She must have seen herself as extremely sexy at that moment and didn't care if others failed to notice her appeal. The Big Russian and Zulphia surely heard different music because he was twisting like a Mayan chieftain summoning the demons, while she was moving her hips in the most noble and economical way.

It was the last I wished to see of the Malbork disco. I thought enough was enough and silently left the group of onanist onlookers.

When I got to the hotel, I thought I saw Helena.

Long red carpets covered the corridors of our hotel, the walls and ceilings, as well as the armchairs in front of the mirror halfway down the hall, had a reddish-burgundy hue. While all other hotel corridors were brightly lit, this one was dimmed to the level where you had to rely on senses other than sight. I had already reached my room when I heard a door bang very loudly at the other end of the long passage. I immediately thought I had mistakenly assumed the woman I saw was Helena. Helena, or someone resembling her, banged the door, and entered the room opposite the one she had left.

"Helena," I remember muttering, and heading in the direction she disappeared.

I still see the room numbers: 102, 104, 106, 108 . . .

I didn't dare knock. I literally pressed my ear to the door hoping to hear Helena's voice. But no sound reached me, neither Helen nor Maček's voices. The silence behind the door was complete, just like in the Père-Lachaise tombs. I waited in vain for Helena's footsteps, her sneeze, whisper, cry, or yawn. Any sound at all that would testify to her being there. I listened at the doors of 102, then 104, 106, and 108 . . . The hall ended with those rooms. I wished Maček would at least fart, then I'd know for sure the idiot had the girl locked behind one of those doors . . .

But no, he probably sat reading my story. Or slept like a log, blotto, face down.

If so, why wasn't he snoring?

The silence was eerie. Or else it seemed so to me. I walked up and down the red-brown hall several times, hearing nothing but my own heartbeat. They were silent behind the doors as if to spite me.

I even contemplated calling her, but decided against it, fearing her husband.

What could I say if Maček answered the call?

Once again, I had the feeling I had caught a fragment of something. Another scene had ended. But this time I wasn't at all sure the woman causing the noise was my Helena.

Now I recall how angry I was for putting myself into such a stupid situation. I shouldn't have run like that, up and down, worrying about a person I hardly knew. I already had my fair share of worries: Russian tanks, a bomb dropped on Tbilisi, separation from Elene . . . Wasn't that enough? Mme Roget and the Belarusian Mickey Mouse had fallen for each other, Milena and Vitas were together, Heinz and Rudy strolled hand in hand in the night Malbork. But, unlike Iliko, I didn't have the courage to spit at the entire world and jerk off in the name of all the luckless ones, proudly and assertively!

Who was Helena anyway? I'd seen her three or four times, so why would it be problematic to get her out of my mind? Why did I have to start hating everything around just because of her?

I went into my room with these disquieting thoughts and immediately knew I wouldn't be able to sleep—an energetic frog chorus wouldn't allow me to.

I swore at the musical frogs four times during the night. Twice out of the window, twice without getting up, from my bed. Once I tossed a Coke can in their direction. Then I gave up and set to Borisov's story. Or rather *lay to* it as I was reading lying on the bed. I can't say the pastime was particularly relaxing—an anonymous Malbork designer had fixed the lamp immediately above my bed and it attracted thousands of moths and other insects. They burned then and there, dropped dead on my magazine, and others came in their place.

Caught between the croaking and the deathly carnival, I read Borisov's story to the end.

He's leaving. I'm staying!!! I don't care what happens next. I don't care what he wants. I don't care what he thinks. I don't give a damn. He can fuck off! He's got no idea what he's doing. Didn't even argue with me. "Do as you wish." Screw you and your "as you wish"! Thought I'd hit him . . . If I hadn't dashed out, I would've. Old prick! I tell him I'm through and he says "as you wish." What the hell! But what do you want? You personally?

All I can say it was more of a historical chronicle than a piece of creative writing. As opposed to Danuta, it didn't anger me. Actually, I enjoyed reading it. The text once again demonstrated how one should write for foreigners. The story was about a husband and wife at the time the Second World War raged outside their window. It was thanks to the war that the story had reached *The New Yorker*, otherwise I strongly doubt a simple story of a couple from Sofia would have made Borisov so attractive. What did they care for a couple from Sofia?

Borisov was smart: he also managed to incorporate the persecution of Jews and was absolutely right to do so. Of course, if a woman sits at the window in your story and the year is 1939, it's even awkward if she's not planning to hide a Jewish friend and, on the other hand, she's not in love with a Nazi officer. But we face a dilemma here: your local readers are fed up with what foreigners find interesting in your Bulgarian stories. And the other way round: what excites your countrymen remains absolutely impenetrable for the foreign readers.

If I place a woman at the window in my story and set to telling the events of the 1991 referendum, my poor readers will definitely tell me they can go to the library and look through the 1991 newspapers if they wish to refresh their minds. "Give me a pure woman," my reader would say, "and give me some romance. Give me some sex and the probing hands of a man, some rain, bullets, and blood, but keep the frigging referendum out of it! I don't need you to remind me of the Patriarch who came to bless the Opposition Congress—I remember it perfectly well!"

In a nutshell, if you aren't really smart, you're going to lose either your own or foreign readers. Borisov, I'd venture to claim, has already lost his loyal readers. He must have made a handful of snobbish countrymen happy though ("Oh, our writer's published in *The New Yorker*!"). So, following Danuta's advice, one should ignore your own (except the local snobs) and write for foreign readers only! If not, you'll end up with half a dozen readers of your native literary village for eternity . . .

Borisov could have been stuck with a handful of Bulgarian readers if he hadn't placed the history and problems of his native Bulgaria above his own interests. Isn't it right that a region is much more important than you? The region has more chances to draw the attention of a healthy foreign reader because it's more attractive than your talent. The region is big, it is full of problems (there is no region without problems), the region is exotic, it is (or was) riddled with conflicts, the region has gone through a war, it is shocking, emotions are running high in the region, while you . . . You are small. Try telling your story along with that of the region and one day you might become Boris Borisov!

Why can't Danuta describe her regional problems? Aren't there plenty? Or is it that Bulgaria holds particular interest for *The New Yorker*? How should a writer predict which region is going to be fashionable, say, next year? Is there a war planned anywhere I should know? Are they going to behead a hostage anywhere?

It should be publicly announced: in 2020 we are going to be interested in the parliamentary elections of Kyrgyzstan, while the year 2030 will be devoted to the novels featuring the UN . . .

If not for Zviad fumbling with the keys, I wouldn't have put down the magazine for quite some time. I was too weary to talk to him, so before he stepped inside, I switched off the lamp (saving thousands of brainless kamikaze-insects from sure death) and feigned sleep.

He was followed by the smell of vodka or rather he followed it. First it was the smell (which I suspect killed the surviving insects) and then came Zviad.

"Are you asleep?" he asked loudly. Had I really been asleep, I'd have certainly woken up, but as I wasn't, I didn't answer, keeping up the pretense.

"Asshole," he said. He positively meant me, assured I couldn't hear him.

Frankly speaking, I wasn't insulted in the least. I actually took pity of the chap for his pathetic fury. He probably wanted to chum up and drink with me, read poems and spitefully laud the aging writers ("The old prick's cool. He's got these fucking great lines . . ."). And all the while, I failed to render my support, praised him only once when he read his poem in Madrid. I completely ignored the well-established practice of perpetual praise—you need to curse their rivals telling the poets how great they are and begging them on your bent knees to read more of their master-pieces . . . If you don't, they start to hate you: they sneak up on you when you're asleep, unprotected, and call you an asshole.

Zviad bumped into the wardrobe three times, possibly on purpose. I reacted with a grumble as if I were bothered in my deep sleep. He went into the bathroom, pissed noisily, didn't flush and got into his bed without washing his hands. His immediate snoring made me suspect he had gone to sleep while pissing. Coming to bed was purely automatic.

Unfortunately, when I really fell asleep, I was woken by loud banging and a heartrending scream.

"What's going on?" Zviad asked. He was as startled as me.

Something extremely large and heavy was hitting the wall above us. A woman was screaming as if her throat was being slit. Occasionally, though, she produced grunt-like sounds, which must have made me think of a slit throat. But also, her head was being bashed against something large and heavy . . .

At least those were my thoughts before I fully woke up. The victim was crying, squeaking, and singing, I believed.

Zviad saved me from the nightmare.

"It's Milena screwing," he uttered with the voice of a medium in a trance: the netherworld deep.

"How do you know?" I asked.

"I'm a poet, boy, I've got a good ear. Can't fool me!"

I popped up and stretched my neck. If I could prick up my ears, I'd have certainly tried that too. I was determined to identify Milena among the moans and cries and grunts.

I thought I did. "Heinz asked you," "Heinz is waiting," "Heinz wants,"—yes, it was her voice beyond any doubt.

How amazingly a woman's voice changes when she yells . . .

"That banging is the bed hitting the wall," Zviad explained.

"I'm not an idiot, I've guessed that much." I was offended.

What force that petite girl had, what voice . . . The whole hotel must have woken up. What normal person could have slept through the pounding and screaming?

"Vitas's trophy." Zviad sounded sad. Then he added, truly sorrowfully, "Poor thing's a real animal."

"Shall we jerk off?" I suggested.

"No." He sounded stern, dead serious.

That night I woke up twice more: first, aggressive grunting kept me awake, then, at dawn, it was a mewing groan . . . It could have been either Mme Roget or self-composed Zulphia who had rejected the Big Russian, but had succumbed to the frog king . . .

It was a hellish night: the women revealed their true nature.

In the morning we were herded to the Malbork castle.

"I have to look into Milena's eyes," Zviad told me.

However, she didn't show *any signs* of the exciting night. Neither were her vocal cords damaged. Quite the contrary, she sounded remarkably energetic:

"Wake up, the coach is leaving in three minutes!"

How could we wake up if we hadn't slept a wink?

In short, she was the same old Milena (we hoped against all odds that sex would have changed her for the better). Busy handing out red umbrellas in the hall, she didn't so much as smile at Vitas.

There was a steady drizzle outside and we were all supposed to have them.

Zviad would have never carried such an umbrella in Tbilisi because it's still considered a shame for Georgian men to have one. No one forbids it but we still shun umbrellas in general—we get drenched, catch cold and pneumonia, but absolutely refuse to carry one around.

There, in Malbork, we took them as nobody would have taken us for gays if we walked around with umbrellas in our hands.

"Iliko's going to take two, you'll see." Zviad pointed at our disheveled overseer.

Iliko's complexion and sour expression clearly indicated he was the victim of the previous night. His unshaved cheeks were greenish-yellow. He had gummy eyes and looked like a boy suffering from conjunctivitis.

"What's this?" he asked Zviad, pointing at the umbrellas.

"A fridge," he replied.

"Are they free?" Iliko eyed them with disgust.

"The black ones are, but we are to return the red ones."

"Can't see any blacks here." He looked around.

"There were few of them and all are gone . . ."

"You're in a joking mood, are you?" Iliko hissed—not ironically, but with genuine, unveiled repulsion.

"Did you have a bad night?" I asked him.

"I don't remember," he shrugged. "They keep me in a hole. I leave my pants outside, otherwise I can't get into my room. It's a pigeon-hole, not a room! I'm hanging upside down like a bat. Do you know where my tap is? Right at the bed! If I raise my head suddenly, it can snap in two!"

"What about your bath?" Zviad laughed. Strictly speaking, he shouldn't have, but he did.

"Haven't even looked inside. The door's so flimsy, I'm afraid to touch it. I haven't used the toilet in two days. This air must have caused constipation. And a woodpecker has drilled my brain."

"With me it's frogs," I said.

"A woodpecker with me."

"And her." Zviad looked at Milena.

"What did she do?" Iliko turned too.

"Offered herself noisily."

"What? Was she screwed?"

"Yeah, very much so . . ."

"She deserves it. The healthy girl."

The information visibly improved his disposition. However, his face clouded as soon as Irmel and her grasshopper Serb came into the hall.

As opposed to Milena and Vitas, these two didn't try to hide their joy. They stood holding hands and, later, kissed openly on the coach.

"She's abnormal. Poor chap, she'll drive him crazy," Iliko said and headed toward the umbrellas. He took ages choosing, thoroughly and scrupulously inspecting each one. Finally he called out to us:

"Will this one do?"

"Yeah," we nodded.

I'll never forget how painful it was for Mme Roget to get on the coach. She definitely showed signs of the previous night. She was absolutely worn out! The Mickey Mouse Belarusian followed her like a bodyguard, helping her climb aboard the bus. The aim of the literary bodybuilder was clear as day—he meant to secure his future with his tireless muscles, attention, and consideration for her: "I'm going *to punish* you over and over again, Mme Roget. I'm going to please you many times, take your breath away with my punitive operations. I'll make you feel younger, make you forget about your pension, make you hate your grandchildren. You're going to fall in love with me, marry me and then, with God's help, you'll invite my family too: Mum, Grandma and Tanya—we'll all live in Paris. I'm going to slide into the European literature scene using your old back as a springboard. And then I'll get myself new T-shirts: Belarusian Cinderella, Belarusian Cinderella."

"Yeah, he's surely set on marrying her," Zviad agreed and immediately added, "but she's not that naïve. Her generation is pretty tough, you know."

I can't speak for Mme Roget, but the Malbork castle triggered human feelings in someone as cynical as Iliko. Quite unexpectedly we found ourselves in the magnificent medieval times. The castle was built of red brick and from afar it looked as if a red lake was placed in the middle of a forest. It seemed a fantastic reality: the forest gray from rain, the river covered in ripples and a red reflection of the castle. Why do they bother with Disneyland when kids can be brought here?

"This is real Malbork!" Zviad couldn't hide his admiration. Iliko poised his plastic camera and asked us to stand at the castle wall:

"The nation should have evidence you've been to museums because they think you're uncultured."

It was a stupid snapshot: Zviad and I, both red-eyed, standing with red umbrellas against a burgundy-red wall. We looked like a pair of bona fide vampires at the Kremlin wall.

We suggested taking Iliko's photo too but he declined our offer:

"I haven't washed."

In a little while we were taken into a large hall decorated with red-and-white flags. The poems were to be read there.

"If it was me reading, I wouldn't care," Zviad was visibly nervous. "I'm pretty good at dealing with the public. But I fear the reader will fuck up."

Before reading the poetry, the Little Russian was invited to the microphone.

"Mr. Pushkov has a statement to make," Heinz said.

The Little Russian's statement concerned us as we soon found out.

"Our colleagues, our Georgian friends are not allowed into my country," he began. "Russia refused to issue entry visas to the writers Ilia, Zviad and Zurab (?) . . . No, they aren't terrorists, neither are they criminals—you know them quite well by now. Their only crime is that they were born Georgians! That's what the Russian authorities believe. That's how the Russian government punishes Georgians! But in truth, it's us, non-political common

Russians who are punished, we—the intellectuals who condemn our government's position, condemn the war, condemn the policy of not issuing visas to the Georgians. We appeal to you to sign the petition written by my colleague Vladimir Varlamov and myself. It says we sympathize with our Georgian colleagues, object to the Kremlin visa policy discriminating against the Georgians and invite the Russian cultural elite to support the petition. The text is going to be on the Internet and can be found at: no-visa-no -democracy.ru."

The Little Russian expected appreciative applause at the end of his speech. Only Heinz thanked him, others remained impassive. Some of them, I guess, didn't even understand what his speech was about. Aliev sitting in the front row, however, turned to us and lifted his thumb. Although his raised thumb referred more to the Little Russian's speech, I felt grateful. It was Heinz's words that I thought unpleasant (at least at the time):

"True, our colleagues are refused entry visas to Russia," he said. "Unfortunately, they will have to stay in Malbork, but only temporarily as we are meeting in Warsaw again."

"Can't they move me into another room at least?" Iliko growled.

"But we will be with our colleagues all this time. We're not going to forget about them for even a minute!" Heinz raised his voice toward the end.

He talked as if we were dead. Unlike the Little Russian, though, he received his share of clapping. As I said, he had a hypnotic effect on us!

"These Europeans are impotent idiots," the Little Russian told us later. "They should adopt a more severe approach to us Russians. Actually it's best if they trample us down, introduce new sanctions against us . . . But not us, the common people. I mean those sluts in the government, ministers, their wives, and the whole gang . . . If they can't rest at the western resorts, they might slow down. Or throw bombs into each other's houses."

Zviad was so impressed by him that for a while he spoke correct Russian with more or less proper pronunciation (which was a genuine Orthodox miracle!), thanked him profusely and hugged him at least five times though he was sober. One Pushkov outweighed all Russian sins. That minute Zviad was ready to forget all that the Russians had sinned against us: starting with whale-sized Iskander rockets that had flown into people's flats and stuck in their wardrobes and finishing with the hysteria of August 10th when people waited for the tanks to take over Tbilisi.

And more:

Refugees with a stock of toilet paper, empty ATMs, dead airport, the Russian soldiers sleeping on the bridge in Gori—miserable tramps, undressed and hot; mattresses, linen, clothes, and chairs looted from the locals' homes piled high on their tanks; dead bodies strewn on the town square—mainly reporters and taxi-drivers; and a woman in a pink gown with her forehead smashed.

Zviad was ready to swallow his pride and discard his hard feelings only to express his gratitude toward a decent Russian. The Little Russian indeed was a decent chap, sincerely worried that we were denied entry into his country. The Big Russian seemed concerned too, having contributed to the protest against the Kremlin visa policy, but unlike his colleague Pushkov, he wasn't inclined to self-criticism. Encouraged by Zviad's ecstatic thanks, he carped at the Georgian authorities and then reminded us of the Kremlin propaganda "facts":

"Raving mad! Scum and bastards! You killed two thousand Ossetians, bombed Tskhinvali, ran over a three-year-old boy with a tank, drove women and elders into a church and burned them alive!"

"Varlamov is a chauvinist," I said when the Russians left us. "The Little one is quite decent though."

"He's as bad as the other," Iliko muttered with disgust. "I hate their intellectuals more than anything! It's them who deliver the final blow. If they really loved their Russia, they should have killed Stalin, allowed Hitler into the Kremlin and then broken his neck too . . . Together with the Aryans, definitely not on their own. Do you think the Aryans would have tolerated theirs for long? Adolph would have followed Joseph pretty soon. And again, the Anglo-Saxons messed up."

"Oh, my," was all Zviad managed to utter.

I opened my umbrella and walked into the garden. I still feel guilty, but I just couldn't face his poems at the time.

Had I been Zaza of three years ago, I'd surely have lit a fag. Smoking would have been extremely appropriate to my mood.

The ground was sodden with rain, the flags hanging down from the turrets looked like dirty towels. But still, it was fine. I liked being there . . .

Helena came in through the main entrance.

At first I froze, then I thought I was ridiculous with my red umbrella . . . She approached me and stopped right in front of me. It might have been my sick imagination, but she looked as if we had done something wrong and were now embarrassed in each other's company.

I remember telling myself, "*The girl is yours.*" I also guessed it wasn't worth bothering with the umbrella and that I had to say, directly and immediately:

"So good you haven't left."

Commonplace words, but so heartfelt and so significant . . .

. . .

23 October, Malbork

"I sat in Khachaturian's lap when I was three. At the age of twenty-three I took a trip through Parajanov's dreams . . ."

This is the beginning of my text I'm preparing for the Simplicis-simus *competition. I always write what I experience and feel. I don't live in the reality. My existential environment is the aesthetic space. The raging elements of a dream. The microcosm of sounds and images. This is my true "homeland" . . . That's why I felt so at home in Perge's carnival reveries . . .*

I remember the snow. Abovyan Avenue . . . Perge Gukasyan, young and good-looking . . . in his yellow muffler, with violets in his hand . . .

"Perge, where did you get those violets in mid January?"

I recall my life in musical-visual fragments:

Karina's birth . . .

Perge's death . . .

Naira's wedding . . .

My text will also be written in the same kaleidoscopic manner. Like dropping tear-words which were emotions once.

God, please keep my Karina healthy . . .

Artur has gone to the disco for the night . . . I feel he's been getting old right before my eyes. I've been observing the process for the last 20 years . . .

Yes, he's getting older and older but not to the point where he'd stop going to discos. He doesn't dance, just stands there watching others . . . Though we're always together, we seem to be avoiding each other . . . We talk about everything except the most important issue. And it's extremely tiring . . . I often feel the urge to tell him to his face: "Take off that mask, Artur! Calm down, no one demands anything from you."

I've got a recurrent dream: Perge is in the coffin, red candles are lit in the room, my face is painted white . . . The mirror is covered with a cloth with green roses, which is utterly inappropriate for the occasion . . . I take it down and look into the mirror, but I'm not reflected in it.

I've made Artur sick with my dreams. Possibly he found refuge at the disco from me . . . He wants to be engulfed by life . . . He's had too much of my colors, style, my melancholy . . .

*These days women are so shameless. As if they're devil possessed . . .
They've jumped at men like wild bitches in heat. I'm not even sure if
Artur got lucky. I just don't fancy looking for him in hospitals.*

*Funnily enough, I can't shake the feeling these lines will be
published . . . As if I'm not writing only for myself. Consequently, I'm
not absolutely frank . . . I'm kind of showing off, despite myself . . .*

*Today we visited the old castle. No life at all, only the odor of
a museum, the stale smell of desolation . . . Everything's trashed by
tourists . . . No trace of true history, all's fake, make-believe. I betrayed
my principles and was punished (I know I hate museums, don't I?).
The musty smell triggered a severe headache . . . Perge used to say I
brought about my migraines myself . . .*

*I listened to the poetry reading. Enjoyed the Finnish poet. When
she finished reading, she sent a paper plane into the audience . . . Banal,
but a gesture full of life . . .*

*The Russian read a letter in support of the Georgians. Deeply
troubled by the last month war and bombs . . . Both nations have their
hands smeared in blood. Funny.*

*My head and stomach ache. Menstruation at the age of 46 . . . A
miracle. This bit isn't going to be published. That's why I mention it.*

12. IN BED WITH HELENA

That night they all left Malbork at ten, due in Russia at dawn. After exactly one hour there was a knock on my door.

"Can I come in?" Helena asked.

She had a big pillow clutched to her chest and white jogging shoes on her feet.

"I'm alone on my floor," she said. "It's unnerving."

What about Maček? I thought. *Where is he? Has she left him in the room? Have they quarreled again? Is he going to beat me to death? Is she so spontaneous that she doesn't care if she's playing with fire?*

She seemed to hear my questions.

"Maček's gone to Kaliningrad, but I stayed behind," she said.

And he allowed you to? I nearly asked out loud.

Helena sat on a radiator, still clutching the pillow.

Everything was fine. Maček was on his way to Russia, Zviad was offered another room ("The hotel is virtually empty. Would you like a separate room?"), while Helena was alone and decided to visit me . . . *We might even have sex tonight.* When a woman comes to your room at night telling you she's scared of staying alone, it's as good as a promise. Isn't that the case in films? And in novels and the operas unsung by my uncle, and in life too.

I never dreamt it'd happen to me. I never thought the girl I was crazy about would walk into my room carrying a pillow, at midnight . . .

Who's going to carry her own pillow in Georgia? It's a lot of let's-have-tea and don't-worry-it's-okay before you lure them into the bed, waste precious time on psychotherapy and lies only to feel morally spent and drained in about a second and a half (or two seconds at most) if you're lucky . . .

Quite unlike Helena who came of her own accord, with *her own pillow*, sat down on the radiator (couldn't head directly to the bed, could she?) and . . .

And nothing . . .

"Why?" I asked. In theory I wasn't at all interested in why she hadn't accompanied her husband to Kaliningrad. I just had to say something.

I was absolutely sure we were going to have sex. I was so confident of the prospect that I even thought it'd be better if nothing was said at all. I could keep smiling softly, then approach her calmly and unhurriedly and just kiss her.

I was reluctant to risk it, though. I couldn't be sure she wasn't hiding something up her sleeve: suppose poor Maček stayed behind, sitting now in his hundred-and-something room, gathering strength to kill her? I had no idea whatsoever of their family problems!

Believe me, that's what I thought at the time and I'm still pretty cross with myself for it—instead of enjoying the happy moment, I was worried stiff, ready to step back!

"I should have gone with him, right?" she laughed. "You'd have slept peacefully . . ."

"Oh, no, I'm glad . . . Really glad."

Logically, after those words I had to approach her for a kiss. The sudden hoarseness of my voice and that pause before *really* was a sure indication, but I feared to hasten the natural speed of events and resolved not to take risks.

"I'd like to smoke, but I won't because you don't smoke," she said.

Of course I begged her to, saying if she didn't, I'd have a fag myself, but she was adamant.

"Why did you say it then?" I persisted.

"Not because I wanted to hear you beg," she said a little too harshly. Then she tossed the pillow to the bed and added in her usual manner—teasingly and mischievously, "If I wanted a row, I'd have gone to Kaliningrad, Zaza."

That *Zaza* was definitely nearing the moment of sex . . .

If I hadn't witnessed the conflict between her and Maček, or rather the post-conflict scene ("Tearful Helena and the Drunken Pole"), I'd have been tempted to think she was somewhat sluttish (sorry, Helena!): a doormat for a husband, had a quarrel over some petty problem, stayed behind and needed a sex therapist. What else was there for her to do? She could have some fun and return to her husband later.

The problem was that neither was Maček a typical doormat nor was that post-quarrel scene a sign of a conflict one could easily forget . . .

I might have been wrong though.

What I do remember well is my excitement at the prospect of sex and my delight that she—with her dark silky skin, shapely legs, black eyes, burgundy lips, dimples in her cheeks, light pants, and white top—was in my room, sitting on the radiator, waiting for me to make a move . . .

I had one single wish at the time: for Iliko and Zviad to keep away from my door.

It must have been that unconscious fear of my privacy being invaded that pushed me toward the next step. I went near her (and was not only surprised but actually scared when I saw her eyes widen) and said with all sincerity, probably a little comically:

"I might spoil everything by saying I'm delighted you're here. You must've guessed I've fallen in love."

Helena's eyes reflected as much fright as mine. After my confession, she put her hand on my hair (even pulled at it a little) and looked sideways as if she had just discovered something new and interesting in my face.

"Do you always fall for everyone so quickly?" she asked.

Good she was smiling or else I wouldn't have the courage to kiss her.

"No, not really," I said, taking her face into my hands.

That hand touching my hair had reassured me a lot . . .

My words sounded so stupid and the tone was so miserable that by all rules of the genre she shouldn't want to kiss . . .

I believe she didn't.

Our lips touched. She didn't part hers but closed her eyes, which I saw as a good sign. Her lips were soft and moist and I thought I'd thrust my tongue between them.

I craved to touch her breast but had second thoughts. I didn't dare give a lot of freedom to my hands at the first go.

We stood like that, motionless and expectant, for some time. Then Helena turned away.

"Wait, wait, let's not be so serious," she said.

I wanted to kiss her again, but she put her hands on my chest and pushed me.

"Wait! I want to talk . . ."

If I hadn't been fearful, I definitely would have shown some stubbornness by holding her face and pulling her to me. And if she resisted, I'd wriggle a bit as the custom is. But I'd do that only if I didn't care to lose her. I was afraid—still am as I remember those minutes—of making a grave mistake.

Strangely enough, I was only *partially aroused* when I was kissing her. In purely medical terms, there was no erection, which scared me more than anything else. It meant I was extremely nervous, which in its turn meant I was facing a total failure if we had sex (it was coming to that, wasn't it?).

Why no hard-on? Deeply troubled by the question, I sat down on the bed and looked at her pillow.

"Have you brought it from Greece?" I asked.

My heart was racing, so my voice sounded unnaturally hoarse.

"No," Helena laughed. "I just had to bring something from my room, right?"

Then she sat on Zviad's vacated bed, crossed her legs Buddha-style and looked around.

"It's not bad."

"Frogs are," I said and told her the story of the previous night.

It was a classic example of sublimation: if we weren't having sex (which I craved for), I could at least talk about it.

One of my friends, a sex-crazy chap, was telling me that you have to occasionally mention sex to the woman you are hopeful about. In that way she kind of gets used to the idea. "You've got to drop the right words," he instructed me. "Orgasm, anal and oral sex . . . The terminology is going to do the job." However, I doubt my story had any effect on Helena as Milena's dolphin-like squeaks and twitters would have discouraged even experienced perverts.

"How awful," Helena laughed. "Good thing she didn't wake me up or I'd have killed her."

"There's nothing wrong with screaming, if you think about it." I wanted to move from Milena to more general sex-related issues.

"Yeah, but some only pretend, right?" she went along with me. "The need to scream should come on its own," she laughed, and her cheeks flushed, to my utter surprise, as if she was embarrassed.

"Some men scream too," I said.

"In Greece they talk and talk and talk without stopping."

"While having sex?" I was genuinely baffled.

"Yeah, and as a rule, they get so excited they can't stop—ten words a second . . . You'll be surprised at the things they say!"

Instantly, I was jealous. I envisaged a whole ghost army of Greek men, tanned, good-looking, excitedly talking during sex. My heart ached at the image. Was she referring to her personal experience?

Have you had a lot of them? I nearly ask. *Isn't one Maček enough? What the hell?*

I also thought of joking—*And do the Poles talk too?*—but didn't voice that foolish remark either. Only a complete idiot would remind a woman of her husband.

At that minute my worst fears came true—there was a knock on the door.

It's Maček, I thought. *She's been lying.*

"Is it your wife?" Helena whispered.

"What wife?" I shrugged my shoulders.

It was Iliko.

"Are you up?" he asked, but seeing Helena he recoiled. "Oops!"

"Hello," she greeted him, raising her hand.

"Hello," he sang back.

I stood with my back to Helena and told Iliko through my clenched teeth:

"Go away. I'm at the final stage."

My attempt failed—in a few long strides he was in the middle of the room. He addressed Helena in his harsh, German-like English:

"Okay, so you're also a Georgian if you haven't gone to Russia."

"Actually, I wanted to go but Heinz forgot about me," she answered laughing.

Heinz, she said, not *my husband.* She was reluctant to mention Maček.

"Okay, okay," Iliko nodded like a clockwork toy. He didn't know what to say. Neither did we help him. It was the first time I had come across such an insensitive person—he just couldn't get it that he was unwelcome. What's more, completely ignoring me, he reclined on my bed and set on the organizers:

"They've left us here as if we're junk. Instead, they should've kicked the Russian's ass! They still live with the complex of the two lost wars."

"Have you had two wars with Russia?" Helena was surprised.

"I mean Germany, not us . . . No courage to contradict them . . . As for us, we can't fight big wars."

"But you had one, didn't you?"

"Nope," Iliko winced. "How could we? They came with their tanks."

As if my clenched-teeth plea wasn't enough, he now set to describing the August war. Eventually, when I thought he had finished, he demonstrated more inadequacy and insensitivity— he slapped his belly and barked at us:

"Why are we sitting in this stale cell? Shall we go to the downstairs bar for a beer or two? Frogs don't like beer drinkers."

"A bar? I'm not too keen," I believe I shouted. "Besides, there's no bar here."

"It's not just a bar, it's the temple of kitsch." He turned to Helena, "Why can't we go? Are we dead or what?"

Running the risk of offending Helena, I was about to tell him in Georgian: "Get lost, you stupid prick! We were about to have sex. Can't you feel you're not welcome?" But I immediately realized speaking an unknown language in her presence would have been bluntly rude. I might have been severely punished for my overconfidence. So, I glanced at her with a pained expression, accompanying it with a helpless gesture.

"Shall we?" Iliko sprang to his feet.

"Would you like to?" I asked her.

"I'm not sure," Helena said, "but let's go."

She wasn't looking at Iliko, only me, as if waiting for my final decision. What did I do? Nothing. In fact, I complied with him, ignoring my own desire, which could have coincided with Helena's.

I took her down as if leading her to hell.

And it was! I was reminded of my school canteen. There were chocolate bars and salads in the glass fridge-counters (the Soviet shop-type). The TV fixed to the wall was tuned to football. Staring up at it were a fat bartender with a golden halo (his hair and beard were perfectly blond) and a very tipsy Zviad.

How utterly out of place the canteen and the Georgian poet were in the European Union!

Neither Iliko nor I were thrilled at seeing Zviad, but before we could shuffle back out, pretending we hadn't seen him, he raised his hand in greeting. Bad luck.

"Who's she?" Zviad looked at Helena who, as if she understood Georgian, stretched her hand and smiled:

"I'm Helena."

I decided it was high time I started looking after her and asked anxiously:

"Would you like anything?"

"Who is she?" Zviad persisted.

"No." Helena shook her head.

"Shall we try their salads?" Iliko asked.

It meant he wasn't particularly hungry. If he were, he'd hate to pay (he had to be absolutely famished not to be sorry to part with money). As a rule, he urged others to order food and then, he'd lightheartedly say "Can I join you for a bite?" in a clownish begging tone.

"I'm not hungry," I said sadistically.

We sat down. Zviad was looking at Helena with glassy eyes, wondering who the woman sitting in front of him was.

"Helena's Greek," I said for their benefit, "but has stayed on as a gesture of solidarity."

"Has she?" Zviad expressed surprise. The he raised his hand in Churchill's victory sign, "Achilles!"

I translated my own words to Helena.

"*Solidarność!*" Iliko yelled in Polish.

We all laughed except Zviad.

It was Iliko who found a topic for the conversation.

"Why don't you do Heinz's homework? Why aren't you writing?" he asked.

"I only write when I'm fucking screwed up," Zviad replied.

"Don't translate that," Iliko whispered to me.

"I should be really screwed up to write anything," Zviad went on lamenting. "I can't write a word if I'm not fucked up. I should feel fucking bad, be screwed by everyone in order to write a poem. I can't write on someone's orders."

"What did he say?" Helena asked me.

"He said he can't write when he's fine. He can only write when he feels really bad."

"And is he okay now?"

It was a good question.

"Do you write?" Iliko turned to Helena and slapped her thigh.

Yeah, just slapped lightly, but it infuriated me.

The prick's flirting! I thought, and looked at Helena.

Seemingly unperturbed, she answered she wasn't a writer and pulled a packet of cigarettes from her pocket.

I was immediately swept by another wave of horror, imagining I was losing her. Actually, I did nothing to win her. Suddenly I doubted her interest in me as I began to think that being alone, she was just looking for a man (a one-night stand or for revenge) and if I didn't show more attention, that awful Iliko would take my place . . .

Yes, that Iliko who was faster holding out a lighter to her cigarette.

I even thought it'd be better if I rose and told her, "Let's go, Helena."

But suppose she said no or that she liked it there or, worst of all, if she let me feel unwanted? Would I have to commit suicide? Would I have to hit both Iliko and Zviad?

I was scared. I didn't know her and that kiss wasn't passionate enough to give me confidence. That lip-touching was too weak to build anything between us. So far I was suspended in midair . . .

That's why my spirits dropped. I felt low and tense.

Helena didn't look high-spirited either. Iliko whined about the stamina of the foreign writers and Helena yawned twice. She covered her mouth and half-closed her eyes when she yawned.

"I'll be back soon," she muttered, more to herself than to me, and went out.

I rose somewhat irresolutely.

We followed her with our gaze.

And Zviad uttered horrible words:

"I'm going to screw her."

And what did I do?

"You're late, chum," I whispered. "I've already screwed her."

For some reason I believed I'd be able to better *protect* her.

"Good boy!" Iliko rapped my shoulder.

Admiration, distrust, and envy—all could be read in his rapping.

"What about passing her on?" Zviad asked pleadingly.

"No, not yet," I beamed in a disgusting manner, I guess, and heard how bitterly my guardian angel wept behind my right shoulder.

Quite some time had passed since Helena left us when Iliko asked:

"What happened to the broad?"

"I don't know," I looked toward the door. I was sure she was in the toilet, but because she wasn't coming back, I rose to my feet determined to find her.

"Don't give it to her in the toilet, boy. The pricks will fine you," Zviad called after me.

Helena was nowhere to be seen. Neither was there a toilet. Only the hall.

She had outsmarted us. She sneaked out.

Without exaggeration—I nearly cried.

I didn't go back to the canteen. I rushed upstairs to my room as I thought she might have been waiting at the door or at the corridor mirror.

There was only her pillow waiting for me. It was on my bed, with the creases left by Helena. I neither clutched it nor dug my weeping face into it. I tossed it onto the other bed, undressed and got under the covers. I immediately realized I wouldn't be able to sleep.

Incidentally, the frogs weren't croaking and if Milena was screaming, it was somewhere very far from me, on the train heading for Russia. Her former room as well as the whole hotel had sunk into a tomb-like silence. Dismal and depressing.

The realization was sudden and alarming—if I reconciled with the silence, I'd forever lose the girl who came to my room with her own pillow only an hour ago. Going to sleep was as good as erasing her from my life. If I slept, the next day would be much worse: I'd see hatred or indifference in Helena's eyes. I'd see the *demise of interest* toward me in her gaze. No doubt, that would make my stay absolutely impossible, I would fall hopelessly in love, and begin making innumerable inexcusable mistakes.

She's going to join Maček, I thought. I sprang up as if hit by lightning, got dressed in seconds like a private during the army drill, grabbed the pillow, and dashed out.

The woman of the previous night that I thought resembled Helena went from room 102 into 104 or from 104 into 106 . . .

I ran down the passage but unlike that night, I wasn't only listening to the sounds behind the doors—I was knocking on them.

"Helena!" I called first at room 102 and then at 106.

An old voice came from one of the rooms and practically simultaneously the door of room 104 opened.

Helena was wearing a long white man's T-shirt (probably her husband's). She was barefoot and looked sleepy.

"I've brought your pillow," I informed her happily.

She opened the door wide, turned, and slip-slapped back to her bed. The fact that she left the door open I took as an invitation, so I followed her inside. I put the pillow on the empty (ex-Maček) bed and sat down.

Helena lay in her bed but I believe she wasn't under the blanket. I can't be sure as it was dark and I could hardly see anything. She reached out her hand, found my knee, tapped it, and said in a husky drowsy voice:

"Lie down."

I rose, slowly and quietly undressed, and took a step to her bed.

Helena kind of groaned but didn't object when I crept next to her—even made room for me—and put my hand on her hip.

"Mmm," she protested feebly.

I pressed closer, against her back and her round buttocks, and kissed her below her ear.

I couldn't get it whether she was sleeping or not. She didn't seem to mind me, but wasn't going to give in. It was a strange slumber, partly yielding, partly stubborn. But because I was there, in her bed, I paid no attention to her complaining purrs and slipped my hand under her shirt. First I touched her tight belly, then stroked her round breasts which were slightly tilted to the left. The minute my palm touched her nipples, I felt myself harden. I pressed myself even closer against her back, hips and buttocks. I was about to pull her panties, turn her head, force my tongue into her mouth and cup her breast, but Helena suddenly moved away, rolled over and hid her head under my armpit.

"Let's sleep," she said.

Her eyes were closed.

I attempted to kiss her on the lips.

But she pushed her head lower and embraced me.

"Please," she muttered.

I was completely lost—she was embracing me but refused to kiss.

I tried various strategies but the more I persisted, the more she resisted. Eventually, she curled fetus-like somewhere between my waist and armpit, and fell into a deep, proper sleep.

Her warm breath pleasantly tickled my waist and occasionally her nose touched me.

That night I felt totally baffled: she was mine, but she wasn't.

I didn't know if I was supposed to be happy.

13. KALININGRAD

Maybe Kraus should be summoned when the fourth victim is killed? Or is it better if Kraus himself discovers the fourth victim? What if he remembers Murad's stories and goes looking in the "red" district?

And what if the prostitute lies in the shop window with her throat slit? Bloodstains on the glass (palm marks), an upturned chair . . . a leg in a torn stocking . . . Yeah. Not the whole body, but only a leg in sight. The fourth one can be called—Marietta. A twenty-three-year-old whore . . . Does she need a family name? Mansurova? Marietta Mansurova? I'm not sure.

We're in Kaliningrad. I've been taking notes for my next book. The hotel is on the outskirts, overlooking a lake. Calm, pastoral environs. Haven't seen any whores. Talked to the doorman who told me they'd come after eleven at night and call my room. They charge 100 dollars, but if I haggle, he said the fee might be reduced. Waiting for eleven o'clock. I couldn't find girls only in Frankfurt. Didn't miss the chance in other cities. Even found them in that remote Polish town. I've got huge hopes for Moscow. Can't say I'm dissatisfied with Brussels or Paris— the girls were really cute. I liked Brussels in terms of the "histories." She got scared when she saw me writing in my little book. Thought I was the police. Had a hard time convincing her I wasn't, even told her about Kraus. She was afraid I'd jinx her with my novel and she'd be killed too. She was quite nice. Thought I'd remain "a writer" and show magnanimity, but her skin was so white I couldn't resist. And small firm breasts. Strangely, she had a child. The stretch marks on her belly betrayed it, not her breasts. I'm too tired of their depressing stories though. Such dismal biographies. They can be only twenty-three but have gone through hell. Kraus must note this. The cheapest whores as well as the high-class ones should narrate their stories. At the same time, it's the least unhappy one who gets murdered . . . The pivotal point of my novels. I've spent 1,700 dollars on whores since I've been here. In Poland I even had two of them, but they turned out to be the least interesting respondents. Only "yes" and "no," nothing more forthcoming. Drove me mad. I'll kill them first. Take my revenge. What if Kraus discovers them first?

I am promised an escort service in Moscow. Only models, but not less than a thousand dollars each. Shall I risk it? Will they tell me anything new? Would my crazy lad kill them too?

So far I haven't found midget whores. Curious as I've heard such a lot about them. I was told to look for them in Paris, but I only discovered small and short ones, not midgets. Not the same. Can I make midget whores my lad's accessories? Suppose they belong to his gang. Not sure yet. No clear plans in this respect. Will decide only after meeting the real characters.

Kraus must visit prostitutes but not touch them. He should keep his distance. In order to trap the guy, he can—if it's not too comical—dress up like a woman. Let him try being in their shoes. And Vinogradov should see him in female clothes. The episode could bring a slightly dissonant streak into the otherwise grave atmosphere of the novel.

My head is occupied with whores only. Can't write for the competition. I doubt I'll produce anything, as I don't want to be humiliated by worrying along with the others. Let them write in peace and get their prizes . . .

At four o'clock we're being taken to see Kant's grave. I'll go. Pretty sure there's no chance of coming across girls at Kant's grave.

The Georgians were refused entry into Russia. Poor souls are stuck in Poland. Hope they're still given the subsistence of two cities.

I'm waiting for eleven o'clock! Don't let me down, Russians!!!

14. MOSCOW

Dear Sis Jeannette,

Under different circumstances I would regret being in Moscow and not in Saint Petersburg shrouded by the angelic-demonic genius of Dostoyevsky. I'd have chosen Petersburg. However, at the moment I have neither time not energy (funny!) to complain about my intellectual dreams that haven't come true . . . I'm in Venus Grotto, not attempting to get out. Quite the contrary, I feel restored after the sterile conflicts of Paris, after your absurdly irresponsible behavior—to my great surprise and probably to the astonishment of the Bishop! God almighty! Who obliged you to rewrite poor Mum's letters? There's no end to this conflict between "lucky" and "unlucky" sisters (sorry, Jeannette, but it's so!). Keep writing, but let me live! I'd like to forget all that rubbish—shoes, dresses, bags, even furniture (my God, what madness!), all this false appearance, including Henri and the likes of him (are you surprised?). I'd like to end this pathetic parody! I'm fine, Jeannette. I feel I've cleansed myself of Paris entirely. In Poland, a lad offered me a romance (please, don't go to Poland looking for a similar adventure!). I call him a lad but rest assured it's only an epithet, not a case of pedophilia, as he is thirty-two years old. But since he seems to crave for me as only a youth with a newly awakened body would, I refer to him as "a lad," not mentioning his name (which I find equally appealing). I call him a lad due to his fervor, his primeval passion, not his personality . . .

Oh, Jeannette, if you only saw what interest he shows in examining my aging body (no, I'm not in the least ashamed of saying this!) . . .

How he wants me at least twice a day . . . How I don't want him to crave for an old body. I shudder at the thought I'm dealing with a gerontophile (I nearly wrote a necrophile!). So what if I myself am the object of gerontophile's interest? The lad's passion is pathological as I'm twenty-five years his senior. I hate to admit I'm falling in love with a pathological person. On the other hand, I don't want to complicate things. I just want to be happy, Jeannette. I deserve it. I don't need more drama in my life.

Today he told me, "Let's go to the mausoleum to see Lenin" (not Lenin's mummy, but Lenin himself). I asked him (remembering Antoine Coqueluche's novels) if he was going to take me there too. Obviously, he had no idea what I was talking about (he speaks no French—we communicate with the help of our instincts) and answered in your English: "There's nothing else to see in Moscow except Lenin."

I don't know if this is humor or not. I can't guess when he's joking and when he isn't. I don't know what he wants. And I definitely enjoy being in the dark, this biblical confusion, this logical chaos, all these misunderstandings . . .

I've discovered how pleasant it can be to share your life with someone without talking . . .

Even now I'm in a state of supernatural, divine confusion: sitting here not sure if he's going to demand sex, take me to the mausoleum or out to dinner. It's good when you don't know . . .

Jeannette, how I pity you and how I love you . . .

I hope God will give me enough sense not to post this letter to you.

15. WARSAW

We were taken to Warsaw in a minibus. We were supposed to runite with the other ninety-seven writers returning from Moscow.

What did I gain last night?

1) Sitting next to Helena for five hours;

2) Helena's legs resting on the empty seat and staring at her shiny knees from close (very close);

3) The chance to put my head on Helena's shoulder and pleasant (thanks to the chance) as well as tantalizing (because of the seats) state of half-sleep;

4) Befriending Helena, telling her my biography (fragments of it—I can't keep my mouth shut!), the impressions of the three-months-ago war, the episode of bombing (Elene and I with our passports);

5) Something like telling her about my love; describing the clothes she wore ("This is what you were wearing when I first saw you . . .");

6) Not a single kiss;

7) Holding hands with her;

8) Iliko's gaze full of admiration, doubt, and envy;

9) Helena's words (1): "I don't believe falling in love is so quick. You're going to forget me when you go back to Tbilisi";

10) My frustration at the realization of the impossibility of convincing her of the reverse;

11) The presentation of personal attractiveness and appeal: self-irony, a grotesque description of one hundred writers, and my sense of humor;

12) Helena's soundless laughs, her slapping my knee when laughing;

13) A lighthearted depiction of the previous night;

14) Helena's words (2): "Thanks for not wrestling with me";

15) Helena's words (3) said with a laugh: "I'd commit suicide had I woken up pregnant. I don't remember a thing about last night";

16) Helena's words (4) said seriously: "I hate sleeping alone. Sleeping alone after twenty is a crime";

17) My fear and jealousy (at hearing these words);

18) Stubbornly avoiding mentioning Maček;

19) Helena's banal and lovable short narratives: "I love the sea," "Can't stand November," etc.

20) Helena's story of her father's death;

21) Helena's iPod: one earphone in her left and one earphone in my right ear. The music: I don't remember . . . Shostakovich bought in Brussels? Dead depressing;

22) Helena's words (5): "I'm a good girl for staying with you, aren't I?" n.b.: not *here*, but *with you*;

23) Sensual impulses sent by me;

24) Watching Helena (while she dozed off), falling in love with her features—lips and nose;

25) Zviad's whisper: "Don't fall in love, dude";

26) Kissing Helena's temple;

27) Coming to the final decision: "That's it, I'm falling in love";

28) Helena's physical closeness when our bodies touched;

29) Thinking about Maček's return ("What will she do? What will he do? What will I do?");

30) Losing peace of mind;

31) The fear of arriving in Warsaw;

32) Watching her rub her eyes; her purred "I'm hungry";

33) Carrying her bag.

The main group of our Literature Express gang was arriving two days later, which meant I had two full days, peaceful and Maček-free, at my disposal (my mum's favorite expression).

In contrast to Malbork, in Warsaw we were taken to a spacious, well-lit, modern hotel.

It was already dark. There was a tall, multi-turret Stalin-era edifice in front of our hotel, glowing like a gigantic rocket. The armchairs in the hall were occupied by an army of overdressed prostitutes. I had never seen such a number of fallen women together in my life. They looked like exotically colorful birds.

While on the bus I began worrying about the possibility of Helena not staying in the hotel. It was highly probable that she and Maček had a place of their own in Warsaw too. Okay, she hadn't accompanied him to Moscow, but why would she stay in a hotel if they had a house? Because of me? She could take me home, or was that wishful thinking? She couldn't humiliate him so much.

All my worries were groundless. She didn't hesitate for a second (apparently there was no Warsaw house), put her bags on a trolley (with my help), and adroitly pushed it to the reception. After checking her room number, she turned to me:

"Are you going to sleep?"

"No, why would I?" I asked in surprise. "Shall we go for a walk?"

"We might," she shrugged.

I insisted on carrying her bags upstairs (I had to know which room she was in) though she didn't really oppose me—I carried our luggage to the tenth floor and sweated spectacularly.

Before she opened the door, she turned to me bright-eyed:

"Every time I open a hotel room I think there's something extraordinary waiting for me inside. I love entering hotel rooms!"

What did she expect to see? The same things one can find in

any four-star hotel: a large bed (designed for two), a locked (?) fridge with little bottles, nuts, crisps and chocolate bars, completely useless armchairs, and small bars of soap neatly wrapped in paper . . .

"I'll call on you," I said and picked up my bags.

"Yeah," she nodded.

How soon could I come back? In fifteen minutes? In half an hour? In forty minutes? Or in an hour? Should I have kissed her good-bye? With the previous Elene I got used to definitiveness. I can't stand making decisions!

How much calmer I'd feel if women gave precise instructions: "You are to come back in forty minutes, you won't kiss me because you're sweaty (or 'It's okay that you're sweaty, I like/love you the way you are'), we can find a cafe, have something to drink, then kiss on the way back, further development is a possibility, in other words, if you wish, under favorable conditions, you can take me before we get to the hotel: in a dark park corner/café toilet. Impatient enthusiasm is permitted. If the outdoor conditions are adverse, I'll be yours/I won't be yours. I won't make you guess under any circumstances—I'll be straightforward: 'Today I'm yours,' or 'Not today, but tomorrow you can take me. I'm not going to change my mind till tomorrow, so go now and sleep tight!'"

One day, I'm sure, women-robots will be invented. You will recharge them at night by simply plugging them in. They won't have souls, just a mechanical heart which will store all the information about you—your name and biography. "You must love this one," you can order. "You must be loyal to him, support and praise him, argue with him once a year, and turn a blind eye when he flirts with women." On the other hand, why would she need to turn a blind eye if you can switch her off? Just unplug her or take her battery out when need arises . . . The robot can be called "Patriarchal Dream 001" or even simpler "Slave-Clitoris 2177."

Frankly speaking, at the time I wished to be an unfeeling robot myself, possibly called "Dismal Penis 2008" or "Nothing

Doing 21." I had never worried so much before, even during the war. Being plugged in for recharging would be preferable.

In short, I left without kissing her or agreeing on time. I can't say she was overexcited but she did move around in a slightly agitated way. I thought she wouldn't rest until she unpacked and made the new room her home. So, content with her "yeah," I went looking for my room.

I've fallen in love, I have. I don't want to be in my room. I want to be with her, I thought as I got into the lift, feeling even more miserable.

As soon as I got under the shower, I immediately remembered Helena of the previous night, lying so close to me. My hands kept the memory of her body . . . as if I were still touching her breasts.

I became unbearably aroused. Couldn't ignore the fact. I was genuinely terrified: if Helena as much as touched me, I'd come, just like a teenager. I even thought of practicing Onan's method to ease myself. But jerking off when a gorgeous girl was waiting three floors away seemed a criminal offense and a deadly sin. I set to vigorously drying myself—a dry man is better protected from temptation then a wet one . . .

I had to distract myself once and for all, so I decided to phone Tbilisi, my most asexual home city.

I didn't anticipate (as usual) hearing anything particularly pleasant from Mum, but I certainly didn't expect the piece of news she hit me with:

"Your dad was beaten at the rally."

Incidentally, with hindsight, I was more astonished by Mum's tone rather than the information itself. She said it with pride. I couldn't detect either fear or concern. She sounded proud, and yes, definitely reproachful ("Your dad was beaten at the protest rally for your future while you don't care in the least."). She can't forgive me for not being interested in politics, whereas Dad can't reconcile with his age. He is furious he can't sing as well as he used to, that his aging buddies don't have the same income they used to have, that his sex life is far from what it used to be—so he goes to all sort of rallies. He wears a massive gold cross on a chain round his neck ("It's a present from the Patriarch, Sonny."), a ring with a sizeable ruby on his finger, his mobile on his belt and goes to rallies with his old boys . . . The chaps wear white shirts with their gray chest hair showing at the unbuttoned collar, some have hernias, others have traveled to Moscow for the fatal diagnosis of cancer but here they are many years later, but still, they're cool, they're tough guys. True, their bones have thinned, but had they been younger, they'd instigate mayhem, wreak havoc on the city, blast the sleepy streets . . .

Now I feel angry about it (because I'm back in Tbilisi and everyone and everything drives me mad), but when Mum told me the news, I nearly had a heart attack.

Or am I lying now too?

"They were standing at Lagidze Waters when the riot police attacked them from the upper street," Mum told me. "Poor Rezo Pantsulaia was squashed to the shop window and his hip is broken. Your dad's arm is swollen . . . Otar Vadachkoria's glasses were smashed. His wife is beside herself!"

Groaning and panting, the boys had managed to reach the Opera House where, together with twenty-year-old lads, they swore at the police. Then they took Rezo Pantsulaia with his broken hip to the hospital in Soso Siradze's car.

A considerable adrenalin rush, no?

Dad appeared to be the luckiest—he was hit with a bludgeon only once. Wishing to believe she had a heroic husband, Mum said he was beaten, but who'd give him the pleasure of being valiant? It was Rezo Pantsulaia, the former director of the smithy, who was the unrivalled hero of the day!

"What's he doing now?" I asked.

"We visited Rezo and have just come home . . . Haven't you watched the news?"

"What?"

"What 'what'?"

"Oh, I'm not sure. I don't watch TV. It's forbidden here."

"It was a shame, really the last straw . . ."

"Come on, who wants to know?"

I might be an awful person but when I imagined my dad and his chubby friends being chased by the riot police, instead of feeling indignant I became cheerful. It certainly was unpleasant but I couldn't help laughing. I simply had the impression I was listening to something that happened to a complete stranger, someone quite distant, actually to someone so remote, they seemed not real at all . . .

Mum reminded me of returning back to Tbilisi. First she reassured me, then made me laugh, and finally depressed me.

I had to resist the poison and just enjoy the paradise. I was determined to forget about beaten Rezo Pantsulaia and rush to Helena.

By then 40 minutes had passed.

I should have shaved, I thought. *I might scratch her skin with my stubble.*

I have to admit, I felt more confident than ever before.

First I knocked, then heard Helena's voice (exactly as I had caught in the final scene of the conflict between her and Maček). Had it been the other way round and had I heard her first, surely I wouldn't have knocked. I'd have gone back to my room, giving her time to calm down. The timing was wrong: I was there to catch her shouting into the phone.

Yeah, I was standing on this side of the door, while Helena was quarrelling inside. I wasn't sure what language it was (I suspected Greek), but it was a quarrel all right. I decided to tiptoe away. I guessed I was in the wrong place at the wrong time. Something extremely important was happening over her phone.

However, I couldn't take the knock back, so I froze at the door, awaiting my fate.

Helena stopped talking and came to the door, still holding her mobile. She had taken a shower—her black hair shining wet (first time I'd seen her hair loose), her face pale, and a deep, angry frown. She looked like a beautiful vampire.

As if I had woken her up—she was angry and dazed. She looked at me as if I were a ghost or an alien.

Momentarily, I was taken aback.

"What's up?" I managed to say.

My voice seemed to bring her back to reality.

"I can't come now," she told me. "I'm on the phone." And she looked at her mobile.

"Okay, no problem," I smiled.

She smiled back but not in the way I liked, not as she did in Malbork. This time it was coldly formal. She closed the door and said:

"Sorry."

Utterly wrong time, I fully realized that very minute.

I knew she was talking to Maček. I swore at him silently, whispering obscenities which just about reflected my loathing for him.

I recall weighing other possibilities—I could knock again, rap loudly at the door, even make her hang up. She might have wished me to do it. I might have been meant to be the person shouting the loudest that day. God, how I needed my previous wise Elene that minute to give me advice: "Don't sneak away, make her open the door. She should realize you're sensitive, that you aren't after sex only. You have to free her from that Pole, help her make the decision. You must dash into her life, don't hesitate—can't you see she's confused? She doesn't know what she wants." Or else,

Elene might have been more rational: "What has all this got to do with you? Leave immediately! Are you sure it isn't only sex you're interested in her so much? How can you love a person you hardly know? It's just a passing infatuation because she seems gorgeous compared to Mme Roget and Danuta, so you believe you're in love. In truth, it's an illusion. Don't you dare interfere with the Pole—they're a husband and wife and can take care of their own problems. Who are you to get in the way?"

Fair enough. It was none of my business. And if I was uneasy, it was Helena I was afraid of, not Maček. I was terrified she would yell at me and slam the door in my face. And be dead earnest, not softly apologetic as she had been. What if she and not virtual Elene told me to sod off? She could, I was sure, if she chose to . . .

At least I was sure at the time.

So, I resolved to ignore (for the umpteenth time) my interest, tried to push Helena and her old husband out of my mind. I went to see Iliko. I didn't want to be alone.

Iliko and Zviad were planning to take a walk in the city.

"Why haven't you told me?" I asked Iliko.

"You've sold your soul to that woman," he replied in his typical tone seasoned with a mixture of friendliness and aversion.

"Doesn't she have a husband?" Zviad asked me.

"I believe they're separated."

I remember my reluctance to discuss Helena. They might have come up with some foolishly lewd remark, which would prove to be the last straw. Then I might have hit the roof—I was pretty pissed off with myself for my own confessions of the previous night . . . I suppose they sensed it wasn't sheer sex that drew me to the girl. As opposed to the night before, they were quite reserved when questioning me about her.

I also noticed they were much friendlier toward each other than ever. Earlier, they wouldn't consider going sightseeing without me, but now they didn't even tell me. We had regrouped, and not only physically (like in the minibus), but psychologically as well: I had a new partner, while they had each other. They were like spinster sisters—smiled at me unnaturally (hypocritically, with a touch of hatred), completely disregarded my wishes (for instance, I wanted to see the old part of the city, while they preferred to sit in a nearby café) and seemed to be having a private joke at my expense, but rather subtly, so I wasn't sure. It was just a hunch.

In short, they were envious.

"A rally has been forcefully dispersed in Tbilisi," Zviad told me.

"Was it on TV?" I recalled Mum's question.

"No, I talked to my family."

"Good job!" Iliko enthused. "If I were the riot police, I'd give them a sound beating every single day, put them in barrels full of shit, and roll them down the streets, like the Ottomans did."

"My dad was hit."

I said it on purpose. Wanted him to feel embarrassed.

"Screw them! Are you serious?" Zviad sounded indignant.

"You don't say so!" Iliko blushed.

I had a hard time reassuring them, but succeeded in creating a rift in their coalition. My dad's news made Zviad side with me if only briefly, because soon I discovered their tandem was much stronger than I had imagined. It transpired that Iliko had translated Zviad's text into German.

"Who knows, he might be the winner," he chuckled. "If he does, he's guaranteed a publication. And when he gets the Nobel Prize, he's going to toss one or two percent in my direction. He's not cheap."

"Have you written anything?" Zviad asked me.

What could I? And when?

"I can't," I said frankly.

"Crisis?" Iliko wanted to know.

"Infantilism."

"That's good," he laughed.

"Don't worry, you will write," Zviad yawned, and turned to Iliko. "He's got some time, doesn't he?"

They were discussing me as if I were a hopelessly lazy, absolutely incapable schoolboy. Now they weren't spinsters—they were busybody teachers, seemingly caring but wicked in reality.

"I'm going to write your denouncements," I said. "Traditionally, nights are for writing them, aren't they?"

"Yeah, easily." Iliko was strangely gleeful.

We couldn't find a single café. There were only banks and bank-like buildings in the quarter where we stayed. And we didn't want to go too far. It was getting dark and all we could see around were drunken locals.

"Where did they manage to get drunk?" Zviad wondered. "There must be a place around here. It can't have been in the banks they drank."

"It's a grand drinking night," I said with false regret, just to annoy Zviad. "Isn't it Friday today? The European Union is getting stoned tonight. We just don't know where exactly."

"It's a Monday for us," Iliko hissed.

"No, it's a Wednesday!" Zviad followed suit. "I hate Wednesdays most of all. Neither here not there . . ."

"Yeah, Wednesday is a clinical death," Iliko agreed with a grave face.

Anyway, our "Wednesday" soon finished. We returned to the hotel only to find a larger number of colorful whores in the hall. Two hours earlier there were fewer of them. We stared appraisingly.

"There'll be a crowd after midnight," Iliko said.

Some of them looked pretty scary, so we decided they were men dressed like women.

"You've got to look at their throats," Iliko explained. "It's the Adam's apple that betrays them."

Not all of them were ugly. Some were quite attractive. I could imagine our detective writer Eldar Aliev's joy at stepping into the hotel.

"It's Aliev's paradise," I said.

"Shall we fool around?" Iliko beamed at us.

His words sounded like those he used to say when he was hungry. I noticed he was once again torn by his natural meanness and desire.

"Ask them how much they charge," he asked Zviad.

"How can I? I don't speak their language!" The latter got angry.

"If it's a three-digit number, we can start fasting," Iliko suggested.

He was horny. He had to be, otherwise he wouldn't have insisted. It was his body and not his mind that prompted him to act. He was ready to spend his creased euros, so painstakingly saved, on the whores only to experience some semblance of the victory the Serb grasshopper had. He had to substitute a whore for Irmel.

Some of them looked so alluring and my celibacy had been so lengthy that I also started to contemplate getting physiological compensation.

Helena was too far away, on her phone, while these women were right here, tangible and corporeal (we could touch them if we wanted), attracting us like magnets. As soon as they sensed our open interest, they stared back at us. One beckoning gesture would have been enough for them to surround us like vultures.

I also remember thinking: *If I take one of them, I'm going to lose Helena.* And, like an ancient Greek fatalist, I felt terrified of Aphrodite's wrath. Whoring around automatically excluded winning Helena.

It wasn't that I was sorry to part with money—I've never been a miser. Neither was I afraid of venereal diseases. I just wanted to be loyal to Helena (or rather my choice). I bade hasty farewell to undecided Zviad and Iliko and went back to my room. I was sure Helena would visit me that night.

I thought I might even try writing, but the minute I glanced at the paper, I was gripped with my usual fear. It was six months since I had written anything short story-like, and even that was a draft. Not only the idea of rewriting but even rereading it sent terror waves down my spine. All my energy seemed to have been consumed by the war, then Elene and finally Helena. The organ (or organs) responsible for writing was occupied by the Russian tanks, and the previous and present Helens.

Heinz, my foot! I couldn't write, period. They could publish Zviad in German magazines. He was a good poet and fully deserved winning the competition . . . I was ready to pray for his success.

I didn't write a single word that night. I went to bed, lying in wait for Helena.

It was more or less fine until I was awake. The most difficult part was waiting in my sleep. It was ten times worse realizing Helena wasn't coming again. I believe I woke up every five minutes, looked at the door and sank back into sleep. The tiniest sound coming from the passage jolted me out of my troubled sleep. I seemed to be stuck on Helena. I dreamt of episodes related to her but completely illogically linked to each other (caressing Helen, Helen at the cemetery, Helena in Tbilisi—in the house Elene and I rented, Helena at my door, Helena in Elene's green jogging shoes). It was a feverish dozing, as if I had a flu. I was overexcited, but in quite an unfamiliar way. I was suffering from Helenovirus.

Several times in such near-coma wakefulness I resolved to go up to her room, but as soon as I fully woke up, I changed my mind. Sometimes I found sensible pretexts that stopped me ("She's had a hard day. If she wanted to see me, she'd come on her own."), at other times they were ridiculous ("If I go up, I'll find Iliko in her bed. I'll be obliged to kill him and poor Mum will go crazy.").

Neither did I see her at breakfast. I came across sour Iliko who had spent the night quite differently from his initial plans. His expression clearly showed how sorry he was for the wasted money.

"Recently I was advised to try midgets," he told me. "Circus directors have regular sex with them. You'll be surprised how many families have broken up because of this . . . Apparently, they're experts in fellatio . . . Know who told me? Aliev! Two or three are at it together. He said his relative used to lift them and carry upstairs so that his neighbors would take them for children. Can you imagine? Isn't he a classic maniac? I'm going to read all his books . . ."

I didn't understand what he was driving at. I even asked him how he came to consider midgets in the first place.

"Yesterday I chose the shortest of them, with short arms and legs," he spoke in a conspiratorial whisper. "But she was absolutely useless. A log. I was fooled by her bra. You pay for the bra but discover a flat chest . . . Said she was into black magic, amazingly inane . . . Why did I waste money? I had to jerk off anyway . . ."

I couldn't stand his gibberish any longer. If he didn't stop, I was ready to spit into his tea (why couldn't I be shocking for once?). He seemed to guess I was preparing a terrorist attack and asked me with an amiable interest, just like an experienced psychologist:

"Are you in a bad mood?"

I nodded (had I been eight and not twenty-eight years old, I'd have wept).

"Have you fallen in love with her?" He continued his friendly interrogation.

"I don't know yet," I lied.

"You do," he laughed. "You can't fool me, sonny. It's me who gets along with the likes of her, while you're more of a traditional type. How do you know how to talk to a non-Georgian woman? What you need is someone young, living in a posh Tbilisi district, with a small bum and an extended family."

"You don't know me at all." I got angry.

"Neither do you." He also became angry.

By midday I had exhausted my patience and went up to Helena's room, but was met by a chambermaid changing bed-sheets and towels. Suddenly it struck me that Helena had left, not just went out, but disappeared for good. She might have quarreled with her husband again—for the last time—and dashed out. I decided to check it with the maid, but she didn't speak a word of English. The poor woman just smiled and nodded. She didn't allow me into the room to see if Helena's luggage was still there. It was only at the reception that I calmed down when I was told someone called Helena hadn't checked out.

Incidentally, the fact that I didn't know Helena's surname also transpired at the reception.

I was in love with a nameless person.

"She's Greek, with black hair," I had told the reception clerk. "She's my colleague."

Helena's non-final disappearance cheered me up a little. But she didn't show up at one in the afternoon, neither at one thirty nor at two. Then we went to see the old city.

At the hotel we were met by a group of Georgian girls studying in Warsaw.

"We heard you were here and immediately came to see you," they told Zviad.

Generally speaking, they were his fans.

Probably I shouldn't be writing this but I had never seen such strange-looking people. Or, maybe, I was grim at the time and saw things in gloomy colors. The girls (nine altogether) seemed all right if one planned to be their friend, but the problem was they didn't look like humans, resembling objects more. It might have been my impression considering the Polish women's shapes (had I seen the girls in Georgia, I'd have thought differently), but what we saw that day was very far from feminine outlines. We were accompanied by a radiator-girl, an iron-girl, a washing-machine-girl, a vacuum cleaner-girl, an aquarium-girl, a Brezhnev's portrait-girl, a some-unknown-scientist's bust-girl, a wardrobe-girl, and a hair-dryer-girl . . .

They behaved like objects too. All their questions were about the Georgian politicians and the celebrities that regularly appeared on the national TV channels. At that, they mentioned the names and referred to the events I had never heard about ("Did N get married?" "Has X kept his promise to live in a cave as a sign of protest?" "Has the Patriarch really baptized 600 babies in a day?"). Neither did I find out where exactly they studied or worked. Their answers were so vague, I thought there was something fishy in their reluctance. The radiator-girl was most forthcoming (and the most active):

"There's a Russian Orthodox church here and that's where we, the Georgians, mostly meet."

They were familiar with Zviad's poetry thanks to the Internet but had no idea who I was. But still, they were pretty plucky while talking to me, giggled a lot and even flirted somewhat mockingly (?) with me.

I had no doubt one or two were already infatuated with Zviad, who was flattered (it was clear as day) that a bevy of object-girl-fans met him in Warsaw. He sprayed platitudes with the face of a tired, experienced genius and went an extra mile to further impress not only those two, but the remaining seven as well.

It was the first time I had seen him so elated. Up to that point, if he wasn't drinking, he had been a cautious onlooker. Now that he was surrounded by his fans from his home country, he had regained his confidence, naturally (without any alcohol) feeling cheerful.

When I told him the girls looked like various household objects, he was so offended that he seriously sulked at me.

"They're great," he said. "Crazy about poetry and can easily slit my rivals' throats."

Finally, it was the real Georgian poet speaking through him!

"Is he screwing any of them?" Iliko whispered to me.

"No idea," I shrugged my shoulders. "I don't actually think so. Probably kisses at most."

"Yeah, he's going to tease them a little, make them cry a little, suffer himself and then write a poem," he gurgled Mephistopheles-style.

Their coalition was disintegrating right before my very eyes.

If there were a reputed, proper writer in my place, with what relish, false tears, and pseudo-patriotic phrasing he'd describe meeting the girls: "Our lassies have been driven by the Georgian gray reality to the faraway lands where they study and work, toiling in the name of their home country, assisting their economically deprived families, financially supporting their aging parents . . ."

I was direct with Zviad:

"You're not going to get rid of them for quite some time. I'm off."

He looked at me with a stunned expression but didn't say anything. I took a stroll through the streets of old Warsaw, looked at the buildings painted red and yellow, even discovered the bust of Pope John Paul II. I didn't know what else I could do in this city and returned to the hotel. Without going to Helena's room, I sat in the bathroom, moping, with a pen and paper, in yet another attempt to write.

I wrote twice and crossed out twice the same opening phrase: "The Russians bombed us in August . . ." Then I gave up.

. . .

Moscow–Warsaw. Train

It was incredible: she had tattoos on her ass. 2 tattoos, both signatures. I asked what they were. She laughed . . . "It's a long story," she said. What could it be? Someone had left their signatures on her ass for eternity! I insisted she told me. She was laughing but I felt she was uneasy, even upset about the foolish, undeletable scar. I refuse to understand why she hasn't got rid of it. As I suspected, both belonged to men. One was her ex-boyfriend. Said they had thought they'd never part. He had her signature, had them done at the same time (!). But she absolutely refused to talk about the other facsimile, so I let her be. It might have been forcefully made, how do I know? Or could it be linked to some psychological trauma? I didn't insist—took pity on her. How awful! How would it feel to be literally carrying your love life on your ass? Your past is on your ass—permanently! You can't hide your exes and each new one knows who you have been with once upon a time. What if you don't wish to disclose everything? What if you're trying to hide their identity? Obliged to go into lengthy explanations, feeling guilty and being miserable . . . Isn't it better to cut off such a chatty ass? Why do you need an ass that can't keep secrets? I'd burn my skin or try plastic surgery. For all I know she might be really proud of the names. Or she wants everyone to see what men have been with her. But who were they anyway? Big fish? Was it Borges or Neil Armstrong who left their signatures on her ass?

No, it wasn't my imagination. She was embarrassed. She was pitiful. Not wishing her to feel lonely in this respect, I wrote on my arm in capital letters: MILENA. With a felt-tip pen of course.

. . .

The Literature Express arrived in the evening. Iliko phoned my room.

"They've arrived," he said. "Rudy's wearing a Russian shirt."

Then he moved on to the bit that really interested me:

"Your girl's husband has come too. I bumped into him in the elevator." His tone and heavy breathing made me think he waited for my reaction with a kind of hidden sadistic pleasure.

"Did you? Fine." I had difficulty keeping disappointment out of my voice. "Hope he's not going to hand me to the police in his native country."

"No way," Iliko said. "That's not the Polish method of revenge."

On hearing the news, I found it even harder to stay in my room. The thing I wanted the least was happening to me: I had fallen in love with an elusive stranger. I hadn't experienced such bad luck or felt so confused since I finished school. With Elene, for instance, all was simpler and pretty straightforward. How did I, a fully grown dullard, end up feeling like I was just out of school? I shouldn't have allowed myself to be lured into this stupid trap I set for myself. I had to get out while I still could. I had to get away from Helena . . .

Sleeping together did it.

My head was full of the questions:

Would they make up?

Would I be obliged to watch them sitting side by side?

Did I have to reconcile with my utter failure?

Was I to forget Malbork?

Was I to erase the memory of the minibus trip we did together from Malbork to Warsaw?

And my thirty-three-item list too?

I dashed outside. I hated my room, my clothes, my writing pad and my bags.

I decided to have a drink. Drink, smoke, and attack Zviad's object-fans. I had to entertain myself one way or another, didn't I?

I went into the hotel restaurant and found the Chechen Raul Aldamov drinking red wine.

"Will you have some?" he asked.

"A little," I said with a squint and sat at his table.

"Did you have fun without us?"

"Did you?" I asked in return.

"We . . . we were castigated. Depreciated as worthless. They said self-respecting writers would have never agreed to participate in such an idiotic tour."

"Oh, my . . ."

"Yeah, only the authorities received us in a civil way, but our colleagues stoned us."

"Felt envious, probably . . ."

"No. In theory, they were right. A writer should stay home, wear slippers and sit at his computer, hitting the keyboard. What is he doing on a train? A whole month? Is he an ordinary tourist?"

"Did they say anything about us?"

"The Georgians? No! Didn't give a damn," he laughed. "Pushkov read his protest letter at one of the literature evenings and that was it . . . There was clapping, though. Something like the Communist Party meeting applause. So, we've brought you the sound of applause."

He was okay. Laughed at his own words. It wasn't my intention to spend the entire evening drinking and talking to him. On the other hand, I had no alternative plans. No idea what I wanted to do in the next two or three hours before I went to bed. Then I could sleep at least (I feared to even think about the following day). We sat there, sipping the wine and talking to each other. Or rather, I was listening as most of the time it was him who talked. When I sat down, he was already drunk.

Occasionally I glanced at the door—I was sure Maček would walk in. Didn't he drink himself unconscious in the Madrid restaurant when Helena and I had to carry him upstairs?

"What are you looking at? Are you expecting anyone?" Raul asked me.

I vigorously denied anything of the kind (for some reason I was confident he'd have felt insulted if it were so). Later, when I already was quite tipsy and brave enough, I asked him directly:

"You're a Muslim, how come you drink wine?"

"I'm not a Muslim, I'm a sham," he chortled. "Do I look like a genuine Muslim? If I weren't a sham and didn't have a 20,000 dollar bank loan . . . Listen . . . If I didn't have to pay 600 dollars every month, I'd not only be an ordinary Muslim, but the Hezbollah! The loan's keeping me in check as well as my wife, children and the car . . . A five-year-old Mercedes, by the way . . . Otherwise I'd definitely be a fundamentalist . . . I feel it in my guts! My word! I'd believe that if I killed the Russian president—or, okay, the prime minister—I'd get to heaven where I'd have an army of virgins for sex slaves! How does that sound, huh? But I'm tied up by the loan, Zaza, do you get me? Zviad was right—wine is just a link in this chain."

I wished I hadn't asked. Suddenly I felt horrified at the prospect of spending the night with him rambling on. Besides, I wasn't at all sure he wasn't serious. From time to time he laughed at his own words, but sometimes his face was so livid, I didn't know how to react. Was I supposed to laugh or fall into fury like him? Eventually, I chose the mirror effect: if he laughed, I echoed him; if he frowned, I also frowned, because the only thing capable of destroying our amity of the moment was asynchrony. My reactions had to perfectly match his facial expressions in essence and time, or else we could have a fight. Yeah. It seemed a sure thing. However long he prattled on about his bank loan, I was still suspicious of his ultra-liberalism and humanism. Yes, I admit I'm a slave to the stereotypes and misconceptions. I refuse to believe in the North Caucasian liberalism. I'm incurably ailing from the South Caucasian skepticism.

Now I try to recall my emotions of the time and I don't agree with my past self. I'm not apologizing. Honestly, I've changed my mind.

At least about Raul.

"Have you read Borisov's story?" He suddenly reverted to a murmur (in truth, he had to whisper when he was talking about assassinating the Russian president).

"I have," I nodded.

"And? Isn't it crap? I can write dozens a day like that. *My mum was a nice woman, my dad fell down from a tree.'* What the hell is this? Is he making fun of us? But no, he's not that simple. Don't you see what he was aiming at? Say something . . . You've read it, haven't you? Aaah! You can't! He's wormed his way into politics! Between you and me, what politics do they have in Bulgaria? My ass!" Raul pushed the glasses, plates and the bottle to the sides, clearing the table to give room to his energetic gesticulation. "Do you know what's going on in Bulgaria? I haven't got the faintest idea. It's our politics which is interesting, it's in our countries that politics is dynamic! It's the Caucasus, brother! Fire and brimstone for twenty years. But, Zaza, it needs balls, you know what I mean?"

How tired I was of hearing similar banalities! First it was Danuta drivelling on about Borisov's plot, now him.

"How many times have you fought since the Soviet Union disintegrated?" he said, raising his voice.

"I'm not sure. Three or four times," I mumbled.

"We had two wars. And the Bulgarians?"

"No idea."

"Not even once!"

"Right."

"Exactly! But the bastard's in *The New Yorker* with his story about the Second World War. And you had one a month ago . . ."

"Three."

"Doesn't matter. You had a war! Know what Borisov would have done in your place? He'd write about the first, the second, the third and finally about the last one."

"How do you know I'm not writing about it myself?"

"If you are, I want to see *The New Yorker* here!" he banged his fist on the table. "Give me a good translator, give me a praising review!"

"Should I write about the regional problems?" I pretended to be angry (in reality, his "give me" made me laugh).

"Do that!" he snorted at his own words. Then he clinked his glass against mine, "Let's drink to your four wars! It's a terrific topic."

"Here's to your two," I smiled, "which makes it six. Six novellas . . . The Caucasus wrapped in fire. Super!"

"And sex in Paradise for an epilogue."

I don't remember how I managed to get away from drunken Raul.

No need to say I didn't even try going to Helena's room. I returned to mine and dropped on the bed: sulking, drunk and abandoned. I can say it again: had I not been twenty-eight, I'd have wept. That's what I did after my graduation party. I was in love with my classmate but she was going to marry some freak. I had kept my emotions in check for the day, drank and had fun, but as soon as I walked into my room, I buried my face in the pillow and wept bitterly. I was nearly choking but I couldn't and didn't want to lift my head. It seemed as if I were swapping that girl for my muffled howl.

I didn't weep in Warsaw. There was a twenty-eight-year-old egotist on the bed in a Warsaw hotel and not a seventeen-year-old masochist. I knew I had to start hating Helena.

If I didn't, how could I fall out of love?

Two things happened that night.

First Zviad phoned asking if I had a condom. He was expecting Inga (the hair dryer girl or possibly the bust-of-an-unknown-scientist one). I said I was sorry for not having one and warned him that it was forbidden to sleep with a fan, but if he did, he'd hide from her the following morning and she'd curse him.

"These girls are Europeans," Zviad told me. "It's not one of our villages."

Then there was a knock on my door.

I certainly thought it was Helena.

It was Maček.

"Have I woken you up?" he asked.

Helena has told him everything and he's here to beat me up, I thought.

"Sorry, I seem to be regularly waking you up," he laughed. "I'm a typical owl, so I don't sleep at night . . . I've brought you this," and he handed me my stories. "It's interesting. I think I'll translate 'The Pillars'. We can talk about it later."

For some obscure reason I was sure he was aware of something if not all.

Helena and I had shared a bed, and yet he praised my story! How absurd! Sheer injustice. The couple took me for a complete idiot. They were toying with me.

Raul, here's a good translator you asked for . . .

· · ·

Letter home

I'd have never done it back home: I put The New Yorker *with my story here and there in all carriages. Initially, I asked Ursula, my assistant during the tour, to give a copy to several "writers." She also passed my humble request to come back with their impressions. One whole week after handing them out, and no feedback yet. Do I demand admiration? God forbid! I'm not that old to expect only praise. Oh, no! I expected natural, professional, amiable comments, interest and criticism from my colleagues, which is vital for maintaining a healthy atmosphere in literature on the whole. But what do we have here? Interest is zero. Ursula tells me one can't talk about liking or disliking* it as no one has actually read it! And all the while, the magazine copies were handed out eight days ago! What can one expect from doctors, engineers, artists or physicists if "writers" themselves don't read their colleagues' works? How can we demand that schoolchildren read if professional writers don't? Reading writers are extinct and I am a living witness of the sad result.

The people here call themselves writers but demonstrate utter indifference toward their, I can modestly suggest, slightly more successful colleague. If my story is so uninteresting, why was it published by The New Yorker? Don't they want to know more about the current creative processes in what they call their sphere? And they don't have to go very far—it's right next to them, in Bulgaria.

Are we so uninterested in each other?

Those "colleagues" who were given the magazine copies but haven't yet reacted are, naturally, added to my "blacklist" (I've got no patience for illiterate writers!). But I'm quite prepared to give another chance to those who might still show some concern with the fate of their associate, some interest toward success or failure of their colleague. As the first group of the select failed to reveal a true professional, I'll wait for someone else. Let's see who it is that the river of providence washes ashore . . .

The New Yorker copies are in various carriages and compartments. Ursula and I watch from a distance, waiting for the professionally inquisitive gold fish to take the bait.

Is anyone going to read us in Europe?

Please don't condemn me for the game. I've got to have fun in this circus, don't I?

16. BERLIN

The passengers of the Literature Express said good-bye to each other in Berlin. I suspected our train would be painted different colors, all inscriptions linking it to literature would be erased and then it would be sent to run in the underground. I was fully aware that while I was still on the seminar, it would be absolutely impossible for me to forget Helena or stop loving her. I had already figured out that I would cool down only when seeing Helena was impossible. I was still obsessed with her—I kept looking for her everywhere. If all followed the natural course of development, within three weeks (a month at the most) of my arrival home I would get her out of my mind. It was my personal experience that gave me the confidence. The first week would be the hardest— the Tbilisi winter would set me contemplating suicide—but, if I managed to live through that difficult period, I would accumulate enough energy to write new stories. In short, if my calculations were correct, Georgia would be able to welcome neo-Lazarus at the end of December or nearer the New Year. Even if it was only me. Even on a pretty local scale.

Nothing noteworthy had happened before our departure for Berlin. I spent the entire day lying on the bed and watching TV. Helena didn't turn up. Neither did her husband. I also found out that Zviad had no luck with his fan Inga. He told me she played with him, teased him, but refused to go further. Apparently, they even had a tug of war at the traffic lights in front of our hotel—he pulled her his way, while she stood rooted to the cycling lane. Zviad invited her to his room, saying she had come that far and needed to take just one step. But when he was fed up with begging her, he told her with a mixture of aversion and irony: "I was your chance of becoming part of history, you freak."

No wonder they parted then and there.

The family of the Lithuanian Vitas—four fair children and a two-meter-tall wife—arrived from Vilnius. Outwardly, Milena showed no signs of distress, but I was sure she was seething with fury. Her skin round her mouth was covered in red spots. She reached half the height of the wife and her complexion—in comparison to the fairness of the rest—was Asiatic yellow. To me she always looked fair enough, but I changed my mind as soon as I saw Vitas' white family. He hugged and kissed his children with a kind of animal passion. And all the while, as if by some vicious coincidence, Milena had nothing to do. She stood there, watching the happy family reunion. "That's how it had to be. Did you expect something different, Milena? It's only natural, isn't it? I'll suggest a business meeting to Heinz and Rudy," she must have thought at the time.

In contrast, Mme Roget was truly happy—no one had come from Belarus to see her Mickey Mouse (they'd arrive later, when he was naturalized French). They were kissing nonstop. She wasn't what you'd call young, but spent most of the time on the knees of her homo-muscle creature.

Compared to me, everyone including the hundred-year-old Mme Roget seemed luckier.

Later that evening Iliko arranged an exhibition of the items taken from various hotels. He had presented quite an array: bathrobes (3), disposable slippers (2 pairs), a telephone (!), spoons, a leather folder (bearing the inscription *Hotel Maritim*), a German Bible ("It's Luther's translation, was in the drawer."), a reproduction Modigliani ("Reminds me of my ex-girlfriend, the same breasts and the same red skin."), and one light bulb.

"Worth at least 300 euros," he said. "All I need now is a TV set, a wife and the post of the Ambassador of Georgia."

I asked if he had a place in Berlin he called home, where he could keep all these things.

"Yeah, in Kroizberg, forty square meters. I share it with Stefan. He's in Thailand now. As hard up as me," he chuckled.

Obviously, like Iliko, Stefan specialized in collecting things from hotels. I could vividly imagine their place—eclectic, crammed with disposable items . . .

My last impression of Warsaw was Iliko's memorable exhibition. I hadn't seen Helena anywhere, not in the hall and not in any of the passages, elevators, or streets, not at Zviad and Inga's traffic lights, and not at the railway station.

We left for Berlin and I still had no idea where she was.

Until then our train journeys had been silent and somewhat drowsy, but the last stretch of our trip turned out to be unnaturally animated. On the way from Lisbon to Madrid everyone had started writing as if by an agreement and something similar was happening now too. But instead of just writing down their impressions silently, they pulled out their laptops and set to reading their texts, editing and noisily changing them. Nearly everyone tried presenting their writings out loud. Unlike me, they had taken Heinz's suggestion pretty seriously, had paid proper attention to the announcement made by Irmel and Milena about the Berlin competition. Irmel popped into our compartment to give Zviad his German translation for proofreading. The final, corrected version was to be handed back in two hours.

"We haven't got your text," she told me sternly.

"He hasn't written anything. His fingers were swollen," Iliko answered for me. He was still flirting with her.

"Sorry to hear that," Irmel mumbled rather coldly. She must have found it inexplicable that a writer showed no interest toward such an important literary competition.

I apologized (not sure if I had to feel apologetic about it all) and immediately felt a surge of hatred toward all participants in the forthcoming contest.

Iliko and Zviad concentrated on proofreading. Needless to say, it was Iliko who was reading, while Zviad looked at unfamiliar words with a clever face. The printed text didn't look like a poem at all—it was too wide, more prose than poetry. He must have written a story.

"No, it's a war diary," Zviad beamed at me. "One full day. From morning till night."

"Our war?" I asked.

"No, the Boer," Iliko laughed.

Yeah, but it's my theme, isn't it? I thought.

"I believe he's added something of his own," Zviad winked at me. "Took advantage as I wouldn't understand anyway."

Iliko neither confirmed nor denied the accusation. He went on reading, moving his lips and following the lines with a pen.

I don't know what came over me, but an urge to disrupt their work was stronger than I could control (I must have been envious for staying out of the literary process). So, I said I was going to write about our recent war but describe events in a way that would make it practically impossible for readers to relate them to the reality. I planned to write my own version of the war when we would be the winners . . . I would describe the victory parade in the Heroes' Square, finishing my story with a nationwide war dance: the triumphant nation dances along with its victorious government.

"Why didn't you write it? It sounds cool," Zviad liked my idea.

"No," Iliko muttered without taking his eyes off the printed page with his translation. "They wouldn't appreciate it. Here they are interested in real facts not your imaginary compensations."

"They'd appreciate it all right," I protested. "They've written so much about the complexes rooted in their own victories and lost wars . . ."

I don't know why I was defending my unwritten story with the plot I had made up then and there. I hadn't even thought of anything close. Fair enough, I always wanted to write an anti-eulogy, but not at the expense of that war. I believe the explanation was much simpler: I was envious of those ninety-nine people engrossed in correcting and editing their texts. That day everyone was a writer. I was the only one not involved.

Across from us, the Armenians, Anait and Zeituntsyan were sitting facing each other. She had a white Mac open in her lap and stared at the screen, while her colleague was talking to her in his characteristic most tragic and solemn manner. In his Armenian speech, Mr. Zeituntsyan occasionally used a word or two which were either French or sounded French (at least to my ear), such as *madam* or *pardon*. He seemed to be commenting Anait's text or expressing his opinion about it. I heard him mention the name of our Bulgarian colleague Borisov and after a short passage in Armenian, also say *"New Yorker."* I had no doubt they were discussing the Bulgarian, carping about his story and using the words *politics* and *our war* as often as the Croat Danuta and the Chechen Raul had before them.

Half of the carriage was busy proofreading, while the other half was trying to get someone interested in their work of letters. The writers were reading to the writers. A listener only a minute ago had turned into a writer. Writers were transforming into readers and readers into writers. The listeners were impatient for the writers to finish being such so that they would get the chance of acting like writers. In this respect, it was particularly painful to watch the presentation duel between the Finnish and Spanish poets, which acquired an air of unpleasant desperation. One read his fragment first, then the other, but the comical part was that neither listened to the other: they fired formal compliments like polite robots, sounding natural only when it was their turn to recite. A month ago, on the way from Lisbon to Madrid, they all had been bitten by the writing bug, now it was the reading virus. It might have been a common practice with them (writers reading their work to each other—what's unusual about that?), while it was me who was pitifully comical. The writers lived their natural lives typical of their literary lifestyle: they offered their colleagues the deepest, funniest, scariest, coolest, the most recent, impressive, original, unexpected, significant, and stunning fragments and waited for their reactions to check if they had really produced something worthwhile. Could it be the creative process proper? Or an unconscious attempt, a battle to win over a reader at least in such an appropriate literary atmosphere (because in a non-literary space the reader is practically extinct)? And if anyone was relatively weak, they could deter them from transforming into a writer and if not for the rest of their lives, at least temporarily turn them into readers, into listeners on the train . . .

There were only writers here. The blood of a true reader was scarce. No one left to bite. We were the ones who bite. We might have even jumped at the train operator (he was bound to be a non-writer) like hungry vampires at a young reader-body, like sailors at a woman they accidentally discover on board. (What? These things have surely happened.) How can a writer get aroused (in purely literary respect of course) if everyone is the same? You might feel stimulated by someone a lot better than you, but definitely not by your literary twin. No way. The train presented a collection of equal abilities. Equally talented and equally incapable. Similar ambitions. Similar fears. Similar topics. Similar problems. Similar originality. Similar lack of luck in literature. Yes, it was the train of the luckless. The Germans had gathered one hundred unlucky writers and drove us to the ultimate goal: eventually we all had to proclaim: "I'm not a writer!" It was only logical as having spent time among such a number of luckless people who were so similar to you, it was impossible to still wish to be a writer. The seminar seemed to be the least literature-oriented compared to others. Anti-literature and inhuman! Even the name *Literature Express* was a joke—we were ridiculed! And that's why we were taken from city to city as if we were a sideshow . . . Of course we were pathetic! One hundred (okay, ninety-nine as *The New Yorker* had secured a certain position for Borisov) writers ecstatic over their own—similar to others—texts, aroused, excited, luckless, and nameless . . .

The fact that I was a passenger on the train for the luckless became obvious the moment we left Lisbon and headed for Madrid, but I didn't have a name for it yet. I still harbored hope for a miracle that would stun me with its divine revelation. I possessed nothing to feel different from my twin-colleagues.

We desperately needed a reader. A virginal non-writer. We couldn't stand each other any longer. We were all trying to murder a colleague in each other with our own histories, with our emotional recital: remain a reader, don't attempt to climb higher!

We just had to screw a reader. It was paramount to take a reader with a strong immune system (free from any reading-writing zeal) straightaway. It was the only way of regaining our profession. I'm not joking, so please don't laugh.

I decided to escape from this writing-reading factory by hiding in the dining car.

"Are you going to eat something?" Iliko asked his traditional question. He couldn't bear it if Zviad or I felt hungry at a different time from him.

"No, just a pee," I answered and headed for the seventh carriage.

Everyone there was suffering from the same literary fever: correcting, proofreading, reciting, editing . . .

A pure miracle of literature awaited me at the end of the carriage.

Helena was standing at the toilet of carriage number eight. She was smoking.

She seemed to exist only on the train.

When she saw me, she squinted, shook her head, smiled and tapped her forehead several times with her fist.

I didn't smile back. I was angry.

"Where have you disappeared to? You can't do this to me . . . Can't you see the state I'm in?"

I quarreled as if I were her husband. But passionately. Like a passionate husband.

She clearly hadn't expected my energetic attack and stared at me for some time. Astonished and smiling.

I went for her lips.

Helena grabbed my arm and pushed me toward the toilet. She didn't want us to be seen from the eighth carriage.

"Where have you been? Have you made up with Maček?" I went on in the same tone. "What's going on between you? I don't understand . . . You can't do this to me. Please explain . . ."

I stopped caring what she might think of me. I said everything that came into my head. She covered my mouth with her hand and growled like a small animal:

"Shhh!"

I'm sure it was that very second she made the decision. A quick decision. She opened the toilet door, pushed me, and followed me inside.

I knew I had to keep up the momentum. I embraced her and kissed her neck.

"No, wait," she said without opening her eyes. She wouldn't have closed them if she didn't want me.

"I love you . . . please . . . I love you," I murmured.

"What? What was that?" she asked.

Unwittingly, I had spoken in Georgian.

"It's love . . . It's love," was my translation of my own words.

I pulled her top up. She didn't resist. I didn't waste time with her bra, just pulled it down. I touched her breast with my palm, licked her nipples. I was fumbling, in a hurry to touch as much of her as possible.

"Kiss me," she whispered.

Where? The lips or somewhere else? I thought.

She meant her lips. She kissed me herself.

I was kissing her . . . kissing Helena.

"Shh! Don't moan," she said.

I didn't know I was moaning. I didn't hear myself moan.

I stopped kissing her. Then I embraced her.

"Don't run away from me, please."

I pushed my hands under her jeans, grabbing her amazingly strong, hot, and shapely buttocks.

Helena pressed against me with her pubic bone. I thought my pants would tear.

I knew I had to hurry up.

I unbuttoned her jeans and pulled them down. She didn't resist this time either.

"Here?" was all she asked.

I looked around. I lifted her onto the washstand. I pulled the jeans so that only her one leg was free—they dangled down her left leg. She pulled her right foot together with her jogging shoe out of them and took off her top. She held her arms up, touching the wall for balance. The rectangular mirror fixed above the basin reflected her arching spine and lean hips.

"Quick, quick," she whispered hoarsely.

She pulled my shirt out of my pants and caressed my chest and belly with her palms.

What did I welcome her with? A wide waistline and a sedentary, sagging belly. There was no time to feel embarrassed anyway: her shockingly attractive body was trying to merge with my far-from-ideal body. I could apologize for my waistline later . . .

I unbuttoned my fly, pulled down my pants and only then remembered I didn't have a condom.

Helena figured it out. Momentarily, her face showed anger and fear—the fear of cautious grannies: a complete stranger, it's your first time with him, you're about to face chlamydia, yeast infection, AIDS, and God knows what else. But it was too late to stop. We couldn't. And before the phobias took an upper hand, before the goddess of rationality and cautious grannies slapped us to bring us back to our senses, we entered each other.

I hadn't pulled her panties down (realizing it would take time), just pushed them to the side and tried to find a comfortable position.

Helena also tried to find a better sitting position. She bent her right leg (with her jeans still dangling down her left) and pressed her hands to the wall for balance. Her breasts lifted and I knew if I didn't hurry up, I could come without entering her.

I stood on tiptoe (the basin was pretty high) and suddenly—and without any difficulty—found myself in the fatal heat that cautious grannies dreaded so much.

Helena bit her knee while I had the patience for only four moves. On the third I said aloud "I'm coming!" and heard her rasping moan. I knew I had to pull out. The moment I had seen her raised breasts, I wanted to come on them. Helena guessed all this, jumped down agilely and gave my dick a yank or two.

"Sorry," she said when I came. "I know what you wanted, but I can't wash till we get to Berlin."

I wasn't sure if her muffled moan meant she had reached orgasm. And I didn't ask. We helped each other into clothes, kissed lightly and then giggled like a pair of idiots.

"What have you done to me?" I asked.

"If I hadn't pushed you in here, you'd have started yelling," she said. She splashed water on her face and straightened her hair. I found it hard to believe this body was mine only a minute ago. When she washed her hands, I stooped to kiss her back.

"I'll go first, you come out in five minutes," she hesitated (took a deep breath—trying to compose herself), gave me a stern look, and went out.

I remember being scared of that stern look. She seemed frightened herself.

Only when left alone did I fully realize what had happened. The realization stunned. How could I imagine she'd bring my dream to life in the train toilet? But what did I care? Why did I have to look for logic in her actions? We wanted it and did it in the toilet. Wasn't it the case with me that all important things happened in the toilet? I think better in there.

I came out completely dazed and by inertia turned toward the dining car. As I was midway down the eighth carriage, I walked past Helena. She gave me a faint smile. I walked on.

Maček was in the dining car.

I remember thinking: if he starts talking about my stories, I'll die of embarrassment.

I was sure Helena was visible all over me. The minute he looked at me, he should have immediately guessed his wife and I had sex ten minutes ago. I believed my sin was too obvious. If nothing else, my red cheeks were pretty telltale.

Indeed, he started talking about my stories.

"Did I tell you I've decided to translate 'The Pillars'?" he asked.

He was standing at the window with a glass of beer in his hand. He felt fine.

"The soldier character is very good, matching my concept of the Caucasus," he went on. "I can only imagine how impressive it is in Georgian. Please don't get it personally, but the English translation is pretty awful. If one isn't familiar with your part of the world, one wouldn't understand a thing."

He seemed to be in the mood for a lengthy discussion while I was absolutely apathetic to what he thought of my stupid story. I could still hear Helena's hoarse moan in my ears. I was mad I wasn't sitting next to her at the time.

The Hauptbahnhof greeted our eyes with a colorful display of our national flags. Our first thought was it meant to honor the Literature Express as we suspected Heinz of any such extravaganza. However, soon we discovered that the flags were there because of the politicians, not us. Berlin was hosting a political summit. The whole city was full of police. Later, I learned on TV that fifteen heads of state had arrived, among them the president of Russia, who was rather reservedly criticized by the media. The focus of their cautious disapproval was the Russian-Georgian war of three months earlier. All I could hear around me was the mention of our war. Even Iliko appeared to take pride in being in the limelight.

"Now's the time to sell your stories," he told Zviad and me. "The war has kind of promoted you, don't you see? From now on anything from Georgia will sell like hotcakes. And all you need do is write ... But you're shying like virgins. I'm too lazy to write—you don't even know how full I am of all sort of stories your colleagues wouldn't even dream of."

In his eyes I could see the reflection of my own ambition and fear: it was clear we had to take advantage of the existing reality—all of a sudden we were incredibly interesting. We felt we had to act immediately as there would be a huge demand for our tragedy. A smart writer could sell the war quite profitably.

Actually, I had decided to write about the Russian attack as soon as bombs were dropped on Tbilisi. I was sure I'd survive to write something about it. I was pretty confident of it even when a bomb fell on Makhata Mount, waking Elene and me. My main horror at the time was that the Russian soldiers would rape Mum and Elene. Yeah, it appeared that the biggest fear of occupation is connected to women. It's a terrible feeling, so I'd appreciate it if you didn't laugh at me.

Iliko was talking about the well-selling war, while we smiled ironically (Iliko was always funny, wasn't he?), but deep down our mood was hopelessly spoiled by the feeling of helplessness: how could we sell and how could we use being in Germany for it? Would Maček push me into European literature? Would Zviad win the competition? Georgia was the talk of the world, but still . . .

"No way a Russian is going to come away a winner," Zviad said. "But if it happens, I'll beat both Russians and screw Rudy in front of Heinz."

He'd do nothing of the kind. He threatened a lot but never did anything. I used to fear his explosive ways till I got to know him better.

Zviad was composed and determined, while I was obsessed with Helena. I knew perfectly well that whatever happened between us didn't mean much. It might sound strange but the excitement of it soon disappeared (might as well say there was none). Though I wasn't as agitated as earlier, I was still far from feeling relaxed. I just wanted to talk to her, to explain how I felt about her. I waited for a suitable moment, but as if to spite me, she invariably was with my translator. It made me mad that they seemed to have made up. I refused to understand why she didn't end the conflict. Why were they fighting and then making up again? Why couldn't they hate each other to the extent as to part for good? I failed to penetrate their relationship. When a woman doesn't follow her husband and stays in an unknown city (with unknown men), it's a serious crisis, isn't it? Aren't I right? Theoretically, it should have been virtually impossible to make up afterward. Or is it that I'm a lousy detective missing the focal point of other people's life plots?

Heinz had booked us into the Unter den Linden, an old, Soviet-style hotel on Friedrichstraße. The winner of the literature competition was supposed to be announced in the enormous hall of the same hotel. But the most fascinating fact was that we, the passengers of the Literature Express, were to be the last inhabitants of the place—it was to be pulled down at the end of January. My humble request is not to look for a hidden metaphor in the above. There isn't any. If you wish, you can check that the hotel isn't there anymore.

The whole hotel was bustling with the preparation for the following day. No one minded me. I phoned Mum to ask after my beaten dad, still sulking at me. Apparently, one of the prominent politicians had mentioned his name in a TV interview—my dad was among those intellectuals who had suffered from the riot police and the authorities. As a result, it was the main topic of conversations not only at home but at the Chess Federation as well.

I guessed that if I talked to Mum for another five minutes, I'd wash my Georgian passport down the toilet of the Unter den Linden and die as an immigrant in Germany.

After hanging up, I went for a long walk in the zoo, staying there till dusk. From time to time, the statues of famous classic writers sprang out from behind the bushes, which reminded me I was walking in no ordinary park—I was in an artistic zoo: among the unique species of composers, the poets on the verge of extinction, and totally extinct romantic writers.

I had the impression I found myself in a school library.

I wanted to stay out of the hotel as long as possible, I wanted Helena to miss me, I wanted her to start looking for me . . .

She should wonder where I have disappeared to, was the principle driving me to cross half of the park (which stretched across half of Berlin). I also saw the Reichstag, retraced the imaginary line of the now-demolished Wall, and walked through the Brandenburg Gate, returning to the hotel as fit a dutifully exhausted tourist.

In the hall I bumped into Heinz busily giving out orders. His tone immediately reminded me of Mum.

"Why haven't you submitted your text for the competition? It's not normal."

"I can't write. I don't feel well," I said truthfully.

Heinz needed a short, clear answer but my explanation was too abstract, too vague. In theory, such a disclosure should have been followed by a short psychologically professional discussion ("Have you got a crisis?" "Don't you like it here?" "Do you find it hard to write elsewhere, away from home?"). However, he didn't have time to open me up, neither had he such a wish, I guess. He just wanted to rebuke me, not give me a psychoanalytical session.

For want of a better word, I can describe my state of mind at the time as a passive disappointment. Strange as it might sound, I felt neither surprised nor frustrated when I realized I was about to spend the night without Helena.

I went into my room, discovered a number of tiny bottles with red wine in the minibar and drank them one by one. Iliko would certainly get a heart attack had he witnessed such an extravagance.

"What I particularly hate in hotels is minibars," he used to say. "The prices are sky-high, orange juice for example. I always swear at those fridges before I even open a hotel room door."

My plan was to drink a little, boost my morale, and probably watch a couple of porn films. I didn't care how expensive it all would be. In truth, I was bored in exactly five minutes, while the wine made me drowsy. In other words, I fell asleep before my mood improved in any way.

I likewise had a drink before going into the conference hall. At four in the afternoon.

Everyone was sober, fully composed and completely self-mobilized. I was the only one without any function. The rules of the genre required Zviad to be in my place. I thought it utterly unfair to have turned into him.

The hall was packed with the Literature Express people and many unfamiliar faces—all Germans.

Heinz was wearing a pair of black trousers and a jacket with turned up sleeves. His hair was a *creative* mess. My colleagues met him with a ten-minute applause, shouting his name and whistling in appreciation. I even heard some chanting which was supposed to express their gratitude for a month of entertainment. He looked down at us as if we were his favorite but naughty pupils—with a tight-lipped smile ("You're back to your ways, imps, aren't you?"), then he shook his head in sham disapproval. He raised his hand a couple of times to stop the cheering, but we didn't obey—for the first time in the whole month! More chanting of "Heinz! Heinz!" came from the hall. In his tight jeans and two gleaming gold earrings, Rudy was standing beside him on the stage, pointing his finger at the person shouting his boyfriend's name the loudest. That minute the pair looked like a president and the first lady.

Eventually Heinz managed to put an end to the cheering:

"We've only rented the hall for half an hour, so if we don't stop clapping and get down to business, we'll be obliged to announce the winner in the hotel lobby."

Though he sounded dead serious, the hall laughed. It was a short but thundering laughter. Just as Heinz would like it. In the meanwhile, he invited the editor of *Simplicissimus* to the stage. He was a rabbit-like, scruffy old man—a stereotypical editor with stereotypically uncombed gray hair. He reminded me of the busts that had ambushed me in the park the previous day.

Quite unexpectedly, the rabbit turned out to have a deep, powerful voice. Apparently he cracked a joke in German as Heinz and Rudy roared with a reverential laughter. Then the editor greeted us in severe English (which I initially took for German), praised us, and finished with a totally insincere whine—he said he'd have given everything for the chance to travel with us.

Then it was Heinz again who took the floor. He assured us that in truth we all were winners (the typical rhetoric of all competitions) but at the end of his lengthy introductory speech he announced the real winner:

"Raul Aldamov, "Hard Talk," Russia."

"Shit," Zviad muttered under his breath. He was sitting next to me, his face red with anger. His high hopes must have crashed at that moment. He might have cursed Iliko for his disillusionment—he was told Georgia was top of the charts and sold well.

Each and every one from the Literature Express was certain in his or her success. However, the applause that followed the announcement didn't demonstrate any hard feelings.

"We would like to ask Mr. Raul Aldamov, the writer from Chechnya, to come up to the stage," Heinz repeated over and over (by mentioning Chechnya, he was attempting to balance the earlier announced Russia). But Raul Aldamov was nowhere to be found.

"Apparently, he's not here," he finally gave up. "But we'll surely pass the news to him," he rounded up with a touch of disgust.

He should have been appalled that the winner failed to show up at such an important event.

Along the wall of the door opening into the hall, there was a row of tables covered with white cloths. Long-stemmed glasses with rosé and plates with euro coin-sized sandwiches were laid out on them.

I was deeply worried to realize I was the first to approach the tables. I obviously started acting in accordance with someone who had been Zviad not long ago.

Together with others, Helena and Maček came out of the

conference hall. Helena and I caught each other's gaze and, like well-trained spies, looked in the opposite directions. Personally, I (considering my condition at the time) didn't care in the least if Maček noticed anything, while she seemed intent on not revealing what had happened. The most unnerving thing was that every time I glanced at them, I saw his idiotically amiable smile. I wanted to meet Helena's eyes, but found his. I even thought they were a couple of perverts. Being quite old he couldn't get sexually aroused, his wife told him about me, so before the departure they would invite me to their room for a collective coitus: while Helena and I made love, he would sit nearby watching us. Voyeurism might be the last resort to bring back his feeble manhood. He might decide to join us with a desperate masturbation. Who could say for sure?

Everyone around was talking about the Chechen writer. Zviad tried to involve me but not finding sufficient interest in me, he set to drilling Iliko's brains. He just couldn't reconcile with the idea that he wasn't the winner. I turned to the couple that held my attention. I wished to be as drunk as that night, three months earlier, when I blurted out all my secrets to Elene. I wished to be so blotto as to talk in my sleep or, even better, talk like an outspoken zombie about Helena and myself. I wished to approach Maček and tell him how I fell in love with his wife, how we lay side by side in Malbork, how we slept cuddled up on the minibus on the way to Warsaw, and how hopelessly I tried to get her out of my mind. I wanted to be able to speak like a robot—heartlessly, without fear or embarrassment. To be capable of an oblivious confession to him, which would destroy his relationship with Helena in the same way as I had wiped out my and Elene's bond with my drunken prattle three months earlier. I wished my lips and my mind to act of their own volition, to own up without any pangs or foresight: *We've slept together, my dear translator!* With my unacceptably transparent confession to him, I had to stamp out the remaining trust in her. The kind, mindless zombie had to free Helena from the claws of the Polish werewolf.

Maček was a civilized guy. I was sure he wouldn't hit me. He might have even chuckled. His reaction would once more prove to Helena that he was a father figure. A father would be able to forgive, but not a husband.

Helena would turn pale, I was absolutely confident. And her lips might become purplish. On the other hand, she might laugh too. I didn't know her. One thing I knew for sure: she wouldn't splash wine in my face.

I clearly remember getting cold feet: I knew myself inside out, especially my inability to hold my tongue. I decided to go to my room. The rosé had already alarmingly warmed my innards.

It was the Czech writer, I recall with absolute clarity. Bumped into him at the lift. He was deeply upset and his eyes were bloodshot.

"The Russian president has been shot," he told me in his elfin English and laughed a little stupidly.

Because he was an elf, I thought I had misunderstood him. Not getting an adequate reaction from me on the piece of the news, he repeated more loudly in English that was close to the real English:

"The president of Russia was shot at. It was on the news."

Till this day I have no idea why I accepted my twisted version of the events. Why didn't I wait for the next TV news to check? Why did I rush to the reception to find Raul Aldamov's room number?

The only explanation is that I was a real zombie by then. Or Heinz's wine must have got into my system. Had I been sober, how could I believe even for a second that my Chechen colleague, Raul Aldamov had shot at the Russian president?

I existed in my own imaginary plot.

I had recalled my conversation with Raul about terrorism,

which I linked to his absence from the award ceremony. I thought the man was a complete fake, his talk about the bank loans was a well-calculated decoy, and that we didn't have the slightest idea who he was in reality.

I was in no state to question the questions in my head. Not suspicious of my suspicions.

I might have been poisoned by the Helens in my life or by the drink, but at the time it seemed pretty realistic that our winner had shot at the President of Russia.

. . .

Hotel Unter den Linden

My story "Hard Talk" is the winner of the competition!

Danuta, Anait, Pushkov, Zaza and Irmel have just left my room. I could hardly believe my ears—I thought they were poking fun at me. And I'm down with a flu! Finally managed to bring my temperature down to 37°C . . . They told me the Germans were calling me for 20 minutes from the stage . . . How embarrassing! But how should I have known? I thought they knew about my fever. They're so well-organized, but failed to check on me? Not my fault really. Zaza said because I wasn't there in the hall, he thought it was me. He had a good laugh at my expense. I said I couldn't possibly fall so low—throwing a cake was too "civilized" for a Chechen. We watched TV together. The whole thing seems absurd . . . First the prize, then the "terrorist attack" . . . Irmel promised to call a doctor. Fine. Heinz phoned but I'm not sure I understood him. I guess he said he intends to visit me. What do I do now? Get dressed or stay in bed? I don't believe it. My "Hard Talk"? And to think I debated whether to submit it or not!

I'd like to remember these seconds, these minutes, the whole day . . . I've left the other ninety-nine behind. I don't believe it.

The cake should have been brought to my room instead.

. . .

The cake was thrown at the Russian president by a Belgian journalist. His chin and red tie were smeared with the cream as he was rushed out by his bodyguards. The footage was televised over and over again. But the things my drunken imagination pictured about Raul! Now that I recall those days I believe I had lost any sense of reality. Especially that evening when I was turning into Zviad.

The cake story had overshadowed Raul's victory.

"Were you upset that it was cream instead of blood?" Heinz asked with a laugh. "You're Caucasian, aren't you?"

"You think the Belgian has taken revenge on our behalf?" Iliko chuckled.

"Sure. These are writers, so someone had to do the dirty work, no?" Heinz looked at Zviad and me.

"Why?" Iliko said. "They can be quite ruthless if they choose. If properly asked, we could have thought of something impressive."

"No," Heinz shook his head. "I know them. I've got sufficient information about them to state with confidence that they're not terrorists. Their problems are of a very different nature." He winked at Iliko, whose face was bright red.

It still baffles me—what did he mean? What kind of information did he have?

I talked to Helena in the morning. I said good-bye to the Literature Express people in the afternoon. And I took a flight back to Tbilisi in the evening.

I saw Helena at breakfast. She was without her husband. She came over to my table with her cup of coffee.

My head was spinning and I felt sleepy. And I sulked at her.

"I failed to split you and your husband," I told her.

I wanted these words to sound grave, tense and cold, but didn't have the courage to. I feared it might be too much under the circumstances. Instead, the words were said with a smile. As if it was a joke.

"We shouldn't have slept side by side in Malbork," she said. "I confused you. I shouldn't have treated you like that. I was mad at something else. Will you ever forgive me?"

She planned her revenge. Her beloved had angered her and she meant to punish him by being unfaithful. Punish him with my help. But she wasn't a cold-blooded avenger. She came to her senses just in time, realizing she was acting foolishly. She duped me and dumped me. And was now finishing the whole thing with apologies because it wasn't about her and me. It was the love story between her and Maček that was significant. The main drama unfolded there. The novel should have been written about them and not me. I was a third-rate character and novels are never written about the likes of me. I had thought I was interesting, but all the while I had to investigate what was going on behind their closed doors. I utterly failed to do so. I had completely missed the main storyline.

The Greek music critic was asking to be forgiven. What could I have said?

Maček joined us. He was ignorant of our Malbork night. He knew Helena loved him. And I was just an obscure Georgian writer.

We said good-byes at that breakfast in Berlin. The farewell was quite friendly. I promised Maček to send him my story as soon as I got back.

When I left the dining hall, Helena was pouring herself coffee from a silver pot.

I refused to believe it was the last time I would see Helena. Something strange happened in Tbilisi airport. Elene met me. Strictly speaking she was there to meet her niece who had been on the same plane with me. But I'd like to believe she was somehow welcoming me too. How many hours we had spent discussing the trip! I imagined how she'd have prepared for our meeting had we still been together. But now we greeted each other like casual acquaintances. I did notice she was glad to see me and I was happy she was there to meet her niece and not a new character in her life.

The central streets were blocked by protestors. Along the airport motorway, there were huge boards with the photos of the August war atrocities. The air itself was heavy with the politics and the aftermath of the war. I hate returning home just as much as I hate leaving. I prefer to be where I've been tamed to feel comfort.

The next day I phoned Zviad. I missed the Literature Express people. I even talked to Iliko over Skype. He said if we collected money for him, he'd visit us.

It was those days that I set to writing this novel. I didn't know have anything more important to describe. And I saw the text as a sure means of getting free from Helena.

I'm much luckier in the novel.

However, I've changed the names of the main characters. They're bound to recognize themselves anyway. Don't I have the right to take revenge? I hope they won't be offended. They'll understand my intention without any hard feelings.

I don't even know if I'm in love. When I'm telling about her, I definitely feel in love. When I'm not writing, I feel I'm forgetting her. If I don't write things down, her face, her features, her body and her voice are disappearing.

I let Heinz know I'm writing a novel about our Literature Express. It's a good topic. Totally un-local. It's about love and literature. I believe it's going to be original. And do you know what he wrote in reply?

I'm giving his reply word-for-word below:

"It's a great idea. The only thing is we'll be obliged to publish volumes. Half of the Literature Express is writing a novel about our trip. I'm getting letters from your colleagues on a daily basis. Everyone seems to have fallen in love with our train. All in all, it looks as if we're going to have a hundred novels about the Literature Express adventures. And I believe all of them will be of equally high quality."

. . .

31 October. Berlin

Today he tells me he's been acting like an idiot. I told him he's been a complete idiot for the whole month. And he says: "I don't want you to love me! I'd like to be the one in love." Is he delirious or what? We've made up but I'm still not sure if it's the right decision . . .

God, thank you for protecting me from a foolish mistake. Good thing we only literally slept in Malbork and nothing more than that! I think I've confused the guy . . . He didn't understand what I wanted, what I was up to. I did go to his room . . . So stupid of me! Who did I want to punish? My God, had I gone further, I'd be utterly miserable now . . . I bumped into him on the train and immediately guessed he wished to talk, but I didn't know what about. Did I promise anything? What kind of plans might he have only because we slept side by side? How absurdly naïve!

Suddenly I thought he'd drag me into the toilet. His look was pretty insane. But no, he's a decent guy, it was just my phobias . . . I ran away from him like a fool. On the other hand, what could he have done? Nothing! Then I felt really ashamed. Today I saw him at breakfast and apologized for Malbork. I didn't explain anything . . . What was there to explain anyway? He's got nothing to do with it, poor him . . . What was it I meant to drag him into? One day I'll probably tell Maček how I planned to take revenge but changed my mind—didn't have enough courage for more than an innocent sleep with a complete stranger. Will he be jealous of just a sleep? Or will he think it daft? The irony of it is that he's going to translate Z's story. In other words, we've both chosen the same guy. We've got similar tastes :) Now I feel guilty as I've noticed infatuation in his eyes. It'd be just great if Z wrote something about me and if Maček was to translate it. Then he'll really hit the roof! And then we're sure to split.

LASHA BUGADZE was born in 1977 in Tbilisi. He is a playwright, novelist, newspaper columnist, and television and radio announcer. He has authored four novels and numerous plays; his works have been published in Georgian, Russian, Armenian, French, German, Polish, and English. His story "The Sins of the Wolf" appeared in *Best European Fiction 2013*.

MAYA KIASASHVILI is a translator of Georgian literature. She co-translated *Flight from the USSR* by Dato Turashvili, which was published in 2012.

Georgian Literature Series

In 2012, the Ministry of Culture and Monument Protection of Georgia collaborated with Dalkey Archive Press to publish *Contemporary Georgian Fiction*, a landmark anthology providing English-language readers with their first introduction to some of the greatest authors writing in Georgian since the restoration of independence.

Given the success of this project, the relationship between Dalkey Archive and the Ministry has evolved into a close, ongoing partnership, allowing an unprecedented number of translations of the major works of post-Soviet Georgian literature to published and publicized across the English-speaking world. Beginning with such contemporary classics as Aka Morchiladze's best-selling *Journey to Karabakh*, the Georgian Literature Series will provide readers with a much-needed overview of a vibrant and innovative literary culture that has thus far been sorely under-represented in translation.

MICHAL AJVAZ, *The Golden Age.*
  The Other City.
PIERRE ALBERT-BIROT, *Grabinoulor.*
YUZ ALESHKOVSKY, *Kangaroo.*
FELIPE ALFAU, *Chromos.*
  Locos.
IVAN ÂNGELO, *The Celebration.*
  The Tower of Glass.
ANTÓNIO LOBO ANTUNES, *Knowledge of Hell.*
  The Splendor of Portugal.
ALAIN ARIAS-MISSON, *Theatre of Incest.*
JOHN ASHBERY AND JAMES SCHUYLER, *A Nest of Ninnies.*
ROBERT ASHLEY, *Perfect Lives.*
GABRIELA AVIGUR-ROTEM, *Heatwave and Crazy Birds.*
DJUNA BARNES, *Ladies Almanack.*
  Ryder.
JOHN BARTH, *LETTERS.*
  Sabbatical.
DONALD BARTHELME, *The King.*
  Paradise.
SVETISLAV BASARA, *Chinese Letter.*
MIQUEL BAUÇÀ, *The Siege in the Room.*
RENÉ BELLETTO, *Dying.*
MAREK BIEŃCZYK, *Transparency.*
ANDREI BITOV, *Pushkin House.*
ANDREJ BLATNIK, *You Do Understand.*
LOUIS PAUL BOON, *Chapel Road.*
  My Little War.
  Summer in Termuren.
ROGER BOYLAN, *Killoyle.*
IGNÁCIO DE LOYOLA BRANDÃO, *Anonymous Celebrity.*
  Zero.
BONNIE BREMSER, *Troia: Mexican Memoirs.*
CHRISTINE BROOKE-ROSE, *Amalgamemnon.*
BRIGID BROPHY, *In Transit.*
GERALD L. BRUNS, *Modern Poetry and the Idea of Language.*
GABRIELLE BURTON, *Heartbreak Hotel.*
MICHEL BUTOR, *Degrees.*
  Mobile.
G. CABRERA INFANTE, *Infante's Inferno.*
  Three Trapped Tigers.
JULIETA CAMPOS, *The Fear of Losing Eurydice.*
ANNE CARSON, *Eros the Bittersweet.*
ORLY CASTEL-BLOOM, *Dolly City.*
LOUIS-FERDINAND CÉLINE, *Castle to Castle.*
  Conversations with Professor Y.
  London Bridge.
  Normance.
  North.
  Rigadoon.
MARIE CHAIX, *The Laurels of Lake Constance.*
HUGO CHARTERIS, *The Tide Is Right.*
ERIC CHEVILLARD, *Demolishing Nisard.*

MARC CHOLODENKO, *Mordechai Schamz.*
JOSHUA COHEN, *Witz.*
EMILY HOLMES COLEMAN, *The Shutter of Snow.*
ROBERT COOVER, *A Night at the Movies.*
STANLEY CRAWFORD, *Log of the S.S. The Mrs Unguentine.*
  Some Instructions to My Wife.
RENÉ CREVEL, *Putting My Foot in It.*
RALPH CUSACK, *Cadenza.*
NICHOLAS DELBANCO, *The Count of Concord.*
  Sherbrookes.
NIGEL DENNIS, *Cards of Identity.*
PETER DIMOCK, *A Short Rhetoric for Leaving the Family.*
ARIEL DORFMAN, *Konfidenz.*
COLEMAN DOWELL, *Island People.*
  Too Much Flesh and Jabez.
ARKADII DRAGOMOSHCHENKO, *Dust.*
RIKKI DUCORNET, *The Complete Butcher's Tales.*
  The Fountains of Neptune.
  The Jade Cabinet.
  Phosphor in Dreamland.
WILLIAM EASTLAKE, *The Bamboo Bed.*
  Castle Keep.
  Lyric of the Circle Heart.
JEAN ECHENOZ, *Chopin's Move.*
STANLEY ELKIN, *A Bad Man.*
  Criers and Kibitzers, Kibitzers and Criers.
  The Dick Gibson Show.
  The Franchiser.
  The Living End.
  Mrs. Ted Bliss.
FRANÇOIS EMMANUEL, *Invitation to a Voyage.*
SALVADOR ESPRIU, *Ariadne in the Grotesque Labyrinth.*
LESLIE A. FIEDLER, *Love and Death in the American Novel.*
JUAN FILLOY, *Op Oloop.*
ANDY FITCH, *Pop Poetics.*
GUSTAVE FLAUBERT, *Bouvard and Pécuchet.*
KASS FLEISHER, *Talking out of School.*
FORD MADOX FORD, *The March of Literature.*
JON FOSSE, *Aliss at the Fire.*
  Melancholy.
MAX FRISCH, *I'm Not Stiller.*
  Man in the Holocene.
CARLOS FUENTES, *Christopher Unborn.*
  Distant Relations.
  Terra Nostra.
  Where the Air Is Clear.
TAKEHIKO FUKUNAGA, *Flowers of Grass.*
WILLIAM GADDIS, *J R.*
  The Recognitions.

SELECTED DALKEY ARCHIVE TITLES

FOR A FULL LIST OF PUBLICATIONS, VISIT:
www.dalkeyarchive.com

Joseph McElroy,
  Night Soul and Other Stories.
Abdelwahab Meddeb, *Talismano.*
Gerhard Meier, *Isle of the Dead.*
Herman Melville, *The Confidence-Man.*
Amanda Michalopoulou, *I'd Like.*
Steven Millhauser, *The Barnum Museum.*
  In the Penny Arcade.
Ralph J. Mills, Jr., *Essays on Poetry.*
Momus, *The Book of Jokes.*
Christine Montalbetti, *The Origin of Man.*
  Western.
Olive Moore, *Spleen.*
Nicholas Mosley, *Accident.*
  Assassins.
  Catastrophe Practice.
  Experience and Religion.
  A Garden of Trees.
  Hopeful Monsters.
  Imago Bird.
  Impossible Object.
  Inventing God.
  Judith.
  Look at the Dark.
  Natalie Natalia.
  Serpent.
  Time at War.
Warren Motte,
  *Fables of the Novel: French Fiction
    since 1990.*
  *Fiction Now: The French Novel in
    the 21st Century.*
  *Oulipo: A Primer of Potential
    Literature.*
Gerald Murnane, *Barley Patch.*
  Inland.
Yves Navarre, *Our Share of Time.*
  Sweet Tooth.
Dorothy Nelson, *In Night's City.*
  Tar and Feathers.
Eshkol Nevo, *Homesick.*
Wilfrido D. Nolledo, *But for the Lovers.*
Flann O'Brien, *At Swim-Two-Birds.*
  The Best of Myles.
  The Dalkey Archive.
  The Hard Life.
  The Poor Mouth.
  The Third Policeman.
Claude Ollier, *The Mise-en-Scène.*
  Wert and the Life Without End.
Giovanni Orelli, *Walaschek's Dream.*
Patrik Ouředník, *Europeana.*
  The Opportune Moment, 1855.
Boris Pahor, *Necropolis.*
Fernando del Paso, *News from the
    Empire.*
  Palinuro of Mexico.
Robert Pinget, *The Inquisitory.*
  Mahu or The Material.
  Trio.
Manuel Puig, *Betrayed by Rita Hayworth.*

The Buenos Aires Affair.
Heartbreak Tango.
Raymond Queneau, *The Last Days.*
  Odile.
  Pierrot Mon Ami.
  Saint Glinglin.
Ann Quin, *Berg.*
  Passages.
  Three.
  Tripticks.
Ishmael Reed, *The Free-Lance Pallbearers.*
  The Last Days of Louisiana Red.
  Ishmael Reed: The Plays.
  Juice!
  Reckless Eyeballing.
  The Terrible Threes.
  The Terrible Twos.
  Yellow Back Radio Broke-Down.
Jasia Reichardt, *15 Journeys Warsaw
    to London.*
Noëlle Revaz, *With the Animals.*
João Ubaldo Ribeiro, *House of the
    Fortunate Buddhas.*
Jean Ricardou, *Place Names.*
Rainer Maria Rilke, *The Notebooks of
    Malte Laurids Brigge.*
Julián Ríos, *The House of Ulysses.*
  Larva: A Midsummer Night's Babel.
  Poundemonium.
  Procession of Shadows.
Augusto Roa Bastos, *I the Supreme.*
Daniël Robberechts, *Arriving in Avignon.*
Jean Rolin, *The Explosion of the
    Radiator Hose.*
Olivier Rolin, *Hotel Crystal.*
Alix Cleo Roubaud, *Alix's Journal.*
Jacques Roubaud, *The Form of a
    City Changes Faster, Alas, Than
    the Human Heart.*
  The Great Fire of London.
  Hortense in Exile.
  Hortense Is Abducted.
  The Loop.
  Mathematics:
  The Plurality of Worlds of Lewis.
  The Princess Hoppy.
  Some Thing Black.
Raymond Roussel, *Impressions of Africa.*
Vedrana Rudan, *Night.*
Stig Sæterbakken, *Siamese.*
  Self Control.
Lydie Salvayre, *The Company of Ghosts.*
  The Lecture.
  The Power of Flies.
Luis Rafael Sánchez,
  Macho Camacho's Beat.
Severo Sarduy, *Cobra & Maitreya.*
Nathalie Sarraute,
  Do You Hear Them?
  Martereau.
  The Planetarium.

ARNO SCHMIDT, *Collected Novellas.*
Collected Stories.
Nobodaddy's Children.
Two Novels.
ASAF SCHURR, *Motti.*
GAIL SCOTT, *My Paris.*
DAMION SEARLS, *What We Were Doing
and Where We Were Going.*
JUNE AKERS SEESE,
Is This What Other Women Feel Too?
What Waiting Really Means.
BERNARD SHARE, *Inish.*
Transit.
VIKTOR SHKLOVSKY, *Bowstring.*
Knight's Move.
*A Sentimental Journey:
Memoirs 1917–1922.*
Energy of Delusion: A Book on Plot.
Literature and Cinematography.
Theory of Prose.
Third Factory.
Zoo, or Letters Not about Love.
PIERRE SINIAC, *The Collaborators.*
KJERSTI A. SKOMSVOLD, *The Faster I Walk,
the Smaller I Am.*
JOSEF ŠKVORECKÝ, *The Engineer of
Human Souls.*
GILBERT SORRENTINO,
Aberration of Starlight.
Blue Pastoral.
Crystal Vision.
*Imaginative Qualities of Actual
Things.*
Mulligan Stew.
Pack of Lies.
Red the Fiend.
The Sky Changes.
Something Said.
Splendide-Hôtel.
Steelwork.
Under the Shadow.
W. M. SPACKMAN, *The Complete Fiction.*
ANDRZEJ STASIUK, *Dukla.*
Fado.
GERTRUDE STEIN, *The Making of Americans.*
A Novel of Thank You.
LARS SVENDSEN, *A Philosophy of Evil.*
PIOTR SZEWC, *Annihilation.*
GONÇALO M. TAVARES, *Jerusalem.*
Joseph Walser's Machine.
*Learning to Pray in the Age of
Technique.*
LUCIAN DAN TEODOROVICI,
Our Circus Presents . . .
NIKANOR TERATOLOGEN, *Assisted Living.*
STEFAN THEMERSON, *Hobson's Island.*
The Mystery of the Sardine.
Tom Harris.
TAEKO TOMIOKA, *Building Waves.*

JOHN TOOMEY, *Sleepwalker.*
JEAN-PHILIPPE TOUSSAINT, *The Bathroom.*
Camera.
Monsieur.
Reticence.
Running Away.
Self-Portrait Abroad.
Television.
The Truth about Marie.
DUMITRU TSEPENEAG, *Hotel Europa.*
The Necessary Marriage.
Pigeon Post.
Vain Art of the Fugue.
ESTHER TUSQUETS, *Stranded.*
DUBRAVKA UGRESIC, *Lend Me Your
Character.*
Thank You for Not Reading.
TOR ULVEN, *Replacement.*
MATI UNT, *Brecht at Night.*
Diary of a Blood Donor.
Things in the Night.
ÁLVARO URIBE AND OLIVIA SEARS, EDS.,
Best of Contemporary Mexican Fiction.
ELOY URROZ, *Friction.*
The Obstacles.
LUISA VALENZUELA, *Dark Desires and
the Others.*
He Who Searches.
PAUL VERHAEGHEN, *Omega Minor.*
AGLAJA VETERANYI, *Why the Child Is
Cooking in the Polenta.*
BORIS VIAN, *Heartsnatcher.*
LLORENÇ VILLALONGA, *The Dolls' Room.*
TOOMAS VINT, *An Unending Landscape.*
ORNELA VORPSI, *The Country Where No
One Ever Dies.*
AUSTRYN WAINHOUSE, *Hedyphagetica.*
CURTIS WHITE, *America's Magic Mountain.*
The Idea of Home.
Memories of My Father Watching TV.
Requiem.
DIANE WILLIAMS, *Excitability:
Selected Stories.*
Romancer Erector.
DOUGLAS WOOLF, *Wall to Wall.*
Ya! & John-Juan.
JAY WRIGHT, *Polynomials and Pollen.*
*The Presentable Art of Reading
Absence.*
PHILIP WYLIE, *Generation of Vipers.*
MARGUERITE YOUNG, *Angel in the Forest.*
Miss MacIntosh, My Darling.
REYOUNG, *Unbabbling.*
VLADO ŽABOT, *The Succubus.*
ZORAN ŽIVKOVIĆ, *Hidden Camera.*
LOUIS ZUKOFSKY, *Collected Fiction.*
VITOMIL ZUPAN, *Minuet for Guitar.*
SCOTT ZWIREN, *God Head.*

FOR A FULL LIST OF PUBLICATIONS, VISIT:
www.dalkeyarchive.com